AF242364

# Beyond the Bucket List

*a novel*

BRIEANNA WILKOFF

**NEW YORK   LOS ANGELES**

Jacket design by Rejenne Pavon
Jacket Copyright 2026 by Winding Road Stories
Interior book design by A Raven Design
ISBN#: 978-1-960724-52-6 (pbk)
ISBN#: 978-1-960724-53-3 (ebook)

Published by Winding Road Stories
www.windingroadstories.com

*To Lenae, for believing this story was worth telling*

# PART I

# MUD RUN

I like winning, more than I mind being uncomfortable.

I've pushed myself to run despite feeling crummy before, but standing in the frigid rain waiting for this 5K to start, I want to race home to my bed.

Mom, Dad, and Bean huddle under umbrellas and offer sympathetic smiles before I stretch. I take a slow, deep breath, but as my chest expands, it's like this illness I can't get over lodges against my ribs to assert, *Nope, that's enough air for you.*

Water drips down my forehead while I touch my toes. When I straighten up, I spot Charlie jogging toward me, the strap of his camera peeking out beneath his jacket. He holds his umbrella over both of us and pulls me in for a kiss.

"Good luck." He moves back, but I grab his hand to grant myself a few more dry moments before getting pelted by raindrops again.

"I wish this were snow," I say.

"Wouldn't that make it harder to run?"

"That would make them cancel the race."

Charlie envelops me with his free arm. "I would give you a blizzard if I could."

I snuggle into his stocky frame, so soft and warm, which makes the elements outside our embrace even less inviting. "It's nice here," I mumble with my face smushed against his shoulder. "I don't want to run."

"You don't want the weather to suck, but you always want to run." He gently pushes me off him and looks into my eyes. "You've got this. We'll all be cheering you on."

As Charlie joins my family, I indulge in a final curse at the rain, then go into competition mode. *Three miles. You're training for a marathon—this is cake.*

The grass squelches under my feet as I walk toward the start and get into position. Down the line is another girl from the school cross-country team, and we nod at each other, fellow sufferers who seek out community races, like this aptly named Run Your Ice Off 5K, to stay sharp in the offseason.

When the air pistol sounds, I take off, water splashing my ankles.

The first leg is a straight shot across the field, which is dotted with spectators. Bean jumps up and down and waves, her little yellow hood covering her head. I lift my hand briefly as I pass, then head into a grove.

Bare January trees offer no protection from the rain, and with their roots close to the surface, there's no grass—just mud.

It sucks at my shoes like quicksand. One foot slips, and I thrust out an arm to keep my balance. The cold doesn't do my lungs any favors, and fighting the uneven terrain saps my stamina. Instead of maintaining a steady pace, I take short, quick steps and practically dance my way through.

My heart is pounding when I land back on the grass and slow to a walk.

I *never* walk.

After a few seconds, I resume running and ignore my body yelling at me. Being tired during a run isn't new. Lately, it's the norm, what with longer runs to train for the marathon and the residual symptoms from being sick.

I push myself past the girl in front of me. Breathe in through my nose, out through my mouth. Then I set my sights on the next girl, the one currently in first place. I bring each foot down with a splash to propel me another step closer, not caring about the mud that splatters my legs. Huffing and puffing, I manage to overtake her just before we head into the trees at the other end of the field.

The next obstacle is a hill so slick, my foot slides down it, dragging my knee through the mud and costing me time. I grab hold of a nearby branch and swear as I toddler-step my way up and over.

I'm still in the top spot as we near the end of the woods, but only because we have to run single file. As soon as we spill out into the open, I can't keep the lead. God knows I'm digging as deep as I can, but my body Just. Won't. Go.

A giant puddle looms ahead, directly in front of the gate we have to pass through to get to the track and the finish line. Four of us reach it at once. One girl makes the fatal decision to dart to the side, which allows the next girl to overtake her as she runs straight through.

I follow, and my feet are submerged. The next several steps are awkward and off-putting as water squishes inside my shoes. Several sounds compete for my attention as I approach the inflatable "Finish" arch: People cheering. Footsteps behind me, coming on fast. Ragged breathing I recognize as my own. *One foot in front of the other.*

The girl behind me barrels past, followed by the girl who sidestepped the puddle.

I come in fourth.

*Fourth.*

Last year I won this race.

To give the vise around my chest time to loosen, I walk a couple laps around the snack tables, then work my way through the crowd until I find my family.

Dad protects me with his umbrella and puts his free hand on my shoulder. "This was a tough one. You were amazing."

Mom gives me a one-armed hug. "We're proud of you."

At the *click* of Charlie's camera, I glare at him. "Not a photo-worthy finish."

He lets the camera rest against his chest but says, "Oh, it definitely is—this is your messiest race by far."

"One girl fell down," Bean informs me. "She was *covered* in mud."

As satisfying as it is to hear that this sludge spectacle amused the spectators, I am desperate to get cleaned up, so we make our way toward the parking lot and head home.

The cascade of hot water from the shower melts away the tension from the race, even if it can't dissolve my frustration at the outcome. I close my eyes and savor the warmth.

Too soon, my legs decide they've had enough of holding me up. Once I step out and wrap a towel around myself, I sit on the edge of the tub until I muster the strength to go to my room. I sit on my bed to pull on fleece plaid pajama bottoms and an oversized sweatshirt of Charlie's.

He comes over in the afternoon. Mom or Dad lets him in, and when he appears in the family room, I peel back the blanket to invite him into the spot next to me.

"You look cozy."

By way of an answer, I rest my head on his shoulder. He lifts the camera strap off his neck and sets the camera in his lap. A second later, he clicks through the pictures of the race.

"Too soon." *Give me 24 hours before I have to relive it.*

"These aren't of you."

I raise my head and look at him.

"You'll like this one."

Bean is in the center of the shot, mid-spin—arms spread wide, yellow raincoat fanned out around her. Her expression is pure sunshine, the joy of a seven-year-old twirling in the rain.

Charlie and I smile at each other. "I know you weren't having fun out there, but I thought it might help to know someone was."

I take his hand. With his other, he clicks through until he finds another picture he wants to share.

My sister was one thing. Why is he taunting me with a runner beaming as she crosses the finish line when he knows I wish he had a picture like that of me? I pull my hand back and stare at him.

"She was the last person to finish."

"So, what? She was mocking the whole thing?"

His brow furrows. "Mocking it? No, she was thrilled."

"Because she lost?"

"Because she finished. I talked to her afterward—this was her first race, ever."

*Oh.*

I take the camera and look closer. Behind the smile, her tiredness shows. The crease in her forehead, the weariness in her eyes. The relief that it's over.

Also, the relief that *she did it*. The pride and excitement.

It's all there—it's always all there in Charlie's photos.

He sandwiches my hand in both of his. I scooch down so I can press my cheek to his chest and ask, "How do you do that?" A rhetorical question I've asked in earnest before. He explains his talent by saying he's observant and patient and always has his camera ready. But it's more than that. Anyone could develop those skills. Only Charlie can so perfectly capture the truth, the whole truth, of a moment.

I pick up the camera and click backward until I find myself.

My race pictures usually show mixed emotions too—resignation at not being the best along with pride in placing higher than expected, or disappointment with the loss plus self-respect for giving it my all. But today is different. I should have won. If I weren't still dealing with the lingering effects of this cold or flu bug I had months ago, I *would* have won. My only emotion is frustration, and that's exactly what Charlie captured in the picture.

"I should have had it."

"The conditions were terrible. That had to throw you off."

"They were terrible for everybody," I counter. "It was an even playing field, and I should have won."

"But you're still not a hundred percent. If—"

"If a 5K was this hard, how will I run the marathon?"

"You've got plenty of time before then." Charlie kisses my forehead. "And you finished a 5K in fourth place even though you were sick."

Pulling my knees up, I grumble, "Fourth place isn't a win."

"You win some, you lose some."

I tilt my head at him. "Is that supposed to make me feel better?"

The corners of his mouth turn up. "Maybe?"

Even though I'm smiling, I shake my head. "Try again."

"It is what it is?"

"Trite—pass."

"Okay, okay. Take the bad with the good."

"Stop spouting clichés. Nothing will—"

Charlie shuts me up with his lips. After he pulls back, he asks, "Did that make you feel better?"

"Not about the race," I tease, and he leans his body into mine so we both fall and lie sprawled on the couch. "But it was an excellent diversion." I tuck a curl behind his ear, only for it to immediately pop out.

He kisses me again before lifting his weight off me. "I should go. I have to study for my chem test."

"Okay. My appointment tomorrow is at nine. Will you send me your calc notes?"

"Sure. Text me after you see the doctor."

I look at him hopefully. Maybe this doctor will have some answers. Maybe soon I'll get back to running at full speed.

# THE C WORD

"**Y**ou have cancer."

The doctor doesn't really put it as bluntly as that. He uses words like *malignant* and *aggressive*, says we'll treat it with *chemotherapy* and aim to send it into *remission*. Therapy should begin as soon as possible, before the disease gets any more *advanced*. He assures us Hodgkin's lymphoma has a good *prognosis* and tells us not to worry.

I have cancer.

I grip the sides of my hard plastic chair and try to ignore the pounding of my heart. *Nope. That can't be right.*

The doctor is still talking, but I don't think the words I'm hearing are the ones actually coming out of his mouth.

"...treatment regimen called (*cancer*), which stands for (*cancer*). It's administered as a series of infusions, and she'll need to come to the (*cancer*). Or she can go to the outpatient clinic at (*cancer*) if that would be more (*cancer*). Each infusion takes anywhere from (*cancer*) to (*cancer*) on (*cancer*), and the whole thing is repeated every (*cancer*)."

*I have cancer?*

Surrounded by the buzzing fluorescent lights and cold, sterile air, I can't stand to be in this tiny room a second longer. I jump up and bolt into the hallway. Mom calls after me, but I run into the bathroom and turn the lock.

I rest my head against the door and close my eyes.

Last night I woke up drenched in sweat again. The first couple times it happened, we thought my fever had broken. But the fever didn't go away, and I kept having night sweats from time to time. It's gross—my pajamas and sheets are literally wet, there's so much sweat.

Not normal, sure, but that means I have cancer?

Mom asked me yesterday if I wanted to meet with the doctor at the same time she talked with him or wait for her to tell me the news. I guess that was the tip-off that we probably weren't talking about a virus anymore, but I was not prepared for this.

*Now what?* The Contemporary Lit paper I'm supposed to turn in tomorrow has obviously dropped in importance. And yet, I'm pretty sure the world isn't going to stop, even though it should. A bombshell like this warrants a pause button for life, something to give me time to process.

After what feels like an hour, I open the door a crack. The hallway is empty, so I beeline to the front.

Mom paces the waiting area while holding my puffy coat. Our eyes meet, and a magnetic force threatens to propel her toward me, but I avert my eyes and hurry outside to the minivan. As soon as it unlocks, I climb in and face the window. Even though I was only exposed to the cold for thirty seconds, I'm shaking. I cup my hands and blow in the space they make to warm them up, then set them in my lap and fixate on the scenery passing by.

Everything is soggy and droopy from yesterday's rain, although the sun tries to peek out before being swallowed by the clouds. Lights still decorate some houses, even though

Christmas was a month ago. The residential surroundings give way to the city skyline as we merge onto the freeway, the van hugging the curve on the entrance ramp.

I sense my mother's glances. Eventually, she says, "Do you want to talk?"

Such a reasonable question, but I shake my head, because I know if I speak, I'll cry. Her hand moves toward me, and I'm afraid she might pull my face to the left, forcing me to look at her. Instead, she picks up my hand and squeezes it, and I swallow a few times to choke down the lump in my throat.

"Let me make you some tea," she says once we're home. When she hands me the mug—the sweet herbal scent familiar and pleasant—I escape to my room and set the tea on my nightstand, where it remains untouched. Even chamomile, my favorite, can't comfort me today. With a parting glance at the steam swirling above the red ceramic, I get into bed and stare at the starburst pattern on the ceiling.

What the hell does this mean? Am I dying? No, scratch that. The doctor talked about treatment, so we treat it. And I beat it. *Right?*

*Right,* I want to say to myself, but even in my head, the uncertainty is palpable.

Now that I let in a few questions, more rush at me: *What will treatment be like? How much school will I miss? Can I still run? What about the marathon? Who will tell Dad and Laine and Bean and—*

Charlie. My phone buzzes with a text from him; he was expecting to hear from me an hour ago.

> Did your appt run long?

This is not something to share via text.

> We'll talk later. Come over after school.

> What's wrong?

When I don't respond, he tries again.

> Dell? Please.

His words drip with fear, and I can't deal with it. I leave my phone in my room and go outside.

Given that the sun won its battle with the clouds, I have to shield my eyes from the brightness. On Bean's play set, I sit on a swing and twist myself around and around, coiling the chains until they're as tight as possible. Then I let go, lifting my feet and spinning freely. Round and round and round. Dizzying. Disorienting. *Fitting.*

Once my shoes touch the ground again, I tap my foot. Spastic, angry, like the earth is responsible for what's happening.

The sun offends me. Bird song frays my nerves. The chilly breeze sets my blood boiling so that when a few remaining leaves rustle, I want to jump up, ball my fists, and scream, "Shut up!" at every single one of them. The day has no right to be beautiful. A day like this demands deafening claps of thunder and heart-resuscitating jolts of lightning. It deserves a torrential downpour, but all I get is a single leaf that falls from the oak above, the lone tear the day will shed for me.

With a huff, I go back inside. As I pass the dining room window, a beat-up blue Toyota Camry pulls into the driveway, and my heart leaps into my throat. Charlie skipped class.

The second the car stops, he throws open the door. Shaking his dark brown curls out of his eyes, he loops his camera strap over his head. After he kicks the door shut with a *thud*, he moves so fast, the camera bounces up and down on his chest.

My heart beats like a hummingbird's wings as I open the door. Seeing Charlie's face, full of concern and fear and knowing, destroys my self-control, and I give him the last reaction he's expecting and the most inappropriate one imaginable: I laugh.

It's more of a giggle, really, and I cut it off mid-chuckle, giving it a pinched, pained sound. Charlie furrows his brows. In the silence that follows, we stare at each other until he says, "Dell, what's going on?"

"Come up." I mount the stairs and leave him to close the door, which gives me a few seconds to compose myself.

Once we're in my room, he sits on the edge of my bed and looks at me expectantly. When I don't speak, he stands again. The closer I am to him, the more nervous I get, so I pace and shake my hands to get some feeling in them, because they're icy even though my armpits are sweating profusely.

"Dell…" Charlie's pleading finally overpowers my resistance.

I lean against the wall. "It's Hodgkin's lymphoma." I can't bring myself to say *cancer* out loud yet.

Charlie's face contorts. Because his pain on top of my own is too hard to bear, I slide down the wall till I'm sitting on the floor and hug my knees. After taking a shuddery breath, Charlie slides down next to me.

I stare at a spot on the carpet, the rough patch where the fibers stick together from the honey Bean spilled during a tea party when she was five. I hate that patch of carpet, because it scratches my skin every time I walk barefoot over it, yet it's blurring before me as tears make their way down my cheeks. Charlie takes my hand, and I meet his glistening eyes. We reach for each other and press our lips together.

When we stop kissing, Charlie rests his forehead against mine. He opens his eyes, cups my face in his hands, and looks at me intently. "You won't go through this alone."

*Was I afraid I would?* Apparently so, because a volcano of emotion erupts inside me, and I bury my face on his shoulder and sob. As he strokes my hair, Charlie says, "I'll be right beside you—like always."

<hr>

That evening, I attempt homework, which doesn't go well. My phone rings, and when "Laine" appears on the screen, I know my mom has told my older sister.

My heart flops around like a fish out of water. I take a deep breath before I answer. "Hey."

"What the hell, Dee? How can you have cancer? *Cancer!*"

Her outburst sets me at ease. Given that my whole world seems to have changed, it's reassuring that my sister has not.

She audibly inhales. "I don't want to say 'how are you,' because that's asinine, but...how are you?"

"You're right, that's asinine."

She laughs, but it's strained.

"I don't know. I mean, I get that it's not normal to be sick for three months, and waking up drenched in sweat is weird, but I still wouldn't have thought...cancer." (*There, I said it.*)

Silence. As I'm checking to make sure my phone didn't drop the call, I hear Laine say, "Shit."

I lift the phone back to my ear as she continues.

"I wish I weren't hundreds of miles away and could wrap you in a hug. Before I called, I spent, like, an hour thinking about what to say. What the hell do you say for this? 'Gee, Dell, I sure am sorry you got cancer. That really sucks.' No, that's supremely lame."

"What you're saying is perfect."

"I'll be home in a month and a half. It's not soon enough, but—"

"You can't skip Rio!" I interrupt.

"Please. Do you seriously think I could enjoy spring break knowing what's going on with you?"

"But you already bought tickets," I protest. The truth is, I'm thrilled by the idea of Laine coming home. Even five months in, I'm not used to her being gone. Sometimes I sit in her room, with the empty hydroponics growing system and her poster of the Eiffel Tower, just to feel a little closer to her.

"Big picture, Dee. Money is not what's important here."

A smile spreads across my face.

# THE RED DEVIL

W e get a second opinion—more tests and needles—then boom, I'm scheduled for treatment.

The ten days leading up to my first chemotherapy appointment, and even the actual infusion, are uneventful, with five notable exceptions:

**1. Shannon Cooper is a bitch.**

One morning, Charlie and I are standing in the hall before first period. He squeezes my fingers and stares at me. After a few seconds, Mr. Zielinski reminds me that we're standing in the doorway where everyone can see us. "Hello, Charlie. Would you care to enter, Adele?"

The pale skin on Charlie's cheeks and neck blooms bright pink, a bodily quirk of his that he hates, and I give him a reassuring smile before rushing to my seat.

Once the bell rings, Mr. Zielinski returns our tests from last week. I cringe as I take the paper he hands me: C+.

I never get Cs.

I rarely get Bs.

Shannon, who sits next to me, leans over and whispers, "Maybe if you spent less time with your boyfriend…"

When I glare at her, she shrugs. "Just saying."

*Why must she comment?* She couldn't be further from the truth anyway.

**2. I have multiple appointments and tests to get ready for chemo.**

In addition to drawing blood, they check my heart and lungs and implant this thing called a port below my collarbone. It's metal, about the size of a dime, and after they stitch my skin closed, I feel a little like a robot, knowing I've got this thing inside me now. *Beep boop.*

**3. My cross-country friends act aloof.**

A handful of us who only like long-distance running and who participate in cross-country in the fall but not track in the spring run together after school a few times a week. When I tell this group about the cancer diagnosis, they turn into deer in the headlights. (*Who knew a person could go so long without blinking?*)

I expect them to hug me or say they're sorry, but everyone just stands there staring at me.

Sheryl finally speaks. "Dell, that's terrible."

More silence follows, until Annie says, "I'm sorry, I have to go." She glances over her shoulder toward where we parked. "We'll talk more tomorrow, okay?"

Without waiting for me to answer, she turns and hurries to her Mazda. The others follow, and I'm left alone, my stomach down at my feet like they punched me in the gut.

Since I thought sharing the cancer news would be the awkward part, I searched "How to tell someone you have cancer." Turns out, the internet wisdom I actually need is "What if your friends bail when you tell them you have cancer?" *What do you say to that, Google?*

**4. I meet the tallest person I've ever seen in real life, in the form of my oncologist.**

He's warm and friendly, putting a hand on my shoulder after

saying hi to Mom and Dad. "You must be Adele. I'm Doctor James Mastroianni, but people call me Dr. Mastro."

With his wide smile and kind eyes, he reminds me of a young Barack Obama.

As he explains what to expect with treatment, I look from him to Dad—my father is six feet, so Dr. Mastro's got to be six-eight at least. When I realize he's talking to me, I pull my attention from the top of his head and make eye contact.

"Our team here is the best there is, and we'll do everything we can to make this as easy on you as possible, okay?"

I nod. *Let's go.*

**5. I'm infused with something that looks like it's from a movie set.**

I remove my ear buds and ask the nurse, "Why is it so red?" I know the color of a medicine means nothing, but that does little to quell the part of my brain screaming, *Warning! Danger! Stop!*

"This is Adriamycin. It's famous for its color, which can be shocking, I know."

It's not just the color catching my eye. It's also the giant syringe it's in, which tempers the hazard associations because it reminds me of a Jell-O shot Laine had at a frat party. Now I get my own supersized syringe. *Woo.*

The next morning, my pee is reddish-orange, and despite the fact I was warned about this, it's unsettling.

Otherwise, things aren't so bad. One of the meds, a steroid pill I take at home, tastes awful and makes me edgy, but since that's not crawl-into-bed worthy, I go to school. The day is oddly normal, as is the day after that. By the next day, I'm tricked into thinking, *Maybe I won't have any major side effects from chemo.*

It hits me ten minutes later, like I've jinxed myself. All at once, my muscles turn to jelly, my stomach rumbles, and my mouth churns out saliva. Of course I'm at school. Forget getting home, I need to get to the bathroom ASAP, before I hurl in front of everybody—that is *not* an option.

As soon as I barge into the bathroom, I drop my books on the counter so fast that one falls off. It hits the floor as I cram myself into a stall. I don't even lock the door before sinking to the floor. Once the wretched sounds from my body subside, another toilet flushes. *Great, someone else got to hear that.*

I lean my head against the wall and grimace at the taste in my mouth. Since it's safe to say I'm done with school today, I text Mom.

> I threw up. Will you come get me? Bring a pot.

Guess I know now why they call Adriamycin the Red Devil.

---

Things go downhill fast, turning my days into a nightmare hellscape that makes me question the distinction between "medicine" and "torture." Any desire to eat, socialize, or move unless absolutely necessary goes out the window. On top of my stomach taking its revenge for some perceived injustice, my taste buds turn on me. Dad tries to tempt me with my favorites, but they don't teach "Cooking for a Cancer Patient" in culinary school—I tell him repeatedly that foods taste off or I can't taste them at all. Eventually, he gets it and makes some steel cut oats with sliced banana and cooked apples that are acceptable, and toast with gouda and mashed avocado that I actually enjoy.

My energy from the steroid wears off, and because it made me restless at night, I'm hit with a double whammy of chemo fatigue and lack of sleep. I've never spent so much time in my bed.

After I miss a third running session, Mom hesitantly suggests waiting until next year for the marathon. I say I'll think about it, but once she leaves the room, I Google shortened training schedules. Twelve weeks seems like the minimum for a first marathon, which I might be able to pull off if I can run during the second half of each chemo cycle. *It can't be like this for the full three weeks, can it?*

Charlie keeps asking to come over. Since I keep saying no, I mix up my reasons: "I'm sleepy." "I'm gross." "I'm throwing up." "Who is this Dell you speak of? I'm the demon that's taken up residence in her body."

Eventually, I feel human again. A sick and tired human, but still. When I finally agree to a Charlie visit, which happens to be on Valentine's Day, he brings me a care package of Sudoku, a jigsaw puzzle, adult coloring books, and colored pencils, plus an adorable velvety rabbit (my favorite animal) holding an "I love you" heart.

"These are great." I set the boredom-busters on my nightstand.

"If you'd let me come sooner, you would have had something to do this week."

"But that would have interfered with my quality puking time."

Charlie smiles wryly. "Your snarkiness suggests you're feeling better." He makes himself as comfortable as he can in my wooden desk chair. It seems designed less for his stocky build than for my lean—and getting leaner by the day—frame.

I open a coloring book to a picture of a butterfly and choose teal for the body. Realism is overrated.

*Click.*

"What are you doing?" I ask, even though I know the answer.

Charlie lowers his camera slightly but doesn't set it aside.

"Please don't."

"Why not? You're cute."

I raise my eyebrows. "I need a shower."

"You looked content."

*I guess.* "This isn't exactly a time I want to remember."

He sits by my feet and puts a hand on my knee, tentative. "As a whole, no." The tips of his fingers brush my thigh as he lifts his hand off my leg, and a shiver runs up my body. "But individual moments?" He scoots up so he's tucked in at my side, then leans down and kisses me. "Might you want to remember this kiss?"

I set the coloring book aside, and Charlie slides his hand under my hair, cupping my neck. He pulls me close and kisses me deeply. My tongue finds his, and by the time he sits back, I'm out of breath.

"What about that one?" He grins. "Would that be terrible to remember?"

I tug on his shirt. "Shut up and kiss me again."

---

Thankfully, the side effects subside over the next couple weeks. And with my next round of infusions, they give me an antiemetic that keeps me from barfing. *Score one for the oncology team.*

A week and a half after my second cycle of chemo, while I'm reading yet again, I turn to reposition my pillow. And that's when I see it: my hair, a brown stripe on the pillowcase.

*Oh God.*

My heart pounds. This isn't a strand or two of hair. It's a clump big enough to hold in my palm, and when I raise a shaking hand to my head, my fingertips find a patch of my scalp where the hair is thinner.

I don't try to stop the tears or stifle the ugly noise that comes out of my mouth.

This isn't a surprise, but it's my *hair*, and cancer is taking it away. *And if it takes this, what else will it take?*

I don't want to have cancer. I don't want to get chemo. I don't want to wonder whether the treatment will work and what will happen if it doesn't (*and I die*)—and I want that damn voice in my head to SHUT UP!

Mom knocks on my door before poking her head in. I'm such a mess that she rushes to my side and wraps her arms around me. I let her hold me for several minutes, and when I finally sit back, I show her the hair as explanation and cry again.

She pulls me close, resting her cheek on the top of my head. "I'm so sorry."

Once I'm down to sniffles, Mom wipes her own eyes and says, "I had a thought. What if we shop for wigs with Laine while she's here?"

Not the kind of shopping I normally enjoy with my sister, but the idea of having her there for support comforts me, so I nod.

Mom puts both her hands on the sides of my face and stares into my eyes. "This will be okay. You will be okay. We will make it okay."

I'm about to cry again, but she kisses my forehead and stands. "Who knows? It might even be fun. It's not often I hand over my credit card."

After the door closes, I turn to the pillow again, but the hair is gone. (*Sneaky mom skills.*) I push back the covers, walk to my dresser, and face the mirror. If I let my vision blur, the thin spot disappears, but when I refocus, I can't not see it.

Careful to not pull any out, I gather my hair and imagine myself without it. Will my head have a nice shape? *Nope, not ready to go there yet.* I drop my hair and stare at the ceiling until the tears get reabsorbed into my eyes.

If my hair is falling out, that means chemo is killing fast-dividing cells, which includes cancer cells too. *This is a good thing.*

Back in bed, I grab my phone and visit the marathon website

for the hundredth time. A flashing message at the top of the page indicates there are fewer than 100 spots left.

My finger hovers over the "Register" button.

I should check the cancelation policy and confirm I can get my money back if I end up not being able to race. I should check with Mom and ask if she thinks twelve weeks of training will be enough based on her experience preparing for three marathons. I should check again tomorrow and track the number of spots still available.

I *should*…but I don't. Instead, I click the button.

When I choose "Minor, Under 18" from the "Who are you registering?" drop-down, it prompts me for Mom's name and email address. I comply with the former but type in my own email address.

Under the "Marathon" box, I pause on one of the bullets:

- Course Limit: 6:30 (14:53 per mile)

That should be nothing.

That would be nothing if I were still running every day and able to train as planned. That will probably be nothing as long as I can get twelve weeks of training in.

*But will running after chemo be the same as running before?*

I fill in all the fields as that nagging voice wonders whether my mother might, perhaps, have a point about waiting until next year.

*What if there is no next year?*

My heart beats faster as I add my debit card number. Footsteps I recognize as Charlie's sound in the hallway. Right as he knocks and opens the door, I hit "Submit" and toss my phone onto the nightstand, like I'm hiding evidence.

"You look perky."

*Perky* is better than *guilty*. "It's amazing what a good night's sleep can do."

"Well, then."

Like mirror images, we slide down until we're lying face-to-face on my twin bed, no space between us. Charlie rests his hand on my waist and moves it over the small of my back as he pulls me close. I squeeze his shoulder.

Kissing is an excellent distraction.

That is, until Charlie threads his fingers through my hair and tugs. I jolt back.

"What?" he asks. "Too hard?"

*No, no, no.* I want to stay distracted. I shake my head and kiss him again, but as soon as his hand goes back into my hair, I can't stop the tears from worming their way into the corners of my eyes. *Dammit.*

I sit up and cover my face with my hands, leaving poor Charlie alone with his confusion.

"Dell, what's wrong?" Alarm colors his voice, but his hands are gentle as he smooths down my hair.

"It's falling out," I manage to say.

Charlie wraps his arms around me, and after a few seconds, I settle into his embrace. As much fun as kissing is, I like this even more. When I'm nestled against him like this, I feel protected, safe, loved. It's because of who Charlie is, because of his heart, but I also love his body. Being enveloped by a skinny guy would feel different, and I'm happy I get a little lost in Charlie. I know the extra weight he carries bothers him, but I wouldn't change it —they're his teddy bear pounds.

Once my crying lets up, he looks at me intently. "Adele Marshall, you are beautiful."

My skin flushes, and I tip my face down, but Charlie puts a finger under my chin and lifts it up. Then he runs his thumb over my eyebrow. "You have soulful eyes—I could stare into them for hours." He slides his finger down the bridge of my nose. "Your nose—" He boops the end of it. "Your nose is sexy."

A giggle escapes through the tears, which makes him say,

"Your smile lights up a room. It is one of my very favorite sights on earth."

Tears stream down my cheeks again, but I let them fall and steady my gaze on my amazing boyfriend.

"Long hair, short hair, brown hair, no hair—I don't care. You will always be beautiful, and I will always love you."

He pulls me close, and I take a shuddery breath. This is the first time cancer has made me feel grateful.

# REVERSE MOHAWK

T he wait on Saturday is interminable—I want Laine to be here now!

She texts with an ETA when she leaves Notre Dame, and I check the clock a million times as she makes her way from Indiana to Ohio. As soon as her car pulls into the driveway, I race out the front door, with Mom, Dad, and Bean right behind me.

"Laine!" I cry.

"Oh my God, Dell!" She wraps me in a hug that's a little tighter than my ravaged body is prepared for, but I wouldn't trade it for the world.

Bean wedges herself between us, and Laine puts a hand on her head.

"My turn," Mom says once she can get in for a hug. "How was the drive?"

"Good."

Dad grabs Laine's bags. "I'll put these in your room."

Laine takes my hand. "How are you doing?"

"Will you have a tea party with me?" Bean interrupts.

"You bet," Laine says as we amble up the walkway.

Once we're inside, Dad comes downstairs. "Are you hungry? Can I make you some lunch?"

At the same time, Mom asks, "How were your exams?"

It's a good five minutes before all the questions get asked and answered and everyone stops talking at once. Dad makes a stack of gooey grilled cheese sandwiches, and we all sit at the table. He may cook fancy food in his restaurant, but he's just as skilled with casual dining—he makes the best grilled cheese in the world (at least, that's how I remember it, when food tasted good). Today, he makes mine on whole-grain bread, which sits better, and adds avocado, because I need to gain weight. I miss the regular version but am surprised when I eat my whole sandwich.

In between chewing, Laine gives us updates about school and classes and friends she's made.

"Any new guys…?" I give her a sly smile.

She raises an eyebrow at me. "No…not really."

"What does that mean?"

She shrugs and too quickly engages with Bean about Build-A-Bears.

Later that night, the two of us are alone on the couch. Dad brings Laine his homemade hot chocolate at her request and sets a second mug on the coffee table for me, even though I didn't ask for it. Its rich smell wafts under my nose as Mom nods at it, since I'm supposed to drink more and the calories from the milk will be good for me. "Don't stay up too late," she says.

After they disappear up the stairs, I prompt, "So, about those guys…"

"There's not much to tell." Laine curls her legs under her. "Just a few dates with a couple different people."

"Ooh. Do you want to see either of them again?"

"One was a dud. The other is all right. We had fun."

I toss a purple pillow at her. "You gotta give me more than that."

She throws the pillow back at me. "Fine. Matt is in my American Lit class, he asked me out, and we got coffee, then another time it was pizza."

I roll my eyes. "Tell me about his personality. Is he funny? What do you talk about? Do you see yourself having his babies?"

Laine laughs. "Who cares about a couple dates? We should be talking about you."

"I don't want to talk about me. In fact, I very much want to talk about *not* me. And I would love nothing more than to hear every trivial detail about these dates with a guy you may or may not spend the rest of your life with."

Smiling, Laine gives in. "As you wish. Matt is tall." Since Laine is five foot nine, this matters more to her than it does to me at five-four. "Brown hair, brown eyes. Good-looking."

"I need a picture."

She nods. "He is funny…maybe a little too funny, though."

"How can you be too funny?"

Laine looks thoughtful. "I don't know if he can be serious when he needs to be—life isn't all laughs."

*Don't I know it.*

Seeming to read my mind, my sister pats my knee and stands. "I brought you something." She runs upstairs and comes back a minute later with a beautifully wrapped box.

"What's this for?"

"Just some things I thought you might need."

I tear off the paper and lift the lid to find several smaller packages wrapped in pale blue tissue paper. The first reveals a tub of moisturizer.

"I read that people can get turned off by certain smells when they're going through chemo. This is unscented and natural."

All my Bath and Body Works products have definitely been neglected lately. "This is great. Thank you."

The next one leaves me confused.

"That goes around a seat belt so it doesn't hurt when it rests on your port," Laine explains.

My eyes get misty, so I don't say anything, just unwrap the last gift—an eyebrow kit to use if I lose that hair too.

I can't stop the tears, and Laine opens her arms for a hug. "I'm sorry. I didn't mean to upset you," she whispers.

"No," I choke out. "It's wonderful."

---

During my shower Monday morning, more and more strands of hair wrap themselves around my hands, and I almost opt to not rinse out the shampoo. I'm in tears again when I finish, my emotions heightened by the fact that my scalp hurts, like when I take my hair out of a high ponytail after having it up all day.

To cover the thin spots, Laine suggests using one of Bean's JoJo bows. I deem it an okay solution until I can get the wig, but as we're filing out of first period, Shannon Cooper bumps me. "Nice bow—welcome to the spoiled brat fan club."

I keep my head down and talk to as few people as possible the rest of the day.

That afternoon, Mom, Laine, and I visit a shop with beauty salon vibes. I guess that's the point, because when the woman who's helping us covers my head with my chosen wig—a brown that's darker than my natural color, shoulder length, with soft waves a bit gentler than Laine's curls—I feel beautiful.

We buy a few brightly colored silk scarves as well, and as we leave, Mom says, "You made some good choices."

Laine puts her arm around my shoulders. "And now you have options, so you can decide what you want when the time comes."

*When the time comes.* The time is here.

I suppose I could wait until so much hair falls out that bows won't hide it, or maybe I could wear the wig over my hair? But the obvious thing to do is…shave my head.

My heart beats faster just thinking about it.

*You can do this.* "Can we shave my head tonight?"

Mom and Laine look mildly surprised. "I'll help you." Laine reaches for my hand and holds it until we get to the van.

Throughout dinner, my stomach is in knots. Once everyone is finished, Laine gathers what we'll need while I change into my bathrobe. When I pull my hair out of the collar, another chunk comes out in my hand—the motivation I need to leave my room.

In the bathroom, a trash bag is laid out on the tile. A pair of scissors and Dad's electric shaver sit ominously on the counter.

Laine smiles at me. "You ready?"

"Ugh." I force my feet forward.

Laine stands behind me and lifts my hair, smoothing it between her fingers, then massages my shoulders.

"Just get it over with."

I close my eyes and listen as she picks up the scissors. The blades slice through my hair, which drops to the floor. Unsettled by the lightness and the air on my neck, I swallow hard. A minute later, a button clicks, and the *buzz* of the electric shaver hums in my ear. Nothing happens for a second, then I feel it—vibrations across the top of my scalp.

After the first pass, Laine pauses. "Want to see yourself with a reverse Mohawk?"

Unable to resist, I open my eyes. A strip of brown fuzz runs down my crown, bordered on either side by what is left of my hair.

She stifles a giggle, and after a second, I smile and laugh too. Before long, we're both laughing so hard we're crying…and then I'm just crying.

"Oh, Dee," Laine whispers and wraps me in her arms.

I bury my face in her shoulder and sob.

"I'm sorry," she says. "I was trying to keep things light, but I should have just gotten it done."

"No. It felt good to laugh. I just needed to cry too."

---

When I close my locker door at the end of the following day, my first day wearing the wig, Shannon Cooper's face appears behind it. "Come with me."

Before I can respond, she pulls me, somewhat forcefully, by the elbow and leads me down the hall.

"What are you doing?" I ask.

Without making eye contact, she says, "Buying you coffee."

Despite the fact that Charlie said I was sexy, I'm unbelievably self-conscious now. "Why?"

"Because I owe you an apology."

This is so unexpected and bizarre that I go along. I shoot Mom a text to let her know I'll be home late and hope Shannon will give me a ride since I'm missing the bus.

We reach Shannon's car, an old, probably-red-but-too-dirty-to-tell Honda Civic, and she tosses a pile of junk from the passenger seat into the back. Once we're moving, I wait for her to say something, but she turns up the music—Adele—and I marvel that we have similar tastes. Based on her overall demeanor, I expected something angrier.

I brace myself against the smell when we enter Starbucks (*nope, can't do coffee these days*) and order steamed milk with a single pump of raspberry syrup, knowing even that will probably be off-putting.

Once we're seated across from each other, Shannon tilts her head and stares at her cup, running her thumbs up and down the sides. I can't help but notice her long, straight, brown hair.

It's a lot like mine—like mine used to be—and I'm again surprised that we have something in common.

I've taken to studying the trail of earrings in her ear when she takes a deep breath and says, "My brother had cancer."

Dumbfounded, I stare at her. After a few seconds, she meets my gaze. "I'm really sorry about the hair comment. I didn't know then. If I had, I never would have said it."

I expected an apology for her general bitchiness—I did not expect this.

"Well?" she prompts. "Say something."

My mouth opens and closes a couple times before I force sound out. "I…I don't know what to say. I mean, that's terrible. Is he…okay?"

She fiddles with her cup again and shakes her head. "He died three years ago."

"Oh my God." I swallow hard. "Shannon, I'm so sorry."

"It was leukemia… He was nine when he got diagnosed… Fought it for two years before…"

"I'm sorry," I say again. I barely hear myself over the voice in my head obsessing over the proof that kids do die from cancer.

"I know we're not close, or friends even, but if you ever want to talk, that's cool." Shannon looks up. "My brother didn't have a lot of people who would listen, and it turns out that was something I was actually pretty good at."

I think about how little I've talked about this, *really* talked about it. I haven't said how scared I am. I haven't asked what will happen if the drugs don't work. I haven't voiced my growing terror that I won't make it through this, because I know no one has a response to that.

"Everyone keeps saying I'll be fine," I blurt out, "but what if they're wrong?"

Several seconds pass. "Everyone told Noah he would be fine too."

I expect this to send a chill through me, her open

acknowledgment that I could be dying. But it doesn't. I actually breathe a sigh of relief.

"Did you believe he would make it?"

"At first. My parents didn't share a lot of details, and they put on a brave face for both of us. Eventually, though, their words didn't fit what I was seeing." Her tone shifts. "They grasped at hope until the very end, always saying he would get better. But I knew he wouldn't. *He* knew he wouldn't."

My hands are clammy, and I push the hot beverage aside. "How did you get through it?"

"We talked—we imagined what heaven would be like. We said what we'd like to be reincarnated as. We agreed how much it sucked." Shannon takes a drink. "I didn't want him to pretend he wasn't dying or that he wasn't scared. He let my parents tell him what they wanted to believe, but I didn't want to do that to him. So, I was the one he didn't have to be strong for."

I nod like a human bobblehead and focus on the repetitive motion in order to hold it together. Shannon recognizes my struggle and stands. "You want to go?"

Another nod is all I can manage as I grab my jacket. As soon as I get in the car, I bury my face in my hands to hide my anguish. Once I can take a shaky breath, I wipe my eyes and apologize.

"Don't sweat it. It's not the first time I've seen someone cry." Shannon gives me a small smile.

Instead of starting the car, she sits with her hands on the wheel, staring out the window. "Was this a mistake?" She turns to me. "Did I make it worse?"

I shake my head firmly. "No. I'm grateful to have someone to talk about this with."

"Okay. Good." She puts the key in the ignition, but before she drives, she gives me her number.

"It won't be too hard for you, talking about your brother, about Noah?"

She shrugs. "It'll be hard. But it's hard when I don't talk about him too. And if talking will help you, even a little, it's the least I can do."

# PROMISE

Over the next week, my heart is yanked around like a yo-yo, with three notable changes in direction—down, up, down:

**1. Laine goes back to school.**

I want to tell her to stay, to skip her last six weeks of freshman year, to screw her academic scholarship. But I don't. I just say I'll miss her.

**2. Charlie is cool with me not wearing my wig.**

In my sadness over my sister, and because I've been inhumanly tired lately, I stay in bed, my bald head buried in the pillow, when Charlie says he's coming over.

He knocks on my door, then sits facing me. I watch as he takes it in, then caresses my scalp. "Your head has a lovely shape."

I smile, and he lies down, squeezing himself into the space beside me. The fleece of his sweatshirt is soft against my forearm.

"Thank you for sharing this with me." He's staring, but his expression doesn't show any of the reactions I feared it might—discomfort, embarrassment, disgust.

Just love.

**3. I undergo a scan to determine whether the treatment is working.**

As soon as Dr. Mastro walks in, I know it's bad news.

"Good morning." No handshakes, no shoulder pats. He immediately sits on the stool and rolls over to us, the wheels squeaking. "There's no easy way to say this. The cancer isn't responding."

Mom sucks in a little puff of air, and my heart speeds up.

"However, that doesn't mean it won't. Some people are late responders after additional cycles. We'll stick with this treatment for (*cancer not responding*), then do radiation and then we'll (*cancer not responding*). If that scan shows a less than optimal response, we have other (*cancer not responding*) that we can (*cancer not responding*)."

My breath comes in short bursts. I focus on the fact that just because the treatment isn't working yet doesn't mean it won't in time, but this is supposed to be a "good cancer," so why can't I beat it? What am I doing wrong?

When Dr. Mastro pauses, Mom glances at Dad. It's quick, but the look she gives him betrays her terror and panic and everything else I'm trying to tamp down in my own body.

My hands turn into a sweaty mess, then on top of hearing my heartbeat in my ears, I suddenly can't catch my breath. And, not to be outdone by my other organ systems, my vision swims. I still see the others in the room, but darkness crowds in from the periphery. My field of vision gets smaller and smaller, Dr. Mastro's voice fades away, and Mom's mouth makes a shape like, "Neil!" before I fall backward—

*It's quiet.*

*Everything in my body has slowed. My breathing is normal, and I am calm.*

*I'm surrounded by snow, blanketing the world. Snowflakes fall. I stand still and listen. They rustle ever so softly as they land.*

*The cold pricks my exposed skin, but it's not unpleasant. It makes my blood dance, my cheeks tingle. I breathe in the clean, fresh air, feel it in my nose and chest.*

*Snowflakes catch in my eyelashes, and I—*

My eyelids flutter open.

I'm on my back on the exam table. Mom, Dad, and Dr. Mastro hover over me. As I struggle to sit up, the paper crinkling beneath me, Dad supports my elbow while Mom entwines her fingers through mine.

A nurse steps forward and offers me a cup of juice. I take a sip, then hand it back—my stomach and I aren't on the best terms today.

I wipe my palms on my thighs as Dr. Mastro squeezes my shoulder. "Don't worry. This isn't terribly uncommon in times of stress. I expect it's an isolated incident."

He leans closer, and I stare at the brown skin between his eyebrows to avoid the intense gaze he's directing at me.

"While this isn't the result we were hoping for, we're still doing what we believe gives you the best chance for a cure, okay?"

It's a little patronizing, but I'm tired, so I nod.

---

Once I've had my fill of Mom, Dad, and Charlie reassuring me (*and themselves?*) that this isn't the end of the world, I text Shannon and invite her over.

She walks around my room, stopping in front of the bulletin board and lifting one of my medals. "You run track?"

"Cross-country. How about you—any sports or anything?"

"Nah. Not really a 'team player.'" She uses air quotes, and I smile.

Not shy about examining my wardrobe, she pulls a hanger from the closet. "When did you think this was a good idea?"

"They were popular for a while," I say to defend the overalls.

"Not in our lifetime." Next, she holds up a mauve, lacy dress. "Now, this I like."

"Me too." It's my favorite piece of clothing, mostly because it reminds me of Charlie and homecoming sophomore year—the first time he told me he loved me.

Once she's done scrutinizing my stuff, Shannon sits in the desk chair and looks at me expectantly.

"I got some not great news yesterday," I say and tell her about the scan.

"I'm sorry."

"Thanks. Everybody—the doctor and my family and boyfriend—is still pretty hopeful…"

*Maybe too hopeful.* I asked Charlie what will happen if this regimen doesn't work, if the next scan shows the cancer still isn't responding. He wouldn't entertain the thought, saying firmly, "It will. You have to believe that."

And when I posed the same question to Mom, she locked eyes with me and said, "Something will. You're strong, we're fortunate enough to have access to one of the best hospitals in the country, and I trust our care team. They're going to find something that works."

So, now I ask Shannon, "But they thought this treatment would work sooner and they were wrong—what if they're wrong again?"

Shannon leans forward and rests her elbows on her knees. "I'm sure they're scared shitless they'll be wrong. And they have to know you're scared too. I don't know why people are so afraid to talk about that fear."

"Was it like that with your brother?"

"A hundred percent. My mom was positive each new treatment was 'the one.' Forget the fact that the last three had failed, this one, *this one* was going to work, she just knew it." Shannon practically spits out the last couple words.

It takes her a moment to come back from the memory. When she does, her eyes are softer. "They *want* it to work, for you and for them. Maybe it will, maybe it won't—and they should be able to talk about that—but it's not wrong to hope."

---

The only traveling I do during spring break is to the hospital for my third round of infusions. It rains most of the week, which lessens the sting of living in a chemo chair or my bed, but I still wish I were doing something fun, even just going with Bean to the zoo.

A week after chemo, I wake up one night drenched in sweat and burning up. I know I have a fever, the thing Dr. Mastro said to be vigilant about. As soon as Mom touches my forehead, she says, "Get dressed. We're going to the emergency room."

Hours later, I'm in a hospital room and getting antibiotics through an IV in my arm to treat this neutropenic fever—a fever with low white blood cells, which makes it harder for my body to fight off infection. I sleep for what remains of the night and on and off throughout the following day.

After one dozing session, I open my eyes and find a basket with a handle wrapped in purple satin ribbon on the table near the bed. "What's that?"

Mom offers it to me. "Cards from school."

I settle the basket at my side and lift out the first note, from Jeanie Sammons, a girl I've known since elementary school: *I'm praying for you, Dell.*

The next reads, *Cancer sucks. But you're tough. Kick its ass. — Chris Corrigan*

*Everyone here is so sorry for you, honey. Hang in there. —Mrs. Davis, Mr. Melton, and the front office staff*

I get choked up as I read through the stack.

*I'm not sure what to write... I don't know you well, Adele, but I'm truly sorry you're going through this. My heart goes out to you. —Samantha Wilkins*

*You're a fighter, Dell. You'll beat this. —Meghan Dilly*

Everyone on the cross-country team signed a card. I study it to see if Sheryl and Annie and the other girls I was running with before I was diagnosed wrote anything personal, but their messages are generic. I move on to the next card and focus on people's kind words.

*Don't tell the others, but you're one of my favorite students. Get well soon. —Mr. Landry*

*Feel better, Dell. I need my lab partner back! —Jenna Myers*

*You're a rock star, but I'm here anytime you don't want to be. —Shannon*

Tears spill down my cheeks, but I brush them aside and keep reading.

*Dear Adele: No young person should have to go through what you're experiencing. Please know you are in my thoughts and prayers daily. I hope you may have a speedy recovery and emerge from this challenge with grace and gratitude. —Mrs. Carolyn Evans*

So many beautiful and heartfelt notes, from teachers and students, people I know well and others I don't. I sniffle loudly, and Mom hands me a tissue.

---

I'm never alone. Charlie comes every day after school. Mom stays the whole time minus one trip home to take a shower, and then Dad keeps me company. Mom brings Bean when she returns.

Bean pauses in the doorway.

"It's okay, Jill," Dad says. "Dell is getting medicine through a vein to make her better faster."

I make eye contact with my sister. "Hey, Jilly Bean. Will you come over here? You don't have to be afraid."

She stares straight ahead.

"Jill?" Mom tries.

Bean blinks and glances at Mom, then takes tiny, tentative steps in my direction. I scoot to one side to make room.

"You can sit next to me if you want. You won't hurt me. All the tubes are on this side, see?" I show her the tubes now coming out of my port, then extend my arm as an invitation.

She's so careful as she climbs into the bed that the stiff pillowcase hardly crinkles when she rests against it.

"I'm glad you came to visit. It's boring here."

"Why?" Her voice is barely audible.

"There's not much to do. I've slept a lot."

Silence fills the room.

"I have an idea," Mom says. "Jill, could you read a story to Dell?"

*Distraction—another Mom skill.* After Bean nods, Dad leaves to find a book she can read. We wait for a few minutes, then he returns with *Green Eggs and Ham.* Bean starts off slowly and quietly, but as she continues, she grows more animated, and I smile at Mom.

The next day, I'm cleared to go home.

In the afternoon, as I'm walking back from the bathroom, I pause outside Bean's room and watch her dress her stuffed tiger, Eliza, concentrating as she pushes a purple fuzzy slipper onto each foot.

"Do you want to play?" she asks.

I settle myself on the floor, pick up Hannah, the pink bear, and smooth her satin skirt, then reach for a sequined headband. Meanwhile, Bean gets Eliza into her pajama top.

"Your birthday is coming up. What do you want?"

Although I expect Bean to launch into the laundry list of Build-A-Bear clothes and accessories she's been eyeing since Christmas, she doesn't. "I don't know."

I raise my eyebrows at her, but she's too busy digging

through clothes to notice. "You probably have all the coolest stuff already." I open a ruffled purse and place a mirror and makeup case inside, then hold up the bear. "Why is Hannah so fancy?"

"She was going to a party." Bean doesn't elaborate.

"*Was?* Is she not going anymore?"

Bean shakes her head. "She can't."

I set the bear in my lap. "Why not?"

"She has to visit Eliza." In addition to pink Hello Kitty pajamas, the tiger is now wearing a white hooded bathrobe. "She's sick." Bean hugs Eliza to her chest, then tucks her into bed.

Despite my discomfort with more sickness, I follow with the bear. "Hannah will take care of her." With her paw, I stroke Eliza's forehead.

Bean shivers beside me. "No," she whispers. "She's dying."

My heart nearly stops. When I turn to her, she bursts into tears, and I pull her close.

"I don't want you to die!" she sobs, her face pressed against me.

Several seconds pass before I can breathe. I clutch her even harder. "I'm not going to die, Bean—I'm not."

She looks up at me, her eyes glassy, her cheeks wet. "Do you promise?"

The emptiness that floods my body is worse than the most painful hunger I've ever experienced. In the seconds before I answer, I decide if I would rather fill my sister with fear instead of hope or make a promise I might not be able to keep.

I squeeze Bean and stare over the top of her head so I don't have to meet her eyes when I say, "I promise."

# WIDE-ANGLE LENS

The next time Laine calls, she says, "I got pictures."

It takes me a second to understand what she's talking about. Then I remember the guy, Matt, and my chest tightens. In the three weeks she's been gone, I haven't asked about him once.

My phone buzzes repeatedly as several pictures come through. The first shows a guy in a baseball cap, then a selfie of the two of them together, and one of him in her dorm room.

"Back to your place, huh?"

"We were just hanging out."

I shift positions in bed to alleviate the pain in my back. "How many dates have you been on now?"

"We spend most of our free time together."

"Sounds intense." The edge to my voice surprises me. I don't begrudge Laine's newfound romance, I don't. It's just, I don't know…I guess it's hard for me to relate to her new relationship energy when all I can focus on most days is my health, or lack thereof. "Is he still funny all the time?"

"He can be serious." She pauses. "I told him about you, and he was very sympathetic."

"Oh, well, good. I'm glad me having cancer helped you figure out if the guy you like can stop telling jokes."

I open my eyes wide, and from the silence on the other end, it's clear Laine is as shocked as I am.

"Dell, I am so sorry, that's not at all what I meant."

My cheeks burn from shame, and I shake my head. "No, I'm sorry. That was a terrible thing to say."

"But I should be more sensitive. You decide who gets to know what you're going through, not me."

"No, really, it's part of your life too. I'm glad he was nice about it. I don't know why I said that…" My voice trails off, and neither of us says anything else until we end the call.

———

While I'm recovering from the fourth round of chemo, Charlie texts that he misses me, and I agree when he asks if he can come over after school.

I regret it as soon he sits on my bed, the bounce from his weight making my stomach gurgle ominously. He talks to me, but my brain can't focus on anything he's saying. The effects of the steroid are wearing off, and I haven't been sleeping well.

"I'm sorry," I interrupt. "I'm really tired."

"Okay. You rest, and I'll keep you company." He puts his hand on my side, and I close my eyes and quickly drift off.

*Click.*

When I realize what woke me, I glare at Charlie sitting in my desk chair. "What are you doing?" The nausea is strong enough now that I glance at my nightstand to make sure the puke pot is there. I can barely lift my head.

"You looked so peaceful when you were sleeping."

Heat bubbles up within me as Charlie returns to the bed. I clench my teeth as he clicks through his pictures, then turns the camera to me.

I stare at the picture. Sure, from the side, with the blanket tucked under my chin, I look downright *serene*.

"Why do you do that?" I demand.

"Do what?"

"Hide behind your camera."

His jaw tightens.

"It lets you see 'peaceful' when you know I feel like shit. It filters out the things you don't want to see."

"That's not fair, Dell. I see the unpleasant things too."

Charlie picks up his camera again, but I practically yell, "Don't."

His mouth is a thin line, but I keep talking. "If you see anything *except* unpleasant things, you're not seeing the truth."

Several seconds pass before he speaks. "I know it seems that way right now. You're tired, I get it."

"Do you?" With the strength the anger is giving me, I sit up and face him. "I don't feel peaceful. I don't feel strong or brave or even human half the time. There's nothing good here, and you shouldn't pretend it's anything other than hell. So...no more pictures."

Charlie fidgets, brushing the curls out of his eyes. "I'm sorry. I'll ask before I take them." He sets the camera on my nightstand, like that's supposed to reassure me.

"No. No more, not until this is over, one way or the other."

He winces. "Don't talk like that. Why don't you rest again, maybe that will help."

A wave of heat rises up my body. "Clearly, this camera is a crutch. Maybe you're not as strong as I thought, if dealing with me without it to hide behind upsets you this much."

The hurt in his eyes tells me I've gone too far, but I don't apologize.

"You know I don't feel like I have to 'deal with' you," he says. "And you know that's not what the camera is about. You don't mean any of this."

"Yes, I do—knowing I might die makes me not afraid to say it."

Charlie swallows hard. "Dell, please stop."

"Why? Am I making it too hard for you to find something good in this?"

He gets up without looking at me. "I'm going to go."

"I'm sorry this is too hard to face without a wide-angle lens to give you distance," I shout after him as he walks down the hall.

I wait, listening. My pulse clogs my ears. I labor to swing my feet over the side of the bed, grip the nightstand to pull myself up, and shuffle to the door. The hallway is empty.

The price I pay for my anger-induced burst of adrenaline is steep. Sapped of every ounce of energy, I collapse onto my bed, face down on the pillow to muffle my sobs.

My phone buzzes, and I know it's a text from him. Probably saying the things he couldn't say to my face—that I'm hurtful and vindictive and petty. That I'm such a horrible person, I maybe deserve to have cancer. That he can't imagine how he ever found anything beautiful in me.

I grope for my phone to get it over with. After I read what he wrote, I fling the phone on the bed, reach for my vomit pot, and try to expel all the ugliness inside me, knowing full well I can't throw it up.

> I love you. I know you're hurting. I'm sorry I made it worse.

The rest of the day passes in a blur. Mom brings me soup— Dad's chicken and dumpling—but I eat only a few spoonfuls. If I cry long enough, I fall into a fitful sleep, but am never rested when I wake, and returning to consciousness brings back memories of the fight. I shouldn't call it a fight. I don't know a word for when you yell at your boyfriend for something you have no right to be mad about and he says he loves you anyway.

At some point, I'm out of tears and settle into a sleep that is blissfully long. When I open my eyes, I notice something that breaks my heart: Charlie's camera. He never forgets it.

I turn it on and hold it in my lap as I steel myself for the pictures. I click to the beginning, one of me in the hospital getting my third round of chemo infusions. Since it was spring break, Charlie came along.

*Do I really want to look?*

Yes—I want to see what Charlie sees, because his way of viewing the world is far preferable to mine right now.

I linger on a picture of me in the chair. My eyes are closed as the IV bag drips medicine into my veins. But I'm not the focus of the photo—behind me, my favorite nurse, Theresa, and Mom are hugging.

A few pictures later, the corners of my mouth turn up into a hint of a smile. Theresa is bent close to my ear, and I stare straight at the camera as she tells me all the nurses are in love with Charlie.

Tension fills my body at the next series—at home later that week, when the nausea came on. The pain is clear, but there's something else too. Resignation? Determination?

Like always, Charlie captured the whole truth, and it's the reminder I need. Yes, chemo sucks. Yes, I would give just about anything to not have cancer. And yes, I do feel terrible far more often than I would like. But every now and then, a good moment appears in between the bad ones. I'm grateful for the people who are the bright spots in this dark situation. And I'm proud of myself for doing what I have to do to beat this.

I pick up my phone and text Charlie.

I'm really sorry. I have your camera. Come by whenever you want.

A half hour later, he stands in my doorway. I hold out the camera. "I shouldn't have tried to take photography from you. I'm sorry." There's so much more I should say to make up for my awful words, but Charlie speaks first.

"It's okay. I know this isn't easy." He sits beside me and strokes my hand with his thumb. "I'm sorry too—I'll be more sensitive."

I pull on his hand so he lies down next to me, then turn so my back is against him. He drapes his arm over me, and his breath warms my neck.

*If we'd had this "fight" about something else, before I had cancer, would Charlie have been so forgiving?*

Cancer is the trump card—I'm going to win every time. I like winning, so this should be a good thing. But I'm not a cheater. I only want wins I deserve, and knowing I'm going to win whether I deserve to or not reminds me how much this disease has stolen from me.

As I'm getting ready for school one morning the following week, I slip a long necklace over my head. When I flip the hair of my wig off my shoulder, my fingers brush against my neck— and I freeze.

*That lump was not here before.*

A shiver ripples through my body. I sit on my bed and bend forward, trying to slow my breathing. The world is closing in again. Because I know what this means—the treatment isn't working. The extra cycles aren't making a difference, and the disease is spreading. I take air in through my nose and exhale through my mouth as tears pool at the corners of my eyes.

*How can everything I've been through not be enough?*

Chemo has wrecked my body, destroying everything from my hair to my stomach to my energy, taste buds, and sense of smell. And even with all that, the cancer cells are like, *What else you got? Seriously?*

Logically, I know life isn't fair. But witnessing it up close, living it, hurts in such a visceral way that it causes actual stomach cramps.

My mind swirls—cycling through *This is the end* doom thinking and an occasional positive message that *There are plenty of other treatment options*. I know this is true, and I want to be comforted by this fact, but it's hard to ignore the tiny voice deep inside me that's so certain as it whispers, *The treatment they'll give you after this won't work either. Nothing will work—and you are going to die.*

# NEW GOALS

Once I'm confident I won't pass out, I sink to the floor, lean against my bed, and stare at the photograph hanging above the door.

Charlie took it, of course. The first race I won. Three-quarters of the way through, I didn't expect to have as much energy as I did, so I pushed myself even harder. When I came around a bend, I saw the finish, but I was neck and neck with two other runners. I gave it everything I had and full-out sprinted the rest of the way to clock in as the fastest girl.

I love running, always have—driving myself to be better, to go faster, to rise to the challenge.

I've dreamt of my first marathon for years. Imagined myself running the Boston Marathon. Three hours and thirty minutes—that's the time I would need to qualify. That was the number to shoot for.

*Was.*

I may never get there now.

The rims of my eyelids fill until the tears spill over the edges.

And what about graduation? College? Cancer was supposed

to be a detour, not a dead end. But now, am I going to miss those things? I'm afraid of missing so many things.

The tears fall harder, and I hiccup. An image of Bean walking down the aisle pops into my head—my family is there, celebrating without me.

I won't have my own wedding. Or kids. And I won't know Laine's kids. I would have been a kick-ass aunt.

I want a dog. I assumed I would get one after I moved out on my own. *Goodbye, Dog.*

I'm crying so hard I can barely breathe over something that doesn't even exist. There is no dog. But there could have been. This can't be it. Seventeen years is all I get? I have too much left to do.

Mom knocks. "You almost ready?" When she peeks in, her face transforms into concern, and she rushes to my side.

As she kneels in front of me, I sob, "I found a lump."

"What? Where?" My mother is generally pretty unflappable, but she can't hide her panic at these medical curveballs—I saw it in her eyes when we found out the first two cycles didn't work, and I see it in them now.

I point to the lump, and she tenderly runs her fingers over it. "Okay." Her voice wavers. "Let me call the hospital. I'll ask if Dr. Mastro wants to do the next scan sooner. If the cancer still isn't responding, he might want to start you on something else."

Solving problems. Moving forward. That's Mom's MO. Not a bad way to be. But cancer isn't like other challenges to be tackled. It's not just a matter of how to come at it—it's also a question of whether it's beatable. Unlike struggling in physics, where working with a tutor was an easy solution, or qualifying for the Boston Marathon, where if I didn't make it, I could try again another year, cancer may not respond to any treatment. We can cycle through one after another, but at some point, we'll run out of options, or time.

"What if that doesn't work?" I study Mom's expression to

gauge how much she's permitted this possibility to exist in her mind.

Her forehead creases in worry, but she says, "Then we'll go to the next treatment."

"What if nothing works?" I press. "I know we have other options, but shouldn't we have a plan C—or D or E or F—too?" When Mom tilts her head, ready to shut down this line of thinking, I continue, "As much as chemo sucks, it'll be worth it if it makes me better, but if I go through all this for nothing?" My voice catches. "Being cured can't be the only goal." My face scrunches, and several seconds pass before I can speak. "I don't want to feel like I've failed," I squeak.

Mom's eyes fill with tears. "You're not failing." She wraps her arms around me. "All we can do is what the doctors recommend. Let's focus on the things that are in our power to help make you well. No matter what happens, that's all you can ask of yourself."

*Is it?* If I won't get better, I want to do *something* other than curse my fate and wait to die.

Before I can say this, Mom takes a deep breath, pulls back, and fixes me with her gaze. Determined. Resolute. "If the day comes when we have to talk about treatments not working, then we will. But today is not that day. I still have hope. I want you to have it too."

Since sharing bad news is draining, I wait until after school to tell Charlie.

It's a nice day—April appears to have met its rain quota, and the last week of the month is sunny and warm. The weather makes it easy to convince Charlie to take a walk, which allows me to take in the surroundings, instead of the disappointment and fear in his eyes.

After I've gotten the worst of the news out of the way, I conclude by saying, "Dr. Mastro wants me to finish the rest of the chemo cycles and get radiation before doing another scan."

In my periphery, Charlie nods. "Then he must still be confident this regimen will work."

"I suppose so." *It still could work*, I tell myself. But it's hollow.

With running, I've tried various mental techniques—visualizing myself crossing the finish line first and repeating things like *I have more in the tank* and *You're going to win this*. Occasionally they helped, but more often, these tricks didn't lead to a win and made me more upset about losing.

Maybe this treatment, or another, will work. But telling myself it will is an empty promise. I need something more certain.

"What if no treatment works?" I ask, then watch a sparrow land in a nearby tree. I inhale and draw in a rich, floral scent.

"Something will." There's no crack in Charlie's armor, at least not that he's letting me see. "We're lucky Hodgkin's lymphoma has so many options. Some cancers don't."

I shake my head, refusing to hide from reality. "What if?"

Charlie runs a hand through his hair, the curls falling right back over his forehead. "Don't think like that. You have to believe you'll get better."

*Am I wrong to pull his head out of the sand?* Maybe he's happier with it buried. But I need him. I can't deal with this on my own.

"Go with me for a minute. Let's say the unlikely thing happens and the cancer doesn't respond to any treatment."

Charlie starts to protest, but I put up a hand. "Please. I need you to listen."

His scowl tells me he's not happy, but he lets me speak.

"If, somehow, that happens, I will have spent the last however many months, or years, or whatever, of my life being miserable from chemo, not getting rid of the cancer, and wasting the time I had by not doing, I don't know, *something*."

"Like what?" Charlie's eyebrows knit together, but at least he's not arguing.

"I'm not sure. But if I only have a little time left—*if*—I want to make the most of it."

"How?" He stops walking. "If we're being honest here—" His emphasis on *honest* stings like criticism. "—how much will you actually be up for doing? Treatment wipes you out."

"The second half of the cycle isn't so bad…"

"You just said chemo makes you miserable. I know it does— I've been there when you feel like shit." Charlie takes my hand. "Doesn't it make more sense to focus on getting better and then do the things you want once you can enjoy them?"

I sigh. "You're missing the point."

"What is the point?"

While I choose my words, I turn my head up to the late-afternoon sun and bask in the breeze as it blows across my face. "That maybe beating cancer isn't the only goal."

He looks at me incredulously. "What else would be the goal?"

"Living my life!" My voice rises, and I pull my hand from Charlie's grasp. "Knowing there's still one more cycle of treatment is bad enough. And now I might need more. I'm tired of feeling terrible. I'm tired of everything revolving around infusion appointments and managing side effects and scans. I'm tired of deciding what to eat based on what's high in calories and won't make me vomit. I'm tired of cancer being in control."

Charlie's expression softens. "I'm sorry, Dell." His tone is sincere, and his sympathy tempers my frustration. As some of the tension leaves my body, I lean forward and let him wrap his arms around me.

Later that night, I text Shannon.

I might be dying.

Like, right now?

I'm not sure if she meant to be funny, but I crack a small smile.

No.

Whew. What's going on?

I explain about the lump, that I know it means the cancer is spreading, that the treatment isn't working, that maybe nothing will.

That blows.

Before I can send another message, she calls. "Figured it would be easier to talk than type. Where's your head at?"

I'm grateful for the question, the permission to feel what I feel. "Pissed. It wasn't supposed to be like this."

Shannon is quiet for several seconds, and I'm not sure if she's waiting in case I want to say more or if she's figuring out how to respond.

"It's a dangerous game, thinking about how things are supposed to be." Given that her voice is gentle, I know she's only saying it to protect me, but that doesn't stop anger from bubbling up inside.

"You're telling me you don't have thoughts about how Noah's life was supposed to go?" Maybe I'm overstepping, but Shannon of all people should know better than to judge my feelings.

"Oh, I do—a hundred percent." After a second, she adds, "But dwelling on it is pretty soul crushing."

Neither of us says anything. Maybe we should have stuck to texting.

Finally, I ask, "So, what do I do instead?"

I wait forever before she replies. All that time to gather her thoughts ought to produce some pearls of wisdom, but all she offers is, "I wish I knew."

---

When my alarm for school goes off in the morning, I don't get up. *Why bother?*

If cancer is going to beat me, acing a calc test won't soften the blow. I was kidding myself to think anything could make up for the time I'll lose.

So I finish another series on Netflix—who cares?

Or I read a few more books—so what?

I'm not going to run a trail at Yellowstone or have a destination wedding before cancer takes me out. If I had a few years, maybe. But if my disease is what's called primary refractory (an ill-advised rabbit hole I went down last night), the odds aren't in my favor.

When Mom checks to make sure I'm almost ready and finds me still in bed, I attempt to convince her to let me stay home without making her worry. "I'm really tired," I explain. Since this can mean a lot of things, I quickly add, "Normal tired—I didn't sleep well."

Mom stares at me a moment longer, indecision on her face. "Should I call the doctor?"

I shake my head. "Really, I'm okay. Just not up for school."

One perk of having cancer is that this explanation is enough for her to agree to a day at home. "Let me know if you need anything," she says before leaving.

After fifteen minutes of staring at the ceiling and tracing the pattern stamped on the drywall, I wonder how I'm going to fill the hours. It's hard to find the motivation for anything when everything seems pointless.

I end up searching "sad songs" on Spotify so at least there's something to fill the silence while I wallow.

Mom brings me toast, which I set on my nightstand once the door closes. When she knocks again ten minutes later, I sit up and take a quick bite to avoid a lecture about not eating. But it isn't my mother who appears.

"What are you doing here?" I ask as Shannon lets herself in.

She pulls my desk chair close to the bed and tucks a strand of hair behind her ear, which reveals a line of studs and hoops. "When you didn't show at school, I thought you might need to talk."

Damn if my eyes don't well up. "You didn't have to skip. We could have talked this afternoon."

"That's a lot of hours to cope on your own."

I wipe away a tear that escapes, leaving my cheek damp. "Thanks."

Shannon nods. "I'm sorry about yesterday. You were searching for answers, and I was no help." She pauses and shifts her gaze to the white dandelion puff balls stitched into my lavender bedspread. "I still don't know what to say, but I'm sorry I didn't come up with something."

"You don't have to apologize." I mean it, but now we're right back where we started.

After a minute, Shannon says, "Cancer fucking sucks."

I give a little exhale laugh. "It really does." This admission lightens my mood. I reach over and pick up the toast, even though I'm sure it's cold and soggy now. "You know what I wish?" I ask before taking a bite.

Shannon raises her eyebrows, a nonverbal *What?*

Once I swallow, I say, "That I knew for sure." At Shannon's questioning expression, I clarify. "Whether any treatment would work. It would be easier to put up with all the crap if I knew the cancer would respond eventually. And if I knew it wouldn't, then I could skip the torture and 'live each day like it might be my last,' because, you know, it might."

"What would you do then?" Shannon leans forward and rests her elbows on her knees.

"If I knew I only had a few months or something to live?"

"Yeah. Realistically, knowing you're sick and you don't have unlimited cash, what would you do during those last few months?"

"Oh. I guess I've only thought about it as a hypothetical. Not in a serious, make-a-list kind of way."

"So, think about it that way." The uptick in Shannon's energy is palpable and contagious.

I sit up straighter. "You mean, make a literal list? Like, a bucket list?"

"Why not? Maybe you only do some of the things on it, but doing some is better than doing none. And maybe you end up being cured and wouldn't have needed the list, but if you're doing things that are important to you, how can that be a bad thing? Win-win."

For the first time since I felt the lump, I smile.

Shannon can tell I'm inspired, so she leaves me to my thoughts and the notebook and pen I ask her to grab from my desk.

The first ideas that bounce around my head are probably too ambitious—run a marathon, see the ocean. I cast about for something more achievable—I've always thought it would be romantic to kiss in the rain. But is that big enough?

I'm not willing to give up on the marathon yet. I write it down, but I also write, *Run one more race.*

Although it's kind of trivial, I would love for my taste buds and stomach to go back to normal long enough to enjoy a few favorite foods again: my dad's deep-dish blueberry pie with a crust so flaky it's like puff pastry; breakfast tacos from my favorite restaurant downtown, with their house-made chorizo and the Mexican street corn served on the side; and a white chocolate mocha—I miss coffee.

Oh, and goat yoga. I want to do goat yoga.

And visit Laine at Notre Dame. She has a little more than a week left in the semester; maybe I could squeeze in a trip. Doubts about the logistics creep in, but I push them aside and keep writing.

My heart flutters when my mind drifts to Charlie. I want us to have sex for the first time. We've talked about it. I wasn't quite ready, then I got sick. But he's been so amazing these past several months—going through this with him has made me love him even more, in a way that's deeper than I ever imagined.

He comes over after school, and when he appears in my doorway, I grin at him and pat the spot beside me on the bed.

As he lowers himself so we're face-to-face, he looks doleful. I temper my change in mood before I tell him about the list. I don't want to imply I'm giving up on treatment.

"How are you feeling?" he asks.

"A little better." I thread my fingers through his.

"I'm glad. I was worried about you. I thought maybe you didn't come to school because you were stressed about the lump."

"I was. But I did a lot of thinking today."

"About?"

"Well, we can't know whether this treatment will work." I head off Charlie's clouding expression by adding, "I understand it might. And if it doesn't, maybe the next one will, or the one after that. But we can't see the future, so we can't be sure. Right?"

Hesitantly, Charlie nods, and I continue. "Since we can't know whether I'll be cured, I want to focus on treatment, of course, but also on filling my time with things that make me happy."

"Okay…" It's clear by his tone that he's far from on board, but what kind of boyfriend would argue against my happiness? "I always want you to be happy. But we're not talking about skydiving or swimming with sharks, are we?"

*No, not those specifically.* "You think swimming with sharks would make me happy?"

Charlie cracks a smile, but his face turns serious again a second later. "You know what I mean. I want to make sure you're careful, that you're not reckless."

*He only wants what's best for me, because he loves me*, I remind myself. But that word, *reckless*, suggests he doesn't trust me. Shouldn't I have some say in what's best for me?

The things on the list aren't reckless. Most things, anyway. Would Charlie consider the marathon to be risky? What about zip-lining? If those are the most daring activities, I see no issue.

"What's the opposite of reckless?" I ask. "My pursuit of happiness will be cautious, sensible, downright responsible."

"You have a way with words."

"I don't get *As* in English for nothing." I sandwich our entwined hands between our chests. "Holding your hand makes me happy, and that's not the least bit reckless." I press my lips to his, which are soft and warm. "Same with kissing you."

"Mm, well then, pursue happiness anytime you want."

# PART II

# BUCKET LIST

1. *Run a marathon*
2. *Run one more race*
3. *See the ocean*
4. *Kiss in the rain*
5. *Eat Dad's blueberry pie*
6. *Eat Katalina's breakfast tacos*
7. *Drink a white chocolate mocha*
8. *Goat yoga*
9. *Visit Laine at school*
10. *Have sex*
11. *Take senior pictures*
12. *Make a candle*
13. *Do a flip on a trampoline*
14. *Name a star*
15. *Stay up all night talking*
16. *Zip-line*
17. *Read the 100 Books to Read Before You Die*
18. *Sing karaoke*
19. *Watch a Roller Derby bout*
20. *Kiss at the top of the Ferris wheel*

# #18: SING KARAOKE

I don't sing in front of people. I've refused to let anyone hear my voice ever since second grade, when Katie Delminico paused "Let It Go" as we were mid-belt to tell me, "You don't sound good," then went about finishing the song while I stood there, stunned, and tried not to cry. But I like singing, and I'm tired of denying myself to please someone else.

A week after I make my list, Mom lets me go out with Shannon, but not without first establishing the ground rules. "Don't sit too close to other people." She stares at me, and I nod dramatically. Does she think I want to snuggle with a stranger?

"Don't push yourself—if you get tired, take a break. And be home by ten."

It's the last week of chemo cycle number four, the week before the next round of infusions. I usually feel my best at this point, and now that the anemia that was making me so tired is being treated, I'm downright peppy. Still, I nod again.

I agree to drink water and forgo fried foods (like I would be tempted). My foot taps as my mother reminds me to use hand sanitizer after I touch anything. "Mom!"

"Okay, okay." She pats my shoulder and smiles. "Have fun."

When Shannon and I walk into Barney's, this local burger joint that does karaoke on Wednesdays, my eyes are drawn to a stage in the back corner. A stool bathed in light is set in the middle, with a mic stand in front. Given the dim lighting throughout the rest of the place, the people singing will literally be in the spotlight. *And...cue the butterflies.*

Since Shannon has been here a handful of times, I follow her through the crowd to an empty high-top table. "Be right back," she says.

While she approaches the guy running karaoke, I people-watch. Judging by the waitstaff hustling to and from the bar, those over 21 are gearing up for their turn on the stage with a little liquid courage. I'm sure I would hate it, but I gaze longingly at an amber-colored beer as it passes. *Where is my courage supposed to come from?*

Shannon startles me by *plunk*ing a giant binder on the table. "The world is your oyster."

My nerves ratchet up further. *Why am I doing this, again?*

With a shaky hand, I turn the cover and scan the laminated pages.

A minute later, a guy's voice reverberates over the speakers. "Let's get this party started! First up, we have Trevor, singing 'Fight for Your Right.'"

*Here we go.*

We scoot our chairs so we're side by side—I feel the wooden legs scrape against the floor, but it's so loud, I don't hear them. This college-age dude, Trevor, mostly talks his way through the song, which strikes me as cheating, but people cheer him on. My insides unwind a tiny bit.

I lean closer to Shannon so I don't have to shout and ask, "How do you decide which song?"

"Don't just pick something you like. Think about how easy it is for you to sing—like, whether it's in your range."

I nod and keep perusing the options. After a couple more

songs, Shannon stands, the many bracelets she's wearing falling to her wrist. "You ready?"

My stomach is lead. "You go first."

She sidles up to the DJ booth and returns a minute later.

"What did you pick?"

"Adele."

"Love her—she has a great name," I joke.

Our attention is stolen by a forty-something guy who sings —no, *performs*—"Sexy and I Know It."

He's not exactly on a short list for sexiest man alive, but he's definitely in the running for funniest. The dance moves alone have the whole place cracking up and screaming. Shannon practically falls into me, she's laughing so hard. I wipe tears from my eyes, then put a hand on my stomach.

"Oh my God," she says when he finishes. "That was the best karaoke performance ever."

"Yes, but was he *sexy*?" I tease, and Shannon scrunches her face at me. "Okay," I continue, "you know what I like in my guy. What's your type?"

She sips her Coke, then plays with the straw wrapper, winding the paper around her finger.

"Come on. Point to some guy here—who do you think is cute?"

Now she stares at me but doesn't say anything.

"Wait, you don't have a boyfriend I don't know about, do you?"

"Hell no."

"Okay, then who? There's got to be someone here you find attractive. What about that guy?" The one I indicate wears a plaid button-down shirt, which does not strike me as her type, but I have to start somewhere.

"Pass."

"Him?" Jeans and a T-shirt, backward baseball cap.

She shakes her head.

"You're making me work for this. What about him?" Tattoos, blue spiked hair.

Her expression suggests my guesses are laughable.

"I give up. Show me someone you like."

A few seconds pass before she scans the room. Finally, she crooks her finger toward a table near the stage.

"Ew, he's, like, fifty."

She shakes her head and jabs her finger forward again. I lean closer to see from her vantage point. There are no other guys at that table, just a girl who—

*Oh.* "Her?"

Shannon raises an eyebrow, amused at my obliviousness.

"Okay, sure." I nod. "That's cool. She is cute." My cheeks flush as I take my foot out of my mouth. "I'm sorry."

"You shouldn't make assumptions about people, you know."

I can't tell if she's mad, until she adds, "JoJo," and grins. I guess now we're even for her "nice bow" comment.

A couple songs later, Shannon's name is called. "Good luck," I say, then yell after her, "Break a leg?" *What do you say for karaoke?*

Although I'm not singing, my hands are clammy as the music plays. I want her to not be terrible, because maybe then I can believe I won't be terrible.

She isn't terrible.

Shannon is the polar opposite of terrible. Like, so good that when I close my eyes, it's as if I'm actually listening to Adele sing "Rolling in the Deep" in this unimposing hole-in-the-wall in Ohio. Everybody around me clearly agrees, because when I scream, my voice is lost amid the cheers.

When Shannon returns to the table, I stare at her. She takes a drink and ignores my eyes boring into the side of her face.

"You didn't tell me you were *good.*"

She shrugs.

"I can't follow that."

"Of course you can. The key to karaoke isn't being good—it's being *entertaining*. Sometimes that means being good, but you can be bad as long as it's the kind of bad that's fun to watch. The worst is someone who's bad and shy about it. You have to *own* your badness."

Doubt must be showing on my face, because she continues. "Come on—'Sexy' was an awful singer, but he totally embraced it."

I tilt my head in concession. For emphasis, Shannon adds, "And the crowd Ate. It. Up," then taps the binder. "So, what's it gonna be?"

"Ugh...okay." I flip toward the back and drop my finger— "Love Story."

"You're a Swiftie?"

"Don't judge. I bonded with both my sisters over Taylor."

"Fine, but you can't do a ballad. Pick something upbeat— those are the crowd-pleasers. Sing 'Bad Blood' or 'Shake It Off.'"

My heart hammers as I go up to the front, take the pen in my sweaty hand, and write my name and "Shake It Off" on the sheet.

And then I wait.

Every time a song ends and the DJ comes on the speakers again, my whole chest cavity vibrates as I wait for the next person to be announced. My ears throb with the blood that's pounding through my veins. And each time some other name is called, my internal systems only semi-relax, because in three minutes, I'll go through this ordeal again.

When the DJ finally says my name, I want to throw up. I plead with my eyes for Shannon to take my place or remember her curfew is right this second or bend time so I can have done this without actually doing it.

"You got this," she says before giving me a little push toward the stage.

I tug my jeans up, then pull down on my peasant top and

take as deep a breath as I can. As I walk forward, Shannon hollers.

I'm afraid my legs might give out while climbing the steps, but I make it and sink onto the stool. I should adjust the mic, but being inaudible is probably a kindness I owe the other patrons, so I leave it alone.

The music cuts through the people-noise, and I stare at the screen. Words appear, the text white, and I wait for them to turn blue when it's time to sing. Thank God I don't have a heart condition, or this might be the end.

*Get it together, Dell. It's now or never.*

After the first couple lines, I tear my eyes from the monitor and look up. Buoyed by Shannon's encouraging expression, I stand on shaky legs and step closer to the mic. A few seconds later, she puts her hand flat in the air, palm up, and urges me to go bigger.

Right, okay. *What do I have to lose?*

I grab the mic and pace. When noise bursts from the audience, I sing louder. At the chorus, I plant myself center stage and channel all my energy into shaking my body to match the lyrics, to the apparent delight of everyone in the restaurant. The cheers give me such a rush that I bounce my way through the rest of the song, knowing it will wipe me out but not caring, because in this moment, I feel great. By the end, I'm sweaty and out of breath and exhilarated. A swell of approval washes over me as I rejoin Shannon.

She throws her arms around me. "You killed it!"

I grin as I take a long drink of water.

"What are you singing next?" she asks.

"Another song?"

"Hell yes, another song."

"What will you do?"

"Katy Perry."

I nudge her shoulder with mine. "'I Kissed a Girl'?"

Shannon side-eyes me. "Please—too cliché. I do a mean rendition of 'Roar.'"

"I thought before about singing 'Firework.'"

After she slaps the binder closed, she stands. "It's settled. We'll do a Katy Perry double feature."

While she adds our names to the list, I marvel over how good she is. "How are you not part of choir or drama club or something?" I ask when she returns.

"I told you—I don't like group activities."

"Okay, no performing. And no sports," I say, remembering our first conversation in my room. "So, what do you do?"

"I go to school, do homework. Sometimes." She shrugs.

"That's it?" Everyone I know is involved in some kind of extracurricular. One of my neighbors devotes her life to dance. An old friend from middle school volunteers with the Parks department. Charlie has photography.

"Do you knit?" I ask jokingly. (Eye roll from Shannon.) "Garden?" (Head tilt.) "Read?" (Noncommittal mouth twitch.) "Seriously, what do you spend your time doing?"

She pulls her phone from her pocket. "Have you heard of these?"

Now I roll my eyes. "You don't want to, like, challenge yourself with something?"

"You make it sound like mastering life hacks from TikTok isn't challenging. I'll have you know I've perfected the art of reheating pizza in a skillet." Before I can respond, she hops off her seat and heads for the bathroom.

In my relative solitude, I try to ignore the heaviness of my muscles and the fact that it's becoming difficult to sit comfortably in this chair. *My bed can wait.*

The DJ calls Shannon first, and she floors everyone with "Roar."

We pass each other as I take the stage. She leans in and asks, "Want a backup dancer?"

I smile gratefully for her understanding that it would be wise for me to move less this time around. But I can't help bouncing on the balls of my feet and pumping my fist in the air at the chorus. And, okay, jumping up and down during the last verse.

After I replace the mic, Shannon puts her arm around my shoulders for the walk back to our table. If she knows I'm leaning on her less out of friendly affection and more because I might collapse if I don't, she doesn't let on.

We leave, and once she parks in my driveway, I offer a deeply earnest "Thank you." She nods somberly, assuring me she knows everything I mean with those two little words.

# #9: VISIT LAINE AT SCHOOL

**B**efore first period starts on Friday, I lean toward Shannon and say, "I figured out what to do next."

"Hit me."

"Visit my sister at college."

Shannon squints at me, uncertain.

"She's a freshman at Notre Dame, and we talked about me visiting, but I got sick a couple months after she moved on campus. If I don't do it before this school year ends…it might never happen." I level my best puppy dog eyes at her.

"What did your parents say?"

"Well…they'll be on board if we tell them I'm spending the night at your house."

"So, we're lying now?" She leans back in her seat and spins the ring around her thumb.

"It's just that my mom will worry about me being too far from my doctor and the hospital, but it's barely four hours from here. We can go tomorrow and come home Sunday, easy. I'll pay for gas—and your food."

Shannon rubs her forehead.

"Come on," I plead, "you're the only one who would agree to this."

"You mean I'm the only person in your life who would approve of you making bad decisions." She narrows her eyes at me.

"No, you're the only one who understands that even though this might, possibly, not be the *best* decision for my body, it *is* a good decision for my heart."

The seconds tick by as Shannon silently holds my gaze. Finally, she tilts her head back and sighs. "Fine."

I move to hug her, but she puts up a finger. "You better not croak on my watch, because if you do, I'll hold a grudge until I die and kick your ass in the afterlife."

---

When Shannon picks me up, I wait while she moves a pile of paper and some textbooks so I can sit in the passenger seat. Before I get in, I raise my bag, and she answers my unspoken question: "Throw it on top of stuff."

Since the back seat is even worse, I set my bag on the floor. *Would I be this messy if I managed to save enough for a car?*

Still, I'm not complaining. Within minutes, we're on the freeway, on our way to visit my big sister at college. We can't get there soon enough.

I wish we had snacks. When I was little, before my grandparents died, we would drive to their house in Michigan every summer, and the highlight of the trip was going with Mom to the store beforehand and picking out candy and chips for the car ride. But food isn't exactly my friend these days.

"Did you and your family ever do road trips?" I ask.

Shannon turns the music down a notch. "Yeah, we used to rent a house in the Outer Banks."

"That's cool. I've never seen the ocean." And probably never will—despite it being number three on my bucket list.

"It's nice. Sand and sun and all that. I was happy chilling, but Noah loved the water. He and my dad would rent kayaks, and the last summer we went, he paddleboarded for the first time. He wanted to learn to windsurf, but..."

"No bucket list."

"No bucket list," she agrees.

"What else would have been on his?"

She doesn't answer right away. "There are two different lists, right? One, like yours, of things he could have done while he was sick if my parents had let him, and one of the big life things."

*The one I don't let myself think about.*

"He wanted to be a marine biologist. I'm sure a lot of kids say that, and he probably wouldn't have pursued it, but I don't know..." She stares ahead for several seconds. "The ocean made him so happy, maybe he would have."

I was leaning toward studying something in the humanities, maybe philosophy or literature, getting a PhD and becoming a college professor. *Was.*

"His dream was to swim with dolphins. We could have done that. Even though it's expensive, we could have afforded it. My parents kept saying, 'Maybe someday.'"

*Someday.*

A someday that never came for Noah. A someday that might not come for me.

Tears prick my eyes, and I crank up the volume on Katy Perry. Shannon takes the hint and sings along until I join in, then we both belt out the words as we make our way west.

Shortly after we cross the Ohio-Indiana border, Shannon pulls off for gas and a bathroom break. She grabs a Milky Way and hands it to me to buy for her. I get in line, then spot bags of sunflower seeds and pull one off the rack. It's a far cry from a candy bar, but it alleviates my snacking FOMO.

As we're returning to the car, Shannon slows to a stop and says, "Wow."

"What?"

She points to a sign on the road advertising the James Dean Museum 5 miles away.

"Who's James Dean?" I ask.

"He was an actor in the '50s, in that movie *Rebel Without a Cause?*"

I nod; I've heard of it.

"My great aunt idolized him." Shannon unlocks the car. "She was a teenager when he was popular, before he died—he died young, in a car accident." We get in, and she continues, "Her whole life, she was kind of obsessed with him. I remember she had these James Dean plates—like, we would go over for dinner and when you finished your meal, you'd be staring at this guy's face."

"That's...dedication." I can't tell from Shannon's tone what her relationship with her great aunt was like, so I'm careful with my word choice.

Shannon snorts. "That's one word for it. She was a kook, but cool. I always liked visiting her, probably because she was nothing like my mom. Aunt Shirley was a badass."

Fondness colors her voice. As we merge onto the freeway, I say, "Do you want to check it out—the museum?"

"It's out of the way."

"Not by much. We can stop if you want."

She shrugs like she could take it or leave it, but her indifference is unconvincing. "You're so obvious. Just say you want to go—you're allowed to want things, you know."

Her eyes don't leave the road, but the corners of her mouth turn up as she takes the next exit.

Fifteen minutes later, we pull up outside this red brick

building with a white porch and a bench next to the sidewalk. When we step inside, we're the only people other than a lone employee.

"Tell me more about your great aunt," I prompt as we walk around. *Shuffle* is more like it, since the room isn't very big and is crammed full of memorabilia. I would be self-conscious about a stranger listening to us, but our conversation is muffled by the James Dean movie clips playing in the background.

"Oh, well, she always rode a motorcycle," Shannon says as we take in the motorcycle standing before us. "She let me ride with her once. I never told my mom—she would have flipped."

On the other side of the motorcycle, black and white photographs line the wall. The guy loved his leather jacket. And cigarettes—a sign of the times, I guess.

"Shirley didn't take shit from anybody. Lived her life the way she wanted to, not the way everybody else thought she should. No kids, never married—she had the right idea."

I look up from a briefcase. "Do you mean that?"

Shannon keeps talking as if she didn't hear my question. "She never had a traditional job. She was a jazz singer and would play gigs in clubs. And a poet—had a couple books of poems published. For a while, she worked in a circus. Her last job was a feng shui consultant, whatever that means." An easy smile spreads across her face.

We pause in front of a *Rebel Without a Cause* script signed by a bunch of people to someone named Fae. "Your aunt sounds like a neat lady." I lean forward and squint to read an inscription: *Love your cottage cheese.* That, along with, *Hope we work together again. Keep the coffee warm.* And, *To Fae, a wonderful, wonderful person. Love ya,* signed by Natalie Wood, whose name I recognize from *Miracle on 34th Street.*

"She was," Shannon agrees. "Forget being a doctor or whatever—my goal is to be like her."

"You'll need a thing, like she had James Dean."

"Obviously."

"But what?"

"I don't know yet. I've got time to cultivate my eccentricity."

We stop in front of a toy bull and a plush tiger. "Can you imagine having your toys in a museum?" Shannon asks.

I picture my old stuffed rabbit Fuffers, my favorite childhood lovey. How weird would it be if, decades from now, people traveled across the country to see him?

"And your birth announcement?" I point out the card with James's name, date and time of birth, weight. It's next to a tiny sweater with an embroidered baby character with a pink face, blue shirt, and red pants.

Farther down, we find his high school diploma.

"Ew, and your report card? No way I want that on display." Shannon shudders comically.

After a full loop of the room, we've covered everything. Shannon pushes open the door, the bell at the top jingling its goodbye, and we step into the bright warmth of spring.

In the car, Shannon picks up her Milky Way, which has melted a little in the sun, pulls down the wrapper, and takes a bite. Chocolate sticks to her fingers, which she licks before grabbing a napkin from the center console to finish the job, then tossing the napkin on the floor in the back.

For the last hour of the drive, we play car games. I kick her ass at I Spy, 20 Questions, and the Picnic Game, in which we take turns saying what we brought to a picnic, starting with each letter of the alphabet and listing everything that came before. In the three times we play, Shannon can't get past *J*.

We're quiet once Notre Dame comes into view. It's clear why Laine fell in love with the campus. Originally, she was going to major in architecture, and even though she switched to accounting, she still gushes about the gothic style of the buildings, the stained-glass windows, and the Grotto, which is number one on my must-see list.

Once we park, I text Laine and ask what she's doing.

Studying.

Unfortunately, I don't know her room number, but I know her dorm is Cavanaugh Hall. That's where we wait.

You should take a break. Get some fresh air.

Why do you sound like Mom?

Just looking out for you.

After a minute goes by without me texting, Shannon says, "What's up?"

"I'm trying to convince her to leave her room."

"She isn't coming to meet you?" Our eyes lock, and immediately, Shannon knows. "Oh my God, Dell! You didn't tell her we were coming?"

"I wanted it to be a surprise."

Shannon shakes her head. "What if we got here and she was gone? That'd be a surprise, all right."

"Where would she go? I knew she'd be here."

"And if she was busy?"

"Then we would wait."

The crease in Shannon's forehead deepens as we stare at each other. In my peripheral vision, I see the door to the residence hall open, and a familiar figure steps outside. I break eye contact with Shannon and run toward Laine.

It takes several seconds for my presence to register. At first, she looks right through me. Even after she notices me, it's like her brain can't compute that it's me, here.

"Dell?"

I pull up short, refraining from smashing into her for a hug, because her face is so serious.

"What are you doing here?"

Since I'm a little winded from that brief sprint, I use the time it takes for me to catch my breath to temper my enthusiasm. "I wanted to visit you on campus, so…here I am."

Her brow furrows. "But the semester is almost over."

My eyes dart to Shannon, who doesn't say anything but whose expression is less than warm.

"I know, but—"

"And Mom was okay with this?"

I stare at my feet.

"Dee! What were you thinking?"

My sister's scold threatens to unleash tears. "It's fine, I've got Shannon." Not how I meant to do introductions, but when Laine looks at her, Shannon gives a half smile and puts up her hand in greeting.

I move closer to Laine and lower my voice. "We talked about this, me coming."

"Yeah, someday. Not out of the blue the weekend before finals, when I'll be home in seven days."

"But—" I'm near a whisper. "What if this is my only chance?"

Laine's scowl fades. She wraps her arms around me and holds me tight. "It won't be."

Her short-sleeve sweater brushes against my arms, the material soft on my skin. We stay in our embrace long enough that I worry it might be awkward for Shannon. Laine pulls back and finally smiles. "But since you're here…"

I throw my arms around her for a quick hug. "Thank you."

"For real, though, I do have to study."

"No problem. We can entertain ourselves for the afternoon —can we hang out tonight? Ooh, is there a party? I want to go to a college party!" I clap my hands together.

Laine laughs, then says, "I might know about a party."

We deposit our bags in Laine's room and meet her

roommate, who graciously offers to sleep at a friend's so I can use her bed, leaving the futon for Shannon. I toss my sweatshirt onto a chair—won't be needing that in here. I forgot this dorm doesn't have air-conditioning.

While Laine and Shannon get acquainted, I take in my sister's digs—the Christmas lights strung near the ceiling, festive even in May; the inspirational quotes on the wall, my favorites of which are *Say yes to new adventures* and *Let your dreams be bigger than your fears*; and of course her hydroponics setup, which is scaled back from home but has lettuce, her favorite thing to grow. This room is different, but it still says *Laine*, which makes me happy.

When she reminds us she has to study, we embark on a self-guided tour. The first stop is the student center, followed by the library (Shannon makes me take her picture with her arms raised in front of the "Touchdown Jesus" mural). Finally, we stop at the lakes on the edge of campus. It's a lot of walking, and I appreciate the pause as we gaze at the water.

"You okay?" Shannon studies me.

"Yep."

We spend the most time at the Grotto. Laine has described it to me several times, since it's her favorite spot on campus, but standing before it takes my breath away. It's not very big, but the stones are medieval and romantic and full of charm, and that's only the outside. The real showstopper is the hundreds of candles inside, flickering within the darkness of the cave.

The mood changes as we approach. Everyone is quiet. I watch one girl standing in front of the back wall of candles, her head bowed, her eyes closed, and I wonder what she's praying for.

Wordlessly, Shannon lights a candle. I do the same, then close my eyes and sort through my thoughts.

*I don't know what to pray for.*

Hope for a miracle flashes in my brain.

*For my cancer to be cured, if any prayer would be answered. But not all prayers are.*

My eyelids flutter open. Shannon stands next to me, her face still.

Did her parents pray for her brother to be cured? Did she?

*I don't want my prayers to go unanswered. It hurts too much. Fixating on what is supposed to happen isn't helpful, but shouldn't prayers to save a child's life count extra?*

As I close my eyes again, the tears that have been pooling spread wetness through my eyelashes.

*I know I may not be cured. If that happens, then I want the time I have left to mean something. Let me do as many of the things on my list as I can. Let me feel good enough for long enough to reclaim some control. Give me a win, even if it's not the big one.*

For several minutes, I stare at the candles, wiping away tears as they come. I sense other bodies nearby, but keep my eyes trained on the flames dancing in front of me. Before I leave, I offer one final *Please*.

Shannon stands outside the entrance. She looks up from her phone, and I don't comment on the fact that her eyes are red, since I'm sure mine are too.

I've hit my walking quota for the day. When we reach the fountain Laine calls Stonehenge, I sit on its retaining wall and let my body rest while the sun warms me after the coolness of the Grotto.

"My sister sent me a video of someone's dog playing in this fountain." I recall the image of furry joy, the golden retriever splashing and barking, thoroughly in love with life. "I laughed so hard I cried."

Shannon smiles and leans back on her hands. "This is the first campus I've toured. Not bad."

"Can you see yourself going here?"

"Don't know that I see myself going anywhere, but if I somehow found a way to pay for it, then sure."

"There are always scholarships."

"Not with my grades."

"Or financial aid."

"Maybe." Shannon, I'm learning, is a master of changing the subject. She does so now by saying, "I'm starving. There was food in the student center—I want Taco Bell."

Once Shannon digs into a Crunchwrap Supreme, I text Laine to ask how the studying is coming.

Give me one more hour.

Since I'm not up for more sightseeing, we camp out in a lounge space in the student center until Laine says she's done.

Shannon and I didn't bring party wear, so we rummage through Laine's closet. Despite our height difference, Laine and I are both slim, and a handful of her shirts could work. I pull out a few to try with my jeans.

The "back" to one of the shirts is nothing more than two strings that tie together. "You wear this?" I ask, slightly embarrassed by my grandmotherly prudishness. "This is a glorified bandana."

Laine swipes it from me. "Nobody asked you."

I hold up a black halter top and stare at it, debating whether I would fill it out enough to not show my bra. My sister is more, ahem, well-endowed than I am.

The last option is a teal, ruched, sleeveless shirt. I try it on.

"Ooh, yes," Laine says. "And I have the perfect necklace."

I sit on her bed, and as she fastens the clasp around my neck, I wonder if she notices the lump. I'm pretty sure it's bigger, but I push the thought from my mind.

This moment of stillness makes me realize how tired I am. But there's no way I'm bailing on the party. I just need to rest for a few more minutes without concerning Laine. I make a show of lounging on the bed and directing Shannon to model various clothing options.

She opts to stick with her own outfit—black ripped jeans with a black and white striped tank—but I convince her to dress it up with Laine's dangly silver earrings.

Once we're all ready, Laine enters Mom mode. "Here's the deal: we go early, we stay mellow, and we leave before everyone gets shit-faced."

As we follow Laine into the hallway, I practically giggle—I can't believe I'm going to a college party.

Upon first impression, the host house is significantly more subdued than in the movies, but most people haven't shown up yet. Laine leads us to the back door, which opens onto a fenced-in yard that's a bit livelier. Twinkle lights are strung across the patio, a group of people surround a keg in the corner, more people hold plastic cups while keeping a beach ball in the air, and a dog scampers underfoot, licking the grass where beer spills, its wheaty aroma permeating the night.

I'm glad we got here early and some chairs are still open. Laine directs me to one and sits on a garden wall behind me while Shannon takes the chair on my other side.

Not long after, a guy sits to Laine's left, and I'm surprised when he kisses her, until I recognize him from his picture.

"Matt, this is my sister, Dell, and her friend Shannon." Given that she doesn't elaborate on our being here, I assume she already told him. "Dell, Shannon, this is my boyfriend, Matt."

*Boyfriend.* I raise my eyebrows in question, and Laine tilts her head in response.

"It's nice to meet you," I say.

"Same. And thanks for coming to visit—if you hadn't shown up, she would have made me study all night." Matt winks, and Laine playfully nudges him with her shoulder.

As the conversation weaves in and out of different topics, I study Matt, who's definitely cute—the pictures didn't do him justice. He and Laine tell stories together, interjecting and trading off. She talks about a time when the professor of a class they share taught for fifty minutes without realizing he had a giant glob of mustard on his cheek. "As the lecture went on, we were literally watching it dry," Laine says through her laughter.

Matt leans forward and puts his hand on her knee. "And the TA kept brushing his fingers over his own cheek, but Dr. Porter did not take the hint."

When the story ends, they reach for each other's hands, and I marvel at how relaxed Laine is. She's had other boyfriends, but with them, she always seemed mildly uncomfortable, like she was in her head, self-conscious. Not with Matt.

Later in the evening, as Laine talks about the two of us as kids, Matt listens with a small smile playing at his lips.

"We were obsessed with *The Wizard of Oz*," Laine says. "Our parents still had the DVD, and we would watch it, what? Once a month?"

"At least," I agree. "I've always loved running," I tell him, "so for, like, a week afterward, I would chase her around the yard yelling, 'I'll get you, my pretty!'"

"I think that's how you figured out you're good at running—or maybe you got good because you had no mercy on me."

I shrug. "Oh, but poor Bean. Our little sister is ten years younger than me," I explain, "and we couldn't wait to share it with her."

Laine looks sheepishly at Matt, knowing where I'm going with this story. "We might have misjudged the age-appropriateness of that movie."

"She was so scared of the Wicked Witch. We said the line to her once, and she burst into tears. Never watched the movie again. I still feel bad."

"You? I was the one in charge. That experience scared me into being responsible."

Matt puts his arm around Laine and pulls her toward him. She rests her head on his shoulder.

The darker it gets, the rowdier the yard becomes. There's steady background noise of talking, shouting, and cheering, yet I still manage to hear "Heads up!" and raise my hand to block an incoming beach ball several times. Multiple Solo cups get knocked over. Finally, Laine suggests we move inside, and we all stand. I stifle a yawn.

"Actually, I should go. I do need to study." Matt steps toward me, arms somewhat outstretched. "Is it okay if I hug you?"

I nod and lean into an awkward embrace. Laine wasn't kidding when she said he was tall, but he bends his knees so he's on my level and gives me a strong but gentle hug.

"Don't let her convince you otherwise," he whispers. "Coming here was a great idea."

I smile at him, and he says goodbye to Shannon before moving toward the door.

"I'll be right back." Laine hurries after him.

Inside, Shannon asks, "Will you be okay by yourself for a minute? I need to use the bathroom."

"Sure." I wave her away and check out the food. Not that anything sounds good, but I'm curious what kinds of snacks they serve at a college party. For desserts it's container after container of store-bought cookies. And next to those, little plastic cups with a sign reading *Jell-O shots!*

Getting drunk is not on my bucket list, but a Jell-O shot at a college party is too delightfully cliché to pass up.

After I work my tongue around the edges, I gulp it down. It has a bite, a welcome tang that cuts through the orange flavor, which I'm sure would taste off to me otherwise.

Against my better judgment, I pick up one of the lime cups. *You only live once.*

"What are you doing?" Shannon appears by my side.

"Jell-O shots."

Her expression is a mix of concern and exasperation. "You know there's alcohol in those."

"Yes."

"Are you allowed to have alcohol? Like, forgetting the fact that it's illegal because you're seventeen, will it mess with your treatment?"

"What, are you my oncologist now? Or my *mom?*"

Shannon clenches her jaw.

When Laine heads in our direction, I turn away and slurp up the wiggly mold before dumping both containers in the trash.

It quickly becomes apparent that there is absolutely nowhere to sit, and even though I don't admit it out loud, it's equally apparent how much I need to get off my feet. The best we can manage is a strip of unoccupied wall—the three of us lean against it, and I strategically place myself between Laine and Shannon so I can prop myself up against them as well.

You'd think being huddled together, we could hear each other speak, but nope. Laine's lips move, but I can't make out what she's saying. "What?"

"Did you have fun tonight?" she repeats in my ear.

"So much fun." Suddenly, my body tingles in a way I've never felt before. My limbs are heavy and buzzing at the same time. Maybe Jell-O shots on an empty stomach wasn't my best idea ever.

We have a few more stilted exchanges, Laine yelling in my ear or me yelling in Shannon's, until Laine steps away from the wall and shouts at us both, "Want to split?"

I'm torn between my body's vote, *Yes, please,* and my heart's rebuttal that *It's our first—and maybe last—college party.*

"Not yet," I beg. "Thirty more minutes."

Laine hesitates. "Fifteen."

"Twenty."

We have a sister stare-down, which I eventually win, but only because a couch spot miraculously opens up. As we squeeze ourselves into it, Laine checks her watch dramatically. "Twenty minutes."

I lean my head on her shoulder, and although I adamantly refuse to grant them permission, my eyelids droop.

The next thing I know, Laine taps my shoulder and says it's time to go. I suspect she cheats me out of several minutes.

***

Despite sleeping later than the others, I'm exhausted the next morning. I groggily accept the banana and granola bar Laine hands me for the road.

The drive is quiet. I close my eyes for a lot of it. At one point, the car stops, and I open my eyes to find we're in my driveway. Shannon comes around to my side and grabs my bag as I muster the energy to stand.

"Thanks." Once I take the bag, I head toward the garage.

"Take it easy today," Shannon calls after me.

Before I punch in the code, I take a breath and try to perk up so Mom won't worry.

"How was it?" she asks when I walk into the kitchen.

"Good. We had fun."

Mom studies me. "Did you stay up too late?"

"Maybe a little."

She pats my shoulder. "Okay, well, why don't you get some more rest."

I nod, then walk upstairs and climb into bed. Once I'm settled, I text Laine.

> Back home. Sorry for springing the visit on you. Thanks for letting me stay. I'm glad I got to meet Matt.

> Me too. It was fun sharing this part of my life with you.

The dots flash as she keeps typing.

But don't do something like this again, k?

I'm fine, promise.

I love you, Dee.

Love you too.

# #4: KISS IN THE RAIN

We commemorate Laine coming home for the summer with a family (plus Charlie) movie night. Bean suggested it once it started raining, and since I'm still recovering from this week's chemo, I was the first to agree.

The lights are low, but that doesn't stop Charlie from lifting his camera to preserve my parents' admitted cuteness: Dad's legs are outstretched, his slippered feet crossed, Mom is curled up next to him on the love seat, and they're holding hands.

I smile at Charlie, and he smiles back, then shifts position so he can capture me, Laine, and Bean snuggled together. Bean holds her stuffed tiger, Eliza, and all four of us are wearing matching pajamas.

When the credits roll, Mom turns up the lights. "Okay, Jilly Bean, time for bed."

"Awww." Bean leans into Laine, trying to hide from her bedtime. "Why can't I stay up with Laine?"

Sometimes I forget I'm not the only one who misses her. "How about the three of us have a tea party tomorrow?" I suggest.

"With Eliza and Hannah?"

"Of course," Laine chimes in. "Maybe we can even have real tea." She turns to Mom, who regards Bean's hopeful face and says, "We can arrange that—*if* you get ready for bed in the next 10 minutes."

Bean pops up and runs toward the stairs, but doubles back to give Dad, Laine, me, and Charlie quick hugs. Dad takes drink glasses and popcorn bowls (*none for me with this stomach*) into the kitchen.

Charlie stands. "I should go."

The steady drone of the rain that backdropped the movie grows to a roar as I follow him to the front door. *Opportunity presents itself.* I was wondering how I'd check kissing in the rain off my list.

Once he slings his camera bag over his shoulder, Charlie opens the door and clicks his key fob to unlock his car. With a kiss, he dashes out.

I dash after him. "Wait!"

He turns and tries to run onto the porch, but I hurry down the steps and meet him on the walkway. Not understanding what I want, he attempts to sidestep me and take shelter under the porch roof, but I grab his hand and hold him where we are.

"What are you doing?" he yells, as we get wetter by the second.

I push myself up on my toes and kiss him, but he pulls away. "I'm getting soaked!"

"I've always wanted to kiss in the rain!" I counter.

His brow furrows, but I smile and shrug, water running down my forehead and cheeks. After a moment's hesitation, he walks past me and sets his camera bag where it will stay dry, then wraps me in his arms, picks me up, and kisses me.

Soon my face stings from being pelted repeatedly. I squint through the water in my eyelashes. Charlie shakes his head, and droplets fly from his curls.

*It looks so romantic in the movies.* But nature isn't as enchanting as Hollywood makes it out to be.

When I go inside, I call to Laine, "Can you bring me a towel?"

She comes to the foyer. "What happened to you?"

"We kissed in the rain."

"Young people," she mutters as she heads upstairs. Half a minute later, she tosses a towel off the landing.

My pajamas are soaked, so once I'm dry enough to not drip all over the floor, I go to my room and change. By the time I'm done, the kitchen light is off, and Laine is alone in the family room. She flips back the blanket, and I tuck myself in beside her.

"So," she says.

"So…let's talk about Matt."

She smiles. "What about Matt?"

"Why didn't you tell me he's your boyfriend?"

"I was going to. It hasn't been that long."

"How long?"

"Three, four weeks."

"A month?" *Have I really been so preoccupied with my own life that she's been coupled up for a whole lunar cycle without me knowing?* "Seriously, why didn't you tell me?"

Laine casts her eyes down. "I don't know. I guess I felt guilty for this good thing in my life when things are so shitty for you." She meets my gaze.

My cheeks flush—from awkwardness, maybe, or shame. "I'm sorry if I made you feel like you couldn't tell me. I am so happy for you, and—" I glance over my shoulder to make sure we really are alone. "I'm glad I got to meet him. He seems like a great guy."

"He said the same about you. I might invite him here at some point this summer."

"You should! Have you told Mom and Dad about him?"

"Yeah. They said he's welcome to come visit. He's spending the summer at home in Tennessee, though. I don't know if he would want to make the drive."

"I'm sure he'll come. The way he acted around you last weekend—he clearly cares about you."

Laine studies me, her eyes sparkling. "I'm falling for him, Dee."

I take her hand and squeeze, excitement dispelling some of the fatigue and general *blah*ness I've felt all week. "Okay, tell me everything. Is he a good kisser?"

Despite blushing, she says, "Yes."

"And is he good at…?" I waggle my eyebrows, and she swats my knee.

"Dee! …But yes." She covers her mouth with her hands, and I squeal, "Laine!"

"Shhh!" She's beet red now. "We've only done it once, right before we left campus." Her eyes have this dreamy, faraway quality. "But I can't stop thinking about it—about him."

I grin so hard my face hurts, and we settle into contented silence. Eventually, Laine says, "Matt reminds me of you and Charlie."

When I tilt my head, she explains. "That boy adores you. It's obvious you would do anything for each other. That's what I want. And Matt is the first guy I've been with who makes me believe I could have it."

I've never thought of me and Charlie as anything besides me and Charlie—I didn't know we could be something to aspire to, but warm fuzzies fill my insides. "What makes Matt different from your other boyfriends?"

A soft smile touches Laine's lips. "You know how I was afraid he used humor as a defense mechanism?"

I nod.

"He is funny, and he knows when I need to laugh, but the

times I've opened up to him, he's been so attentive and compassionate. When I told him about you?" She pauses, and her jaw tenses.

The memory of losing my cool when she told me about telling him infuses my voice with kindness. "You said he was sympathetic, right?"

"Even more than sympathetic. He was so concerned about you, and our family, and how I was handling everything. And after we'd talked about my life for as long as I wanted to, he opened up about his." Laine takes a throw pillow from behind her and rests it in her lap, picking at the gold fringe along the top. "His mom has struggled with mental health issues since he was little, and he shared some about what it was like for him growing up and how things are with her now. Of course I wish he and his family didn't have those challenges, but letting each other in like that brought us closer." She looks up, and I nod to encourage her to keep going. "We've shared more and more since then. Not just the serious stuff, but fun stuff too—we like a lot of the same music, and he's interested in my obsession with hydroponics, and he teaches me about Tae Kwon Do, which is cool."

Her lips remain parted, like she could talk about him for hours. Her happiness is palpable, and my heart swells in response. "He sounds amazing, and like the perfect match for you."

"I know it's only been a couple months, but I've never felt this way before."

"I wish I'd known all this during my visit—I would have seen him through a different lens."

Laine pokes me as she says, "I'm not sure that would have been a good thing."

"What? It's not like I would have gone up to him and said, 'Laine lo-o-o-ves you!' I'm not six."

"I didn't say I love him."

My sister is so transparent. "Maybe not to him yet. But you do, right?"

Her smile gives it away. "Ahhh—yes!"

I lean forward and hug-tackle her into the cushions.

# #16: ZIP-LINE

It's Dad's birthday, and I'm psyched. Not just to celebrate my father's forty-nine years on the planet, but because this year, instead of presents, Dad asked for the five of us to go to an aerial adventure park where we'll complete obstacles in the trees.

We bought our tickets months ago and crossed our fingers for good weather, which is hit or miss in May. Today the sun is shining, and the temperature is in the sixties, with a forecasted high around seventy. Plus, thankfully, I'm enough days removed from chemo to make it doable.

Per the website, I tuck a light long-sleeve T-shirt into my yoga pants and put my wig in a ponytail before going downstairs.

I'm surprised there isn't more bustle in the kitchen. Dad drinks coffee and reads while Mom rinses blueberries for a smoothie. Bean is glued to the TV in the family room, and Laine isn't here.

"Don't we have to leave soon?" I ask.

Mom turns off the water, Dad sets down his book, and my stomach sinks.

"We thought," Mom says slowly, "that given what's going on, it would be best to do the adventure park another time."

"But I feel pretty good today."

"That's wonderful news." Her tone drips with *but*. "Still, we don't want to risk you getting hurt."

"How will I get hurt? There's a whole section on the website about how they keep you safe."

"I'm not saying it's likely, but we're not taking any chances."

Dad shrugs and adds, "They make you sign a waiver for a reason."

Heat rises in my body. "This is so unfair. There are tons of things I can't do because of cancer, and now when I actually feel decent enough to do something we planned for—on Dad's birthday—you're not going to let me?"

Dad stands and walks toward me. "I know you were looking forward to this, but there will be other opportunities." He puts his hand on my shoulder, and I take a deep breath to stop myself from shrugging it off. "And as far as my birthday goes, as long as I'm spending it with my four favorite gals, it'll be perfect."

"We thought we could watch a—"

I cut my mother off. "Do not say *movie*."

"Bit burnt-out, are we?" Dad asks.

"Why can't we go to the adventure park? Whatever risk there is must be small, and you'll be with me the whole time."

"Dell, I'm sorry, but we canceled weeks ago." Mom's mouth is a thin line.

"Do you know if all the spots are filled? Maybe we can still go."

"It's not about whether there are openings."

"What are you afraid will happen?" I face her and put my hands on my hips. "That the trees will make the cancer cells grow? The fresh air will make another lump appear?"

Mom's jaw works before she speaks. "Obviously, we're not

talking about a cancer risk. But, for example, if you broke a bone, that would require a trip to the hospital, with its inherent risk of infection. And any type of injury might interfere with your body's ability to fight the cancer."

"So, my happiness doesn't matter. Got it."

"Adele," Dad says at the same time Mom says, "Of course it matters."

"Well, it doesn't feel like it," I huff. "I could get hurt doing anything—I could trip going up the stairs and bang my head. I could slip in the shower. I could cut myself with a knife or drop a glass on my foot or burn myself on the oven."

Mom raises her voice. "I'm terrified of all the things that could hurt you. That's why I don't want you taking unnecessary risks. As long—"

"This isn't an unnecessary risk! It's something they let seven-year-olds do, and it was supposed to be something fun for all of us to do together."

"I'm sure it would have been." Dad steps between me and Mom. "But that's not the only fun thing we can do together. What if we go on a picnic? You used to love picnics."

I glare at my father. "Don't try to placate me."

"Don't be disrespectful," Mom admonishes, but I continue talking to Dad.

"You're being overprotective. If you'd take a step back—"

"I know you think we're being unreasonable," Dad interrupts, "but it's not your decision. It's my birthday, and I say we find something else to do."

"Then do it without me." I storm out of the kitchen.

Laine stands on the stairs, her pained expression evidence she's been listening. "Dee…" She reaches out a hand.

"Don't touch me." I slap it away and hurry past.

Blood throbs in my veins. Once I'm in my room, I pace back and forth as I text Shannon.

> Are you free tomorrow?

> Sure. Bucket list?

> Want to do an obstacle course in the trees?

> What are you talking about?

> Are you loopy on pain meds?

> You didn't make Jell-O shots, did you?

Shannon's texts keep popping up at the top of my screen while I send her the link to the website.

> AWESOME.

Tickets are more expensive than I realized, but since I probably won't end up buying a car with the money I saved from nannying during school breaks and babysitting, I click "Reserve."

A few minutes later, someone knocks on my door and Dad says, "Can I come in?"

I take a slow breath. "Yeah."

He sits on the bed, where I've settled. "I'm sorry this is so hard."

"I'm sorry I got mad at you on your birthday."

With his hand on my knee, he shakes his head. "Don't worry about it. You do know we only want what's best for you, right?"

"But what if sometimes that's different than what's safest for me?"

Dad sighs. "This is one of the hardest things about being a parent." He shifts to face me. "When you were three, you were so envious of Laine and her tablet. You wanted to play games on it like she did, but we only let you watch educational shows on TV. Laine begged us too—she wanted to share it with you, and we struggled with the decision. Should we uphold our limits on your screen time, or was it more important to foster the relationship between you and your sister?"

I'm not in the mood to talk, so I let silence fill the space between us. Does he think knowing how hard this is for him will make it any easier for me?

"And do you remember when you were ten and some of your friends got cell phones? We wanted to wait as long as possible before giving you a phone, but we didn't want you to be left out by being the only one without one."

Dad looks at me for a response, but I don't have anything to say.

"So many parenting decisions require weighing the pros and cons of complicated questions," he continues. "All you can do is take everything into consideration and do what you believe will lead to the most good and the least harm. That's what we're doing with the adventure park. I hope you understand."

I nod, and Dad kisses the top of my head before he leaves.

*I understand. I just don't agree.*

***

After a half hour of instruction, Shannon and I climb the steps to the tree-house platform where all the courses begin. Most people complete two or three courses in their allotted two hours. We start with a Green course and plan to work our way up through Blue and maybe to Black.

We take turns hooking our safety clips onto the cable using the tweezle (*cutest word I've ever heard*). A staff member ensures we've done it right, then Shannon steps onto the first element, a log bridge that sways as soon as her foot touches it.

"Hope you're not afraid of heights," she calls over her shoulder. She balances by using the cables running along the sides and makes her way across.

*My turn.* Once I get my footing, I gaze between the logs as I step from one to the next. From this high up, the understory appears magical, like I'm a giant towering above a fairy garden.

The suburban sounds I'm used to have disappeared. Instead, I'm surrounded by birds chirping and the rustle of leaves. I turn my attention upward and follow a butterfly as it flits by. It's peaceful.

"We don't have all day, Marshall," Shannon teases.

I take a big step onto the platform and brush past her. "Excuse me for savoring the moment."

Next is a trapeze bar, and we clip onto the cables above it. I don't have to hold my own weight, but it still takes me a second before I muster enough courage to step into the air. I swing through the trees—the breeze blowing on my face and the sound of the zip-line *whizzing* in my ear—and crash into Shannon with a goofy grin.

Since nothing on the Green course is particularly challenging, we graduate to Blue. During the training, they made it clear that each successive level is progressively harder, and the first Blue element drives home the point.

The wooden blocks that make up this Blue bridge are stable individually, but the whole bridge wobbles. There's only one cable to hold onto, and it has a *lot* of give.

For someone who doesn't do much besides scroll on her phone, Shannon is surprisingly athletic. She keeps her balance the whole way, then derives great amusement from my struggle to do the same.

"Ooh, careful."

I don't acknowledge her, but she keeps talking.

"Ah-h, thought you were going down."

I lose my balance and lean back, squeezing all my muscles to try to pull myself upright, but it's a lost cause. Shannon calls dramatically from the other end, "Noooooooo!"

Laughing destroys any hope I had of recovering. I squat, hanging from the cable with my butt sticking out as I crab walk from one block to the next.

My muscles burn and I'm out of breath when I reach the platform. Shannon mocks me by watching somberly. "Didn't know if you were gonna make it."

Fortunately, the following element, a traditional zip-line, lets me rest. After I clip in, I relax into a sitting position and let go, then fly through the forest at the perfect speed—fast enough to be fun but slow enough to take in the view.

This pleasantness, however, is a tease. It lulls us into a false sense of confidence in our ability to traverse the course, but our next obstacle gives us a rude awakening. A dozen four-by-fours, each with a single peg sticking out perpendicularly at the bottom, hang from two cables stretching between the trees. As soon as I step onto the first peg, the four-by-four swings out wide, a gulf away from the peg my other foot is supposed to land on. In a matter of seconds, I'm doing the splits and desperately pulling the four-by-fours toward me.

There's little victory in getting each foot on a peg, because taking a foot off creates the same problem. I flail wildly, trying to find purchase, while I squeeze the two cables under my armpits to keep from falling off, which hurts enough it will likely leave bruises.

Shannon refrains from teasing and watches silently. My legs are on the verge of cramping, my arms shake, and I'm audibly huffing and puffing. But I make it.

I practically throw myself onto the platform, then lean against the tree trunk and close my eyes.

*I did it.*

Our time is almost up, but my achy body is not sorry to skip the Black course and call Blue our win.

None of the remaining elements are as bad as what we just endured. With one, we stand on a bar and glide through the trees. Another makes me feel like a monkey as I wrap my arms around thick, swinging poles and pull myself from one to the next. *Ook ook.*

The course ends on a platform with an auto-belay, which means we clip in and then just—walk off. Onto nothing. Granted, we'll be slowly lowered to the ground, but still. There's a reason they call it the "Leap of Faith."

Shannon goes first and confidently steps into the air. She lands in a crouch, then unhooks herself so the cable comes back for me.

I clip in. My hands sweat. I wait.

One foot hovers in the air before I return it to the solid wood beneath me.

"You'll be fine." Shannon stares up at me. "Take the leap."

*You can do this.* My heart pounds. I inch closer to the edge until my toes stick out.

And I leap.

Well, I don't actually leap, because they were very clear that we're not supposed to jump, just step out like we're walking, only there's nothing to walk onto. I fall, but it's a slow, controlled fall.

When my feet hit the ground, I'm too relaxed and don't push back, so I keep going down—butt, then back, until I'm lying on the padded floor.

Shannon's face appears above me. "Comfy?"

"Yes, very."

She offers me a hand and pulls me up, and I click into the freezle to free myself.

On our way home, we pass a sign advertising self-guided cavern tours.

I point it out. "Let's stop."

"Haven't we had enough adventure for one day?"

"Never."

Shannon side-eyes me.

"Okay, not never. But not yet today. Besides, exploring a cave is on my bucket list."

"It is not."

"Well, maybe it wasn't before, but that's only because I didn't know this was here."

She looks skeptical.

"Come on, please? We're right here, and who knows when—or *if*—we'll get a chance to come back?"

Even though she huffs, she turns in the direction of the sign. "You can't just play the 'I'm dying and don't have much time left' card whenever it suits you."

"Uh, I think I can. That's kind of the point."

"Dammit," Shannon says as she parks.

We only spend a half hour at the caverns anyway. But in the cool darkness, I see stalactites and stalagmites and even tap on a cluster of them to make differently pitched sounds. Who knew nature could be so musical?

Back in the car, I roll down my window and let the wind beat at my eardrums. I scoot the seat back and stretch my legs in front of me. My muscles are sore, but the good kind of sore. I haven't used them like this in way too long. I'm proud of myself for completing two courses. The Blue one was legitimately challenging, but we did it.

I rest my arm on the window ledge and let the sun warm my skin. *It was a good day. And no one got hurt.*

Or so I believe until Shannon points at my elbow. "What happened there?"

I straighten my arm and twist to spot a little patch of dried blood. I lick my thumb and wipe it away. A tiny cut starts bleeding again. "Do you have a tissue or something?"

Shannon waves her hand around. "Somewhere. Check the glove box."

I find a crumpled napkin and hold it to my arm.

"You need to be careful about infections." Shannon's voice is soft, hesitant.

"I'm sure it's fine. It's barely anything."

She nods slowly, keeping her eyes on the road.

# SOCIAL BUTTERFLY

S hannon comes over after our last day of school and drops a yearbook onto my lap.

"What's this?"

"You weren't there the day they passed them out," she says. "I offered to deliver yours, but first I wanted to collect some signatures."

I open the cover and am overwhelmed by how crowded the pages are. Every inch of available space is covered in ink, a wall of black, blue, pink, red, and green, in all types of handwriting, from loopy cursive letters to tiny block print and everything in between. The back cover is the same. Writing even sprinkles the inside pages.

"You hate people. How did you get this many to sign?"

Shannon shrugs. "I can be charming when I want to be."

Despite how touched I am, I quip, "Why don't you ever want to be charming with me?" Shannon reaches for the yearbook, as if to take it back, but I hug it to my chest. "This is amazing, thank you."

We sit in silence while I read the messages. As the magnitude of signatures sinks in, I blurt, "Do you think a lot of people would come to my funeral?" I study Shannon's expression and wonder if she takes this question to mean I'm depressed, which I'm not, or that I've been obsessing over death, which I haven't. Still, should I die, I hope my funeral would have an impressive turnout.

"I think you'd be shocked."

"Really?" It's such an odd thing to be excited about.

"A shitload of people came for Noah's. Half the middle school—kids, parents, teachers, staff; some who knew him, some who didn't—friends from his swim team, neighbors, old babysitters, the whole church congregation, you name it. Nothing brings a community together like a kid dying."

I set the yearbook aside and lean against my pillow. "I figured all my family and friends would come, but I hadn't considered acquaintances or teachers."

"Oh, a hundred percent. Especially now that you're a senior, it would be even more tragic. I can see the newspaper headline: 'GBHS Senior Has Her Whole Life Ahead of Her—Cancer Takes it All Away.'" Shannon smiles wryly to herself.

While I asked the question out of simple curiosity, now the idea has taken hold. "So, what number are we talking about? Two hundred? Five?"

Shannon tilts her head. "Well, there are over four hundred in our class. Let's say half would come. Plus parents and teachers and some kids who aren't in our grade. Factor in your family and other people you know." After some mental math, she concludes, "Five hundred at least."

I picture it, everyone gathered to mourn me, then pick up the yearbook again. Shannon moves the desk chair next to my bed. Once I prop a pillow under my elbow, I open the book and lay it between us.

"What about someone like Caleb?" I ask. "We were in a play together in seventh grade—is that enough for him to come?"

Shannon nods. "Probably."

I run my finger down the pages, tapping the faces of people I'd expect to show. *Tap*—Rebecca Aikley, my lab partner in freshman science. *Tap*—Scott Atwood, the captain of the football team and a sort-of friend from the one year I was a cheerleader. *Tap*—Caroline Beeman, the nicest girl in our class, who would go no matter whose funeral it was. *Tap*—Davey Edinger, who I've known since elementary school.

Almost *tap*. Shannon raises her eyebrow at me, as my finger remains poised over Mike Horowitz, the first boy I ever slow-danced with. In sixth grade, we had a mad love affair that lasted a week, during which we mostly spoke through third-party go-betweens. But in a dramatic skating-rink showdown, he asked Maggie Sullivan to skate and publicly ended our romance.

After considering Mike for another second, I drop my finger to the page. *Tap.*

When I skip Angie Markel, who I don't know at all, Shannon chimes in. "She would come."

"Why? How do you know?"

"She has the biggest heart on the planet." Before I move onto the next person, Shannon adds, "And—beside the point—she's also a good kisser," then blushes.

I widen my eyes and smile at her. "Did you two date?"

"Nah. It was middle school. We just messed around."

"What about now?"

"What about now?" she retorts.

"Do you ever think about starting something up with her?"

Shannon shrugs. "We haven't talked in forever."

"You could change that."

"But I—"

"Don't like people," I say over her saying the same thing.

Once I stop turning pages and close the yearbook, Shannon gives me a satisfied smile. "I'd say your funeral would be the social event of the season."

# #15: STAY UP ALL NIGHT TALKING

Charlie and his parents and brothers visit some family friends to celebrate the end of the school year, but he calls me late after he gets home. I'm in my pajamas, in bed with the light off. I rest the phone between my ear and the pillow and close my eyes.

"So, how does it feel to be a senior?" I ask before yawning.

"I guess we are now, aren't we? I don't know about you, but I for one have big plans for senior year—"

He stops abruptly, like he forgot and then remembered what this coming year could have in store for us.

"Do tell," I prompt.

"Uh..."

"Come on—tell me what you'll do now that you're at the top of the food chain." I pull the sheet up higher and tuck it under my chin.

"Dell..."

"Please? Pretend with me for a little bit." *Pretend I don't have cancer. Pretend I'm not dying. Pretend we're like everyone else in our class and we'll have an amazing senior year.*

Charlie inhales audibly. "Okay. I want to impart my hard-earned wisdom on the lowly freshman, go through an existential crisis spurred by all the deep college essay questions, attend so many graduation parties I never want to eat cake again, and have teary goodbyes with my favorite teachers—Mrs. Kopecki excluded, of course."

"The only tears anybody sheds for her are because her lectures don't end soon enough." The woman is a cross between Dolores Umbridge and Miss Trunchbull. I shudder at the memory of her history class sophomore year. "What else do you want? Something real."

"For real?" Charlie hesitates. "I want to go with you to prom."

We're both quiet. Prom this year was the Saturday after one of my chemo infusions. Kind of hard to dance when you might hurl at any moment.

"And I might put together a portfolio," Charlie continues. "CCAD has a Photography major, so maybe I'll apply there and to OSU."

An art degree at an art school—Columbus College of Art and Design. This is the first he's mentioned it. We've always said we'll go to The Ohio State University together.

"OSU is still my top choice." He sounds apologetic. "But it's good to have options."

*In case I'm not at OSU.*

"That's amazing," I finally say. "I'm glad you're considering pursuing your art more seriously. Maybe you should major in Photography at OSU—it's what you love."

"I like biology too. And besides, OSU doesn't offer a Photography major—just Fine Art in Studio Arts with an emphasis on photography."

*Huh.* Apparently, this isn't something just springing to mind right now. He's been doing research. That's good. He needs photography in his life, no matter what happens with me.

"When's the CCAD deadline?"

"December."

I'm about to ask which pictures he'll include in his portfolio when he says, "So, what about you? How is senior Dell going to take the world by storm?"

"Oh. Well, you know, run my first marathon, *win* my first marathon, possibly travel the world in a study abroad program, get some cool internship at a bookstore or nonprofit."

"All during senior year? Sounds like you'll be busy."

"Never too busy for you, dear."

"I should hope not."

In the silence that follows, my eyelids get heavy.

"Do you want to hang out tomorrow?" Charlie's voice pulls me back from the brink of sleep.

"Yeah, after I go to the park with Bean and Laine… I'll text you once we're home."

"You sound tired. Do you want to go?"

"No. I want to keep talking. I want to talk forever and ever and ever." *All night, anyway.*

"Forever? We'd run out of words."

"Maybe you would. I'll never run out. I know all the words…" My voice trails off.

"Okay, you're sleepy," Charlie declares (not inaccurately). "I'm saying good night."

"No!" It's after midnight—I have a head start on crossing this one off my list and don't want to waste it. "I'm fine, really. Keep talking to me." Before he can say no, I tell him, "I want you to take my senior pictures. You'll be better than anyone we could hire, and my mom will pay you."

"That's sweet of her, but she doesn't have to. You know I'm happy to do it."

"We should do it this summer…" I yawn again.

"Anytime."

"You'll probably hate your senior pictures. You won't like how…" *…they take them, because you would have done it differently.*

"Dell?"

"What?"

"You stopped talking in the middle of a sentence. Did you fall asleep?" His tone tells me he knows that's what happened but wants me to admit it's time to hang up. *Nope, not falling for it.*

"No—maybe you fell asleep."

"I didn't fall asleep." He's smiling, I can hear it. "But I will any second, so let's call it a night."

"Not yet—I like the sound of your voice. It's soothing."

"No one has complimented my voice before."

*Bingo.* Flattery for the win. "You're welcome." The phone is hot under my ear. I move it to the edge of my pillow and turn on the speaker.

Charlie yawns, then asks, "Did Bean have a good last day?"

"Yeah. It was field day—she spent the afternoon jumping on inflatables."

"Ah, those were the days."

"Right? They had way more than we used to… At least half the stations were bounce houses… Plus tug-of-war and…" … *Velcro axe throwing.*

*Velcro. Like when someone wears a special suit and gets stuck to a giant board that spins in a circle.*

*I'm on the board. Stuck. Round and round I go. My head is dizzy.*

*Now I'm on the spinner on the playground, whirling around and around, faster and faster, and I want to make it stop but can't. I stick out my leg to touch the ground, but I'm afraid it will hurt.*

*Faster and faster and faster and faster—*

I startle awake. "Charlie?" My pulse accelerates as I check my phone and confirm there's no active call. Part of my brain must still be in the dream, because my heart pounds, thump-thump-thumping so hard I feel it push against my chest.

My lungs take a cue from my heart and allow only short, shallow breaths. I have a headache, and tears prick the corners of my eyes. *What is happening?*

Is it really the end of the world if we don't talk all night? The logical answer is no, so why is panic rising within me?

With a shaking hand, I call Charlie back.

"It's late," he says by way of greeting. "I'm tired. You fell asleep again."

"We didn't say goodbye." *Ah.* As soon as I say the words, my reaction makes sense.

"What?" Charlie asks.

Despite the tears running down my cheeks, I temper my emotions so I stay coherent. "You hung up without saying goodbye."

"I'm sorry. I didn't want to wake you—I know sleep is especially important while you're going through treatment."

My face scrunches up. *Charlie was being considerate*, I tell myself. But it's hollow comfort for my overwhelming dread at the idea, however unlikely, that I could have not woken up and the last words we exchanged would have been whatever midsentence nonsense I was spouting when I dozed off.

In this moment, I realize I might not know when the end is coming, and every conversation I have with people could be the last. It's too much pressure.

Once I manage to speak, I can barely choke out the words. "We have to always say goodbye. We have to always say I love you."

"Dell, where is this coming from?" The worry in Charlie's voice is loud. "You know I love you. More than anything."

I nod, even though he can't see me. He's right. I know he loves me as surely as I know my own name. Do I actually think if I died without those being the last words I heard, or said, it would change how we feel?

"I'm sorry," I squeak. My nose runs, and I wipe away the snotty mess with the back of my hand. "It's just—I woke up and you were gone. I was alone."

Charlie's breathing is the only sound for several seconds.

"You're never alone." His voice is quiet, strained. "I'm always here for you. *Always.*"

We sit in silence. I check my phone repeatedly to make sure he's still on the call.

As my heartbeat settles into its normal rhythm and my breathing evens out, I sniffle and whisper, "Thank you."

"I love you, Dell."

"I love you too."

# #11: TAKE SENIOR PICTURES

For my senior pictures, we choose three notable locations:

**1. The running trail.**

I wear shorts and a blue running tank. My wig is pulled into a ponytail, and I crouch on the ground with my medals fanned out around me.

**2. A charming barn where we used to visit Santa every year.**

Part of me is sorry we're not doing this in winter—all the white twinkly lights would make an amazing backdrop. But Charlie highlights the summer landscape. He has me lean against the side of the barn, the whitewashed wood panels contrasting nicely with my mauve dress, colorful wildflowers in the background. I gently remove the rubber band from my wig and arrange the hair around my shoulders. We take a few on the porch with me peering around a column and another set where I'm sitting on a low wall next to vibrant flowers spilling out of giant containers.

**3. Inniswood Metro Gardens, which seem to have sprung out of a fairy tale.**

Charlie stops on a bridge. "Let's take some here." I rest my elbows on the wooden railing and lean back.

"Turn a little to your right."

I do as I'm told and adjust my lavender sleeveless shirt over my jeans. Mom and Laine watch from their spot against the opposite railing. When Laine and I were little, we would come here to play "Poohsticks," tossing sticks over one railing, then dashing to the other in anticipation of ours appearing first in the water below.

When Charlie is satisfied, we move on. We take a series by a stream and another in front of an ivy-covered gazebo.

Once we're done, another memory stirs. "Where's the tree house?"

"Oh, yeah," Laine says. "I forgot about the tree house."

"I think it's by the amphitheater." Mom hesitates, then turns and marches forward.

We follow her as she recalls the way from years ago. As we approach, we cross a rope bridge, and I smile to myself—much easier than the one in the trees.

The house sitting atop an enormous tree trunk fills me with an intense nostalgia. I run my hand along the rough bark as I go around and duck inside the carved-out trunk. This was my space when Laine and I played. She always chose the house on top because she loved the little balcony overlooking the woods, but I preferred it here where it's snug and cozy.

Like she did so many times before, Laine knocks on the porch post. I poke my head out of the door, and she offers me her hand. I let her lead me to the ladder, and as we're climbing up, I half expect Mom's familiar warning to "Be careful."

I sit on the platform, and Laine squeezes in beside me. She puts her arm around my shoulders, and I lean into her. Then we grin at each other, Charlie capturing it all.

We milk our sappy sisterly love for all its worth, then

reposition ourselves so we're facing forward. Laine moves my hair off my shoulder so she doesn't accidentally pull it. I put my hand on hers, and she laces her fingers through mine. As our eyes lock, I'm filled with gratitude for a sibling who's also my best friend.

Not that we haven't had our fair share of fights. We can throw down with the best of them. But I wouldn't trade one angry word or one hurt feeling if it meant losing even a single happy memory.

After a brief hesitation, I look at Charlie. He stares back, his head tilted, waiting.

The magic of his photographs is how he captures and celebrates the truth—every bit of it. That's what I want for my senior pictures. To be me, and to have a record of myself exactly as I am in this moment.

Slowly, I remove the wig. Mom reaches up when I hand it down to her. Laine rests her head against mine, her hair soft and tickly against my bald scalp. Charlie gives me a wide smile before raising his camera.

We scout for a couple more locations to shoot without the wig. By the time we've made two loops around the park, I'm tired, and we call it a day.

Back at home, Charlie and I review the pictures in my room. My heart flutters at the bald shots. It's odd seeing myself without the wig somewhere other than the hospital or my bed. But it's refreshing too—like a weight has been lifted.

And while all the pictures with the wig are great too, these say *Charlie* in a way the others don't. They're more real. Even though I was nervous, I like them best, precisely because they show both my nerves and my joy.

"These are my favorites," Charlie says. "I'm glad you took off the wig."

"Yeah?"

He nods. "You're just you. And you're beautiful."

I hold his gaze. "Don't ever stop doing this. Major or no major, this is what you're meant to do."

With a gentle smile, he leans forward, and we kiss. The world around us falls away. Our bodies entwined, we press our mouths together, leaving me the best kind of breathless.

# 15 MINUTES OF FAME

The next time Shannon comes over, she hands me a folded-up piece of paper. "In case you haven't heard about it."

Smoothing it out, I read *Summer Kickoff Family Fun Run* across the top. A 5K and a mile run/walk on Sunday, June 4th—a week from today.

*Run one more race.* It's on my bucket list, as a backup to running the marathon. And even though it's soon, I've been feeling decent. Plus, I won't have another treatment until I start radiation in four weeks. If I do the mile, maybe I could eke out a final win for the record books.

That evening, when Mom comes to say good night, I motion her in. "What's up?" she asks as she sits on my bed.

"I want to talk to you about something."

"Okay."

I hesitate for a second before handing her the flyer. She reads it, then looks up with a "No" about to break free from her lips.

"Not the 5K," I say before she can speak. "Just the mile."

Mom's mouth is a straight line. "I know you miss running,

but there will be plenty of opportunities after you're done with treatment."

Since responding with "What if this is my last chance?" will derail the conversation, I say, "I've had to give up so much this year, and it's not like I'm asking to run the marathon—can't I have this?"

Several seconds pass. The air-conditioning hums. Finally, she says, "I'll agree to the mile if you jog and I go with you."

"Mo-om. Jogging isn't running. I want to push myself a little."

"I understand. But don't lose sight of the fact that you are pushing yourself. Your body is working hard to get rid of the cancer cells."

"That's not the same."

Mom gives me a sympathetic smile. "I'll register us for the mile. It'll be fun." She kisses the top of my head.

After she leaves, I stare at the flyer, dwelling again on the marathon. I wish I had a crystal ball and could know if I ever would have been fast enough to qualify for Boston.

A couple days later, Mom brings two cups of orange blossom tea to the island and sits across from me. "I registered us for the walk."

*I guess we're not even calling it a race.* "Thanks." I wrap my hands around the mug and inhale the citrusy scent as the steam warms my face.

Mom stirs honey into hers, then sets down the spoon, the metal clinking on the saucer. "The event organizer has an idea I want to run by you. She thinks your participation might make a good story and suggested we talk to a reporter she knows."

"A newspaper reporter?"

"Yes, for the local paper. She gave me her name and number, but before I reach out, I'd like to hear your thoughts."

*Okay, not where I expected this conversation to go.* "So, she would write a story about me?"

"Only if you're comfortable with it." Mom takes a sip. "She would talk to you about the race and what you've gone through over the past five months."

*Huh.* I let the idea of strangers being interested in my cancer journey sink in. "What do you think?"

Mom waits a moment before answering. "I think you've handled all of this with such grace, and anyone who reads the story would be inspired by your courage and determination." She pauses. "But I also think this is a very personal struggle, and you don't owe it to anyone to do something you don't want to do."

I'm still not sure my story is newsworthy, but if this woman believes I could inspire someone else, then I'm on board. And it might be fun to get my 15 minutes of fame. "Let's do it," I say, and an idea pops into my head. "If they use a picture, can it be one of Charlie's?"

Mom smiles. "I'll ask."

The next day, Mom, Laine, Charlie, and I meet with the reporter. She introduces herself as Devyn Channing, and I wonder if her name is real. She's friendly and doesn't appear put off by my bald head, which gives her extra points in my book.

After we've all shaken hands, we go into the family room. Devyn sits on the couch, then pats the cushion next to her. "Adele, please." As I sit, she asks, "Do you prefer Adele or Dell?"

"Either is fine. People call me both."

Devyn rests a notebook on her lap, the bright pink of her nails standing out against the black cover. Her hair is blonde, short, and straight, angled down from her ears to her chin. She tucks one side back, then clicks her pen. "Your mom told me a little about you—she said you're a runner. Can you share a bit about that?"

I glance at Mom, not quite sure what to say or how much, but she nods her encouragement. "Yeah. My mom and I started running together when I was…maybe nine? And I started running seriously around twelve."

"Have you been able to run since you were diagnosed with cancer?"

"I ran a 5K right before we found out." *The icy mud run from hell.* "I was training for my first marathon too…but I haven't been able to keep up with that."

I'm relieved Devyn doesn't ask anything about the marathon. I swallow a couple times to make the lump in my throat go away.

"What made you decide to do this race?"

"Well, I won't exactly be racing. But I love running, and I miss the race environment."

Devyn nods as she writes. We talk about school and cross-country and my friends and family. Once she's gotten all the information she wants, she flips her pad closed and pats her lap. "This is great. We'll run a photo with the story—your mom mentioned you might have one you'd like to use?"

I nod at Charlie, who springs up from the chair and sits on my other side. "I've taken a lot of pictures of Dell." He smiles at me. "What style would be best?"

"One of her running for sure." Devyn rests her pen against her chin. "In case we can use two, give me a portrait style as well." She reaches into her bag and pulls out a business card. "Email the pictures to that address, ideally by this afternoon."

When Devyn stands, the rest of us follow suit and walk her to the door.

"Thank you for meeting with me. The story will run tomorrow in the print edition and online."

The next morning, everyone in my family crowds around the paper, which is silly since Dad reads it aloud:

"'George Bellows High School senior Adele Marshall has been a runner since she was nine. But five months ago, her whole world changed: she was diagnosed with stage IIIB Hodgkin's lymphoma. She quickly began chemotherapy and is due to receive radiation soon.

"'A driven, accomplished athlete, Adele—Dell—is a valued member of the school's cross-country team. She ran her most recent race the day before learning she had cancer. Since then, she's had to pause training for her first marathon to focus on getting better. As for her decision to participate in the city's Summer Kickoff Family Fun Run, Dell says, "I love running, and I miss the race environment."

"'Supported by her parents, Neil and Sylvia Marshall; her two sisters, Elaine (19) and Jillian (7); and her boyfriend, fellow GBHS senior Charlie Boyd, Dell is eager to participate in the race this Sunday. Although she'd love to compete in the 5K, she's grateful to be able to jog the mile, with her mom (also a runner) by her side.

"'Event organizers express their admiration for this courageous young lady. "Adele is an inspiration," said Michelle Gandollini, head of the Rotary Club, which is sponsoring the race. "We're so honored to have her be a part of this event."

"'GBHS staff echoed these sentiments. Anthony Melton, the high school's principal, said, "Adele has been so brave over the past year. She always has a smile for the office staff, even when she's not feeling her best. All of us at GBHS will be cheering for her come June fourth."

"'For this race, the time stamp at the end doesn't matter. When Dell jogs across the finish line, she'll be the winner of the day.'"

Dad puts down the paper, and we all exchange smiles. Mom

wipes a tear from her eye and gives me a hug. Despite not getting to run, excitement bubbles up within me.

132

# #20: KISS AT THE TOP OF THE FERRIS WHEEL

Now that chemo is done, I feel the best I've felt in months. Not pre-cancer good, but it's all relative. So when the state fair opens, Mom agrees to let me go with Charlie.

Walking through the gates is like being swallowed by one of my favorite parts of summer—the bright midway lights, the smell of fried foods, the *ding*ing of games. The fair has heralded the end of school and the beginning of freedom for as long as I can remember, and I'm delighted to be in the thick of it all once more.

I tug on Charlie's hand and steer us toward the giant slide. "This will be okay for you, right?" I ask, though you'd think with my stomach, which still has its bad days, it would be the other way around. But Charlie despises roller coasters and any other kind of thrill ride.

"Yeah. Will it be okay for you?"

"Only one way to find out." I smile like I'm joking, but there's some truth to it.

As we stand in line, I close my eyes and savor the breeze blowing across my face, the late-day sun warming my skin. I listen to the joyful screams that crescendo, then fade as a nearby coaster zooms toward us before speeding away.

"You look happy." Charlie's voice in my ear.

I open my eyes. "I am happy."

He wraps his arms around me from behind and rests his chin on my shoulder, his curls soft against my head. Since taking senior pictures, I've been more comfortable not wearing the wig. Despite some double takes, most people have been warm and friendly, treating me like anyone else, which is the greatest kindness.

We climb the ride's steps until we reach the top. Six people slide simultaneously. Charlie and I each take a mat and place them in neighboring lanes.

"Ready?" He places a hand on his camera to hold it to his chest.

I nod, and we push off.

It's a rush, the wind against my skin as the fair goes by in a blur. Everything has a muted quality that is peaceful and welcome.

Charlie makes it to the bottom before me and pulls me to my feet once I come to a stop.

Grinning, I ask, "Want to do it again?"

He hesitates. "Or we could play some games first, give your body time to recover, just in case?"

That would probably be the smarter move.

*Eh.* "One more time, then we'll do something else." I clasp my hands under my chin and give him puppy dog eyes until he relents.

After our second time, I'm content to keep my feet on the ground since my stomach is giving the barest hint of a warning not to push it. *Fine.*

From past years, we know better than to attempt tossing rings onto bottles, but Charlie's not bad at darts. I stare at his profile as he concentrates, licking his lips before letting go of the dart. The *pop* of the balloon is so sharp, I jump.

He hits enough to win a stuffed monkey that quickly becomes cumbersome to carry. At least it has long arms and Velcro hands. I sling it over my back and fasten the hands so it hangs from my neck. Charlie, of course, takes a picture.

This plush primate is dense, and after a few minutes, my lungs protest the extra weight.

"Here, give it to me." Charlie lifts the monkey over my head and drapes it over his forearm.

"I have a better idea." I motion for Charlie to follow me toward the exit. "Are you emotionally attached to our new friend?"

Charlie raises his eyebrows. "Not particularly. But I don't want to be an accomplice to monkey murder, if that's what you're suggesting."

I roll my eyes and open my arms. Charlie pauses before handing it over. "Don't make me regret this."

I scan the area for families who are leaving. No point in saddling someone else with something they'll have to carry all night, but if I can find…yes! I walk up to presumably a mom and a dad, whose daughter is riding on his shoulders.

"Hi. My boyfriend won this, but we'd rather not carry it— would you like it?" I show it to the girl but glance at the parents to make sure it's okay. They smile, and the dad crouches so his daughter can get down and take the monkey. It's as big as she is, but she hugs it tight, its feet dragging across the pavement.

"That's so nice," the mom says.

The dad turns to the girl. "What do you say?"

She beams at me around the monkey's head and screams, "Thank you!"

I laugh. "You're welcome."

When I return to Charlie, he kisses me. As we walk back into the heart of the fair, he says, "Is it okay if I get something to eat?"

"Of course."

"Anything better or worse for you to smell?"

"You're sweet to ask, but get what you want."

Apparently, what calls Charlie's name is a "donut burger" (yep, donuts are the "buns") and fried Oreos, because that's what he brings to the bench where I'm sitting.

"Wow."

"I couldn't decide between deep-fried Oreos and deep-fried Reese's."

"That was the debate? Not whether a donut burger was a good idea?"

"Nope. That was a given." He takes a giant bite and smiles at me, making his cheeks puff out.

After Charlie finishes eating, it's dark enough that I lead us toward the Ferris wheel. It's more romantic at night, beckoning with its dazzling lights and inviting us into its cozy, intimate cars.

We sit side by side, both facing out, and Charlie puts his arm around my shoulders. The noise from below drifts away as we rise. Charlie turns toward me and brushes his hand over the back of my neck. But he doesn't kiss me. Not yet. Not until we're at the top. Because that's the game—building the anticipation.

I put my hand on his knee and inch it up his thigh. I go further than I normally do, and his eyes practically sparkle as he grips my neck. He puts his free hand on my side, then slides it higher, upping the ante to match my play. As our car hits the northeastern most point before reaching the top, it's all we can do to wait.

The second we dip downward, we lean forward and our lips collide. His mouth presses hungrily against mine, and I pull him tight against me. My heart races as my body tingles. It's the hottest twenty seconds of my life.

We grin at each other once we finally sit back and take a breath. But maybe because of the adrenaline and hormones coursing through my system, the motion going down is somehow different than going up. I don't feel great when we step off and pause outside the gate.

"You okay?" Charlie asks.

"Yeah. It's my stomach. I'll be fine, just give me a minute."

Charlie reaches into one of the pockets on his cargo shorts. "Would these help?" He hands me a Ziploc bag of raw almonds, cashews, and sunflower seeds, which generally sit well.

"You're amazing. You know that, right?"

He smiles and shrugs.

I eat a handful of nuts and try to settle not only my stomach, but also the anger at myself that's bubbling up. What did I expect to eat tonight? Did I imagine I'd find something—anything—here that would be a viable option? No, because I didn't give it a single consideration. I was so fixated on the fun parts that I ignored what I might need, so yet again, I'm dependent on someone else.

"Feeling any better?" Charlie interrupts my self-pity.

"Yeah." I pop another nut in my mouth to give myself time to collect my thoughts. After I swallow, I say, "This is so nice of you. I just…sometimes I wish people didn't always have to take care of me."

"I'm not 'taking care of you' like you can't take care of yourself. I just did something nice for you. You do nice things for me all the time."

"I know. But I didn't take care of myself tonight. I did need you to do it for me."

"Okay, so what? I'm happy to."

"But I don't like needing so much." I sigh. "I wish I could care for someone else every now and then."

Charlie stares into my eyes for several seconds. I think maybe he'll kiss me, but in a quick, decisive movement, he demands my hand, then marches us down the midway.

"Where are we going?"

"You'll see." He walks faster as we head into the area with bigger rides, until he plants us at the back of the line for the Infinity—a circular track where you go back and forth, gaining momentum until you're upside down. A thrill ride.

"What are you doing?"

"I'm going to ride it."

"What? Why?"

His face pales, giving him a ghostly quality in the darkness, but he takes both my hands in his. "You've had to do so much you didn't want to do this year. Now it's my turn."

It's a sweet gesture, but not logical. "That doesn't make any sense. Besides, I'm having fun with all the other things—you really don't have to do this."

"I *want* to do it."

That may be what his mouth says, but everything about his body says otherwise.

"You do realize that your suffering doesn't cancel mine, right?"

"Of course it doesn't. But they say misery loves company, so…"

When he digs his heels in, he's kind of hard to win an argument against, but I'm not ready to throw in the towel yet. "I'm not miserable now. And I'd much rather enjoy the rest of the night with you than keep you company while you hurl."

"I won't hurl."

I'm unconvinced.

"I know what I'm doing," Charlie continues. "Just let me do it, okay? And maybe let me hold your hand until we get to the front of the line."

His mind is clearly made up. I shake my head and offer my hand.

As we move forward, he gets quieter and quieter. I give up trying to distract him, and instead lean into him, our arms sandwiched between our bodies.

By the time we reach the front, I'm a little worried. He's breathing fast and squeezing my hand so hard it hurts. "Are you sure about this?" I ask.

"Yes." He sounds anything but sure.

The ride's cars slow until they come to a stop. I wish Charlie had his eyes closed and wasn't watching the previous occupants wobble their way to the exit. Before he steps in, I give him a kiss and take his camera. "I'll be right here." It takes great restraint to not climb in after him since I (used to) love this kind of thing, but given that the Ferris wheel made me queasy, this would be asking for trouble.

He grips the lap bar so hard his knuckles are white, and once he moves, his face is a grimace of surprise, terror, and nausea.

Because it's a loop, he's visible the whole time, during each swing farther up the track, then for the second he hangs before dropping backward. So, I keep seeing his expression. *He shouldn't have done this. I shouldn't have let him.*

My heartbeat accelerates as he nears the summit. Finally, he goes all the way around, backward, several times. Then round and round again facing forward. I want it to be over.

After another full rotation, he gradually loses speed until he comes to a stop.

With shaky hands, he unlatches his harness and steps out. I return his camera and offer a smile, but he can't manage to return it. We don't say anything as we file through the exit. Once we can walk side by side, I take his hand and lead him to a bench.

He puts his elbows on his knees and leans forward, and I rub his back. Without looking up, he asks, "You like this feeling?"

"I don't think it feels like this for me."

Even after a couple minutes have passed, he doesn't change positions. I bend my head closer to his. "You really didn't have to do this, but it means a lot that you wanted to."

He squeezes my hand but says nothing.

I crouch in front of him. When he meets my eyes, we stare at each other for several seconds.

"I love you," I say.

He swallows. "I love you too, but because I love you, I'm trying really hard right now to not throw up on you."

As I return to the bench, I say, "We probably should have done this before the donut burger," and he gives me a little chuckle. "Here, this should help." I lift his hand and rub my index and middle fingers up and down between the tendons on the underside of his wrist.

He draws in slow breaths and, after a little while, says, "That is helping. How did you know to do that?"

"It's a trick for managing nausea they taught me at the hospital."

At last he gives me a real smile, then puts his arm around me. "Thank you for taking care of me."

"My pleasure."

After a pause: "It felt good to take care of me—right?"

I lift my head to look at him. "Yes…" *Where is he going with this?*

"It's not a burden to take care of someone you care so much about." He points his eyes at me, and I tilt my head in understanding.

He knew all along.

Going on the Infinity wasn't about doing something he didn't want to do to even the score. It was about doing something he knew would wreck him so I'd have to—get to— take care of him.

"The satisfaction you got from helping me—you understand I feel that too?" he presses.

I smile. "I suppose so."

"Okay, then you shouldn't worry about needing help. People want to help you—*I* want to help you, because..." He draws it out, waiting for me to say it.

"Because you love me."

"Because I love you." He smiles before kissing me.

*Okay, you win.*

# #2: RUN ONE MORE RACE

Everybody gets up early Sunday, me and Mom so we can get ready to r—*jog*, I remind myself—and Dad, Laine, and Bean since they're coming to cheer us on.

The race starts at the middle school and ends in front of the library. Mom and I accept everyone's hugs, then head toward the start. Even though I'll be jogging and it's only a mile, I still feel the excited flutter in my stomach that I always experience before a race.

People line both sides of the street, filling the sidewalks. The crowd is bigger than I expected—much bigger. I know thousands, probably tens of thousands, will show up for the marathon, but this summer fun run is hardly the same draw. I'm so distracted by the turnout that I pass several signs before they register:

*Way to go, Adele!*

*Dell, you can do it!*

*We're proud of you, Dell!*

I check whether I know the people holding the signs, but I don't recognize their faces. As I continue scanning the crowd, my cheeks flush.

*You're so brave, Dell*
*Dell is #1!*
*GBHS hearts Adele*
*You've got this, Dell!*

And on and on… I turn to Mom. "What is all this?"

She smiles from ear to ear. "It was Laine's idea. She reached out to Devyn, who helped coordinate—some race volunteers made the signs and offered them to people who want to show their support."

I'm speechless.

Once the race is underway, I'm glad I'm moving slowly enough to read more signs as we pass. A lot of people holding them are strangers, but several are familiar—friends from school, some teachers, and a couple girls from the cross-country team…but not my small group. *No matter.* I wave to people like I'm in a parade.

At one point along the route, the spectators stand three people deep. The outpouring of support makes my blood pump faster, my feet itch to move. I contain my excitement as long as I can, but once we pass Graeter's (best ice cream ever), I turn to Mom. "Can I run? Please?"

She tilts her head like she's about to shake it.

"It might be the last time." *Let's lay all the cards on the table here.*

We stare at each other for several seconds. Tears gleam in Mom's eyes when she whispers, "Yes. Run."

I face forward and pick up the pace. People in front of me shift sideways as I come up behind them. Some of the other racers clap and call my name as I pass. People on the sidewalk cheer for me too. It's ridiculous how winded I am after such a short distance, but I pep myself up with the thought, *It's less than a quarter mile. You can do this.*

Just like I've pushed myself so many times before.

As I near the finish, I recognize a greater percentage of the crowd. Shannon, half a block from the end, holds a sign I know she made herself: *You're a rock star.* I wave to her, then with every ounce of energy I can muster, I sprint across the finish line. The cheers that go up are so loud, my ears hurt.

I'm immediately smothered by my family and Charlie. Mom joins us and places her hands on either side of my face, her eyes still glistening.

The love keeps coming, as person after person walks up to congratulate me. Even at my best cross-country meets, the end of a race never felt like this.

Once the adrenaline wears off, though, fatigue sets in. I desperately want to sit, but don't want to miss out on any of the day's joy. Clearly, Mom recognizes my exhaustion. After the last people in our vicinity leave, she puts her hand on my back. "Let's go home and continue this celebration from the couch."

In the van, I text Shannon.

> Hey. Sorry I missed you after the race. We're keeping the party going at my house. Want to come over?

A minute later, my phone buzzes.

> Not up for a party today. But enjoy—congrats.

> By party, I meant my family and Charlie. I know you don't love people, but they're safe. I want you there.

> Just not a good day for me, okay?

> Why? What's going on?

When she doesn't reply, I try again.

We can talk at my house. Please? You made this race possible for me. I want to share it with you.

After another minute, she relents.

Okay.

Mom splurges and orders Duck Donuts. I'm slowly regaining my taste for food, and I enjoy one with blueberry icing, lemon drizzle, and coconut, then lick the sticky glaze from my fingers and settle on the couch.

Charlie shows me his pictures, which lets me read some of the signs I missed. I thank Laine for rallying the troops.

"I'm thrilled it turned out the way it did. Also, Matt says congratulations."

I nod, then raise my mug of tea and toast Shannon, who squirms at the attention.

Once we're all stuffed with sugary dough, Charlie heads out to let me rest. I follow him to the door to say goodbye. When I return to the family room, Shannon meets me with her purse slung over her shoulder.

"Don't go," I say. "We can hang out longer."

She hesitates, but I start up the stairs. "Come on," I call, hoping she'll follow.

As I climb into bed, Shannon closes my bedroom door, then sits in my desk chair.

It's too hot to be under the covers, so I push them off and cross my legs. "You know what I'm thinking we do next? Goat yoga."

"Seriously?" Shannon's expression is off, lacking its usual amused snark.

"It sounds fun. No?"

"If you say so."

Am I imagining an edge to her voice? "Are you okay? What's going on?"

"Everything's fine." Her jaw moves, but her lips stay pressed together.

Everything is clearly not fine. "You sound mad." Is she mad at me? Because I made her come over?

Shannon scoots the chair back and folds her arms across her chest. "Look, I'm glad the race went well and you got to run and so many people came out to support you."

I wait for the *But.*

"But maybe that should be enough."

"Enough how?" I know this race was my win; I'm not asking to run the marathon (*unless I keep feeling better...*)

"Enough that you're not constantly telling me what we should do next."

Heat rises in my body. "What?" Is she calling me out for wanting to do more on my bucket list?

She stands. "Sorry, I should go."

Nope, I'm not letting her off the hook that easily. "If you have something to say to me, then say it."

She doesn't hesitate. "You should be more grateful."

I stare at her incredulously, my mouth opening with a pissed-off exhale.

"Not that you have cancer, obviously." She sits back down. "But Noah didn't get a *fraction* of what you're getting to do."

"And you don't think I'm grateful? I said earlier how thankful I am for today."

"Yeah, and now you're onto the next thing."

"What's so terrible about that?" *The clock is ticking.* "You're the one who said a bucket list was a good idea."

"It is a good idea." Her voices rises as she says, "But it should be for things that matter, not frivolous crap that pops into your head."

I start to object, but she cuts me off.

"Do you know how much it would have meant to my brother to compete in another swim meet, or get a dog? Or have an honest conversation with our parents where they told him they loved him like it might be the last time he heard it?" She shakes her head and stares at the floor.

"You don't think the things I'm doing are important to me?" This is so ridiculous, I can't even wrap my head around it. "I *love* running."

"Okay, but the cave thing? And goat yoga? Really?"

My cheeks flush. "Fine, maybe they're not all life-changing things, but if I didn't have cancer and wanted to do them, would you judge me?"

"I'm not judging you—"

"Yes, you are."

She throws up her hands and stands again. "I told you I was having a shit day, you should've let me be."

As she heads for the door, I stand too. "And you shouldn't hide from your feelings." *Two can play this game.*

She whirls on me, her eyes wide. "Oh, you're one to talk."

"What the hell does that mean?"

"Come on, you haven't considered that maybe you're using the whole list thing to avoid dealing with your pain and anger and fear of dying?"

My lips part, but it takes a second to find the words. "How can you possibly say that? The *point* of a bucket list is to do the things you want to do before you die. It's fundamentally about facing death."

The smirk on Shannon's face is cold. "Or it's about checking things off because that's how you pretend you have some control over this."

"It's not pretending! The list does give me control—if I'm going out, I'm going out on *my* terms. If I can't beat cancer, at least I'll do the things I want to do first."

"And what if your time runs out before you do everything? Then what?"

I don't say anything. I don't like Shannon's honesty today.

"I'm all for the list, but completing it shouldn't be the goal. It's just there to help you prioritize what will make your last days the best they can be, in here—" She pokes herself in the chest so hard I hear it. "It's not about how much you accomplish."

"Accomplishing things makes me feel good in here." I pound my chest too.

"When you're on your deathbed, what are you going to regret? Not doing goat yoga?"

"What will you regret?" I retort. "Being mad at your parents about Noah won't bring him back, you know. At some point, you have to accept it and move on."

Shannon audibly huffs. "Okay, Dell. You believe what you want about which of us is in denial."

She storms out, slamming the door hard enough to rattle the picture frame on the wall, and I'm left staring after her, stunned.

---

Laine sits on my bed and raises her eyebrows. "What was that about?"

I lean my head on her shoulder. Then I tell her about the fight, about the bucket list. Not all of it, but the parts that won't get me in trouble.

"Everyone wants me to think positively and believe I'll get better, but in case I don't, I want the time I have left to mean something." I look up with tears in my eyes. "Crossing as many things off the list as I can is better than just waiting to die." *It has to be.*

"Of course it is." Laine takes my hand in hers. "Maybe

Shannon isn't so much mad about your list as she is sad that her brother didn't get these kinds of opportunities."

I don't know. She sure sounded mad at me.

"Grief is hard," Laine continues. "And it's even harder if you don't have anyone to help you through it." Her voice is gentle, but it's clear she's taking Shannon's side. "I'm sure what you're going through is bringing back a lot of memories of her brother. Cut her a little slack."

*I suppose she has a point.* I nod.

"You two are good for each other." Laine gives me a squeeze before leaving.

Settled against my pillow, I pick up my phone.

> I'm sorry. Not for refusing to give you space, because I'm going to turn you into a people person if it's the last thing I do, but because today you needed a friend, and I should have been there.

The dots flash, but it takes five minutes before her response comes through.

> I'm sorry too. Not my place to judge anyone's coping strategies. Though with the potential for disease, I do think goat yoga is a bad idea.

> Fair point. Do you want to talk about Noah? Really talk? I'm happy to listen.

> Thanks, but I'm okay. Helped to blow off some steam.

> You know you can talk to me, right? Anytime.

Maybe I should call or go to her house to coax her into opening up. But I realize I don't know where she lives. I've never met her parents or seen a picture of her brother. I don't know if she has posters on her walls or how messy her room is (guessing very, based on her car) or what kind of pet she would have if she could.

For everything I've confided in her, she still keeps me at a distance. *She keeps everyone at a distance.* And it breaks my heart.

# #10: HAVE SEX

Charlie and I have been together a long time, so we've done *stuff*, we just haven't done *it*.

But I don't want to die a virgin.

Since a spontaneous, in-the-heat-of-the-moment rendezvous isn't in the cards, how do I bring it up? Although I'm sure he wouldn't turn me down, the idea of texting, *You want to have sex?* leaves something to be desired.

I wish I'd said something the night of our hot make-out session at the top of the Ferris wheel. Maybe if I could somehow recreate that sexual tension...

Turns out, I'm overthinking it.

The next time Charlie comes over, we find ourselves in my room, which means I'm in my bed. I pat the space next to me, which he happily occupies. He slides down until our faces align and we commence kissing.

When there's a break in the action, I reach for his hand and sandwich it between our chests. "I want to talk to you about something."

"Sure, what's up?"

I give a nervous smile as he waits expectantly. "You know I love you, right?"

"This isn't a preface to you saying we should see other people, is it?" The lightness of his tone tells me he's not actually worried. But I still hurry to reassure him.

"No, definitely not. It's, like, the opposite of that."

"We should see no other people? Your family might have a problem with that—they're pretty fond of you." He grins, clearly proud of himself.

"Okay, wiseass, I'm trying to be serious."

"Sorry. Why is it important that I know you love me?"

I thread my fingers through his, giving me something to focus on for a second before I hold his gaze. "I think we should take our relationship to the next level."

The glint in his eyes tells me he gets my meaning. "You do?"

My pulse throbs in my ears. I don't know why I'm so anxious —it's not like we haven't talked about this before. But before, it was hypothetical, a conversation about someday. "I do," I say firmly. *Someday* feels too uncertain now, and I don't want to regret not sharing this with Charlie. "If you want to."

"Oh, I want to."

I laugh as he tries to not sound so eager.

"I mean, if you're sure." He stares into my eyes, like he's searching my face for reassurance. "It's a big step—I don't want to do it unless you're absolutely sure you're ready."

"I'm ready." I squeeze his hand.

"Will it be safe for you?"

"According to Dr. Google, yeah, with protection and everything. The anemia might have been a problem, but now that my red cell count is up, it should be fine."

Charlie's eyebrows unknit as his face relaxes. "Oh, it will be more than fine." He puts his hand on the back of my neck and pulls me close.

We decide it will be best to do this at Charlie's house. His dad goes to the office every day, and his two younger brothers are at camp most weeks. We just need a block of time when his mom will be gone.

Grocery store runs and other errands are too unpredictable. But when she informs Charlie that she'll be volunteering the next day at the Ronald McDonald House downtown, which involves a four-hour shift plus drive time, he texts me, his giddiness apparent.

Tomorrow, 10:00!!!

I giggle.

As the minutes slowly tick by the following morning, I debate whether to tell Laine. *Maybe after.*

When I ask Mom to borrow the van, I keep my voice casual, despite my fear that she'll say she needs it for something. But she says, "Sure, have fun," and I think, *Oh, you have no idea.*

Truthfully, neither do I.

Mom told me once that the first time can hurt a little. How much is a little? And will it be better or worse for me, given everything I've been through?

Regardless, this is something I've wanted for a while. Long before the bucket list. Before I had cancer. It's scary, the idea of being so vulnerable with someone. But it could be amazing too, and I can't imagine anyone I'd rather experience it with than Charlie, even if I were going to live till I was a hundred.

He lets me in, and our fingers entwine as we walk down the hallway. My pulse raced the second I parked in the driveway, but now it rachets up another notch. I know sex can be like a workout, but are you supposed to be this sweaty before you start?

Neither of us says anything as we climb the stairs, although Charlie slides his hand down my side and over my butt, which makes me laugh. I look over my shoulder, and he waggles his eyebrows.

He locks the door to his room even though we're alone in the house. Candles adorn every surface—the dresser, desk, and nightstand. Even the floor and bookshelves. From floor to ceiling, it glows.

"This is beautiful."

"Just like you." He takes my hand and leads me to his bed, where we lie facing each other. I throw a leg over Charlie's and scoot closer, sliding my hand up his back as our lips meet. A minute passes before we come up for air, and we're both breathing hard.

Tenderly, Charlie places his hand on the back of my head and looks deep into my eyes. "You're sure? That this is what you want, and that you feel up for it?"

I nuzzle my head into his hand. "I'm sure. You too?"

"So sure."

With that, I reach for the button at his neck, and he lifts the bottom of my shirt.

We go slow, Charlie careful to move at a pace that's comfortable for me. His skin is warm against mine as he positions himself. He dips his head to gently kiss my collarbone and neck as our bodies become one. It hurts a little, but I keep my eyes on his until the pain subsides.

My heart wells up with a love that fills me so completely, it's like a second circulatory system, running through veins that touch every part of me, from my toes to my fingertips and all the way up to my forehead. I take in a sharp breath, overwhelmed by the true awesomeness of this moment.

In addition to the sounds of our breathing, there's a lot of Charlie asking if I'm okay. I assure him repeatedly that I'm fine —great, actually.

When it seems like we're close to the end, I grip Charlie's shoulders.

After his body shudders against me, he leans down so our foreheads touch. "I love you beyond words, Adele Marshall."

And with that, I'm completely undone. So many feelings compete inside me—love for Charlie, this boy who has been my best friend for as long as I've known him and who has been my rock these past several months; gratitude that I felt good enough to do this, that I was granted enough time for us to share this experience and be each other's firsts; shock at how intense it was, in the best way possible; and happiness, pure happiness to be right here, right now.

Flooded as I am with emotion and tears, it takes me a second to choke out, "I love you too."

As soon as Charlie realizes I'm crying, he pulls back. "Oh my God, did I hurt you? We shouldn't have done this."

"No." I shake my head. "I'm *wonderful*."

Charlie stares at me until he's sure I'm okay, then kisses me again, our most gentle kiss ever, before settling beside me. I scrunch down so I can rest my head on his chest and close my eyes. The beat of his heart is so soothing, I would gladly stay like this forever.

# #1: RUN A MARATHON—PART 1: TRAINING

Given how often Shannon picks me up, it would make sense for her to stop dumping stuff in the front passenger seat. But today is no different than every other time—I scoop up the pile and drop it onto the back seat before getting in.

"Where are we going?" she asks.

"The running trail."

She takes her hand off the gear shift and looks at me, a question in her eyes.

"You were right," I tell her. "I should focus on things that really matter to me. So, I want to see if I can run a marathon."

Her head tilts with disapproval, so I keep talking to try to earn her buy-in. "I'll take it slow, and I'll adjust the timeline depending on how it goes." *Fingers crossed I don't feel as bad with radiation as I did with chemo.* "There are several more Ohio marathons this year, and if the training goes well, I'll figure out which one to run."

With a resigned expression, Shannon says, "I'm guessing your parents and doctor haven't signed off on this?"

Heat rises in me, and I debate whether telling her was the right decision. I considered reaching out to one of the girls on the cross-country team, but the ones I was closest with seem to have forgotten I exist, and it's too much to ask of those I'm less close with.

"I'll tell them, once I know if it's possible." I know this isn't helping my case, so I add, "But I did Google it, and they say exercise is good for people with cancer."

"Yeah…" Shannon adjusts the vents so the air-conditioning blows on her, making wispy strands of hair dance around her forehead. "But what about the risk of infection? What if you fall and scrape your knee or something?"

I narrow my eyes at her. "You're very fixated on infection."

She shrugs. "You have to worry about it with leukemia too. Not to go somewhere dark, but when the end came for Noah, that's what did it."

We're both quiet for a minute.

"Look, I'm not trying to mother you or whatever, I'm really not. I just know how easy it is for you to get an infection because your immune system is shot to shit. Noah got one after another—he ended up in the hospital several times, then they pulled him out of school because it was too risky, and eventually, he went up against a virus he couldn't beat." After glancing at me, she says, "I don't want the same thing to happen to you."

*When people act in my best interest, it's harder to be frustrated with them.* "Thanks, I appreciate that you care." I wait for her to meet my eyes. "But think about how much it would have meant to Noah to swim with dolphins before he died." My tone is soft. I'm not laying a guilt trip on her, only helping her understand how important this is to me.

Several seconds pass before she sighs. "You're going to make me run?"

I smile. "Give it a chance—you might like it."

"I'd rather talk to a roomful of strangers."

As she finally puts the car into reverse, I say, "Do you want to change—we can swing by your house first."

"Nah, this will be fine."

I eye her shorts—they're definitely going to chafe—as I pull off my T-shirt, revealing my sports bra underneath. I grab a running tank from my tote bag and slip it on.

Once we're on the trail, I show Shannon how to stretch, after getting over my surprise that this is something that requires instruction. It's second nature to me.

"How far do we have to go?"

"We'll ease in—let's do a mile."

Shannon straightens up. "That's easing in? I haven't run a mile since they made us in elementary school."

"Seriously?" From my straddle position on the pavement, I look up at her while pulling my toes toward my knee.

"What's so hard to believe about that?" Shannon's gaze follows a woman jogging with her dog. "Not everyone runs. I bet the boyfriend doesn't—am I right?"

As I stand, I picture Charlie running, but the mental image doesn't fit. "You're right." With a nod at Shannon, I take off, and she follows. "But it's so calming."

"Potato, potahto—you say calming, I say painful."

Neither of us says anything for a while. The first quarter mile feels good—moving my body, hearing the rhythmic pounding of my footsteps, being in nature. A chipmunk dashes into the grass along the trail as we approach, and a yellow butterfly flutters in the air up ahead. We pass old men walking and talking, and moms pushing strollers, while bikes periodically whiz by. *This is where I belong.*

About halfway through, the familiar stitch in my side aches, and I breathe in through my nose, out through my mouth.

"You...okay?" Shannon asks.

"Yep... You?"

She wobbles her head in a noncommittal nod.

Despite not being able to fill my lungs, we finish the mile. After taking a few more steps, I put my hands on my knees and lean forward.

"Oh my God, I'm dying." Shannon lies on the pavement.

I kick the bottom of her shoe. "You are not."

"There is no way in hell I will ever run 26 miles."

*You'll have to if you want to keep up with me,* I think but don't say. "It gets easier the more you do it."

"May be true, but I ain't gonna find out."

"Come on." I reach out a hand and pull her up. "I'll buy you an ice cream."

"I want a smoothie."

"Fine, I'll buy you a smoothie."

"A big one."

---

Given how well my first day of training went, I'm ready to go again the next day. But Shannon is not.

Two miles today?

Uhhhhhh...

Baby.

One mile then.

I am so sore. Why do my sides hurt this much? Weren't my legs doing all the work?

That's your core. Maybe you could stand to strengthen it if one mile did you in.

Har har.

I rub my own side, which aches a little too. But not enough to stop me.

Pick me up at 10?

Sorry, Dell. I'm not up for running today. Maybe tomorrow.

Disappointed, I sit on my bed. Even though I don't have a firm training plan since I'm not sure which marathon I might run, it's a waste to not log some miles on a day when I feel up for it. Maybe I should go on my own—I'll be careful.

After I stuff another running tank in my tote and lace up my shoes, I ask to borrow the minivan.

"Going to Charlie's?" Mom asks.

"Yep, I won't be gone long," I say quickly, like I can verbally outrun my lie.

On the trail, I stretch, then gaze out over the path. Thankfully, most of the trail is in the shade—it's already warm enough that my shirt sticks to my back, and it's only early June.

I take a deep(ish) breath and move. But not for long. A side stitch sends sharp pains through my torso after a few minutes. When I can't alleviate it through breathing, I pause and stretch again, but that doesn't help either.

*No pain, no gain*, I think, then put one foot in front of the other.

As badly as I want to get two miles in, I'm winded after a mile and a half. I keep going for another tenth of a mile, but my chest hurts so much, I flat-out stop, sacrificing the cooldown.

While I recover, I watch two squirrels zip past, one chasing the other into a tree. *It will take time to get back to peak running form*, I remind myself.

So, I keep plugging away, logging four notable runs over the next five days:

**1. Shannon goes with me on Saturday, and we run another mile.**

I'm a little disappointed when she texts since I know I could run farther on my own. But it's nice of her, and since she completes the mile without needing to collapse at the end, we celebrate with more smoothies.

**2. I run two and a half miles.**

Despite pushing myself to get to 3.1, to prove I could run a 5K again, my body refuses to go past 2.5. But still—it's the farthest I've run in five months.

**3. My two-mile run Monday is hard, but I get it done anyway.**

It's frustrating to cover less distance than the day before, but given the intensity of this side stitch, I'm proud of pushing through the pain to finish the second mile.

**4. Shannon and I run Wednesday, and a day of rest has done me good.**

"Let's…keep going," I say after a mile.

Shannon doesn't respond but she also doesn't stop. We finish a second mile. I'm ready to go for a third, but Shannon holds out an arm as she slows. "Wait…"

I jog in place as she catches her breath.

"Don't you think that's…enough for today?"

"One more mile… Then you can say…you ran a 5K."

She shakes her head. "No more… I'm done." Like a toddler throwing a tantrum, she sits cross-legged on the ground.

Reluctantly, I join her on the pavement. "You don't have to keep running with me."

"I know it's important to you." She plucks a blade of grass and twists it around her finger.

"It is, but I don't need a chaperone."

The midnight blue of her fingernail disappears behind green stripes. "You shouldn't be out here alone—I don't want you crawling to the car if you twist an ankle."

My cheeks flush.

"Dell…?"

"Right, I know."

Shannon stares at me, and I struggle to hold her gaze.

"You've run without me, haven't you?"

After the briefest hesitation, I say, "No."

"You're a shitty liar, Marshall." Shannon stands, and I scramble to my feet. "I can't believe you," she continues. "I said I would run with you, even though I hate it."

"And I really appreciate it—"

"But it's not enough. You always want more."

I bristle. *I want a helluva lot I'll probably never get, so what's wrong with a little ambition with this?* "I don't know how long I'll feel decent. If I can get enough training in now, maybe I'll actually have a shot at the marathon. I have to try."

Shannon gazes up at the sky, patches of blue visible among the canopy of leaves. "I get it." Though her voice is softer now, her eyes remain steely. "But you have to be smart about it. Before you go it alone, get the okay from the people whose job it is to take care of you. Swear you won't run anymore until you talk to your parents and doctor."

Her tone makes it clear arguing would be futile—she stares me down until I nod.

---

The next time we get together, it's for a Starbucks run.

After we get our drinks, we sit at a table near the door, and I breathe in the scent of coffee, grateful for it smelling good again. I set down my phone, but as I reach for my white chocolate mocha, Shannon grabs hold of my wrist. She twists to get a better view of my palm. "What happened here?"

I look with her at the scratched-up skin. "Nothing. I just—"

"You just what, Dell? How'd you scratch your hand?" Her tone is ice.

Because she knows.

*I went running again, alone, even though I swore I wouldn't and stupidly tripped on a stick, and as I was falling, I kept enough balance that my knees didn't hit, but had to put my hands down to save my knees, so yes, my palm got cut a little.*

Once I confirm her suspicion, she walks out, letting the door slam behind her.

I assume she'll pace outside until she's calm enough to talk to me, but she gets in her car and tears out of the parking lot.

*What the hell?* She's my ride.

A minute later, my phone buzzes.

> Stay there. I mean it.

*Where would I go?*

My mom was never a "Wait until your father gets home" kind of mother—she disciplined us herself when we needed it— but I imagine this is what it would have felt like.

Surely Shannon won't tattle to my parents, right? I mean, if it were Laine who had found out, sure, but I can't believe Shannon would, especially given her relationship with her own parents and the fact that they didn't support Noah the way she wanted them to.

I've talked myself down from a panic to mild unease when she reappears on the sidewalk. No parents in tow.

I let out a breath and wait for her to come in.

She doesn't.

Instead, she stands by the door, looking at her phone, then

glancing around the parking lot. Like she's waiting for something.

Or someone.

My stomach ties itself in knots at the sight of Charlie's Camry. I jump up and dart toward the door. As I push it open, Charlie gets out of his car, and the pressure of my heartbeat thunders in my ears.

I don't know what Shannon's game is, but I know it's bad. *Bad*, bad. Because whatever she said to Charlie to get him here made him concerned or angry or confused or sad enough that he didn't bring his camera.

Stepping in front of Shannon, I meet him in the middle of the parking lot.

"Are you okay? What's going on?" he asks.

"What did she tell you?" I look over my shoulder at the traitor.

He leads me onto the sidewalk, and we stand against the brick wall in the sliver of shade offered by the coffee shop. "She said you were putting yourself in danger."

I tilt my head and narrow my eyes at her. She raises her eyebrows in reply. "Do you want to tell him, or should I?"

Charlie takes my hand, which makes it worse. "You can tell me anything."

My insides are too twisted up in fear and shame for me to take a deep breath even if my lungs would cooperate. I settle for a shallow one to give myself a second. "I've been trying to run again."

"Not trying," Shannon amends.

I glare at her. "I've been running again."

"Did your doctor say it was okay?"

*Stare at the concrete so you don't have to see the disappointment in his eyes.* "I didn't exactly ask."

Charlie's grip on my hand loosens. "Why wouldn't you tell

your doctor? Exercise is good for people with cancer. I'm sure he would have said yes, as long as you're being careful."

"That's the problem," Shannon says, oh so helpfully.

"What…aren't you being careful about?" The glimmer in his eyes is unreadable—is it fear? Understanding?

"…I've run some on my own, which I've done a million times before—"

"But you didn't have cancer then," Shannon interrupts.

Charlie lets go of my hand, but before I can explain, Shannon continues.

"And it isn't just that you were running alone, is it?"

*Ugh, that tone—I want to punch her in the face.*

"You also fell—"

Charlie's eyes go wide, and I cut Shannon off. "I'm fine, I barely got a scratch—"

"But you did get a scratch—" She grabs my hand and shoves my palm in Charlie's face. "Which is dangerous because of how easily you can get an infection and, you know, the fact that an infection could kill you."

Charlie runs his hand through his hair.

"Oh my God, you guys. We're talking about a scratch. I'm—"

"You're being reckless!" Charlie yells. Despite the angry energy that radiates off him, I touch his shoulder, hoping to calm him, and maybe myself too.

After the force of his outburt drifts away, I say quietly, "If I'm going to die anyway…"

"You don't know that! Even if—*if*—you end up being right, what you're doing might make it happen sooner, or maybe it only happens *because* of what you're doing now. I don't understand you—don't you want to do everything you can to beat this?"

Shannon's eyes soften in response to Charlie's words. She knows, like I do, that he still only recognizes the one goal of beating cancer. He won't get the list—not everything on it. He's not ready to accept that I have other priorities too, and sometimes a reward is worth the risk.

I keep my voice even as I attempt to explain. "If I knew playing it safe would mean I'd be cured, then I would. But what if I do everything I'm supposed to and cancer still wins, and I miss the chance to do things I want to do before I die? That's a risk too, one I don't want to take." *Cancer changed the rules of the game—I have to change them too.*

"Is it worth risking your life?" Charlie looks at me imploringly, silently begging me to stop doing what I love because it's not as safe as living in a bubble. "We talked about this. You know I want you to be happy, but you promised you'd be careful. This...I'm sorry, but this is irresponsible."

I'm not sure what to say, which Shannon interprets as an invitation to speak. "Tell him the rest."

My heart drops to my feet, and I plead with my eyes, *Don't do this.*

She ignores my appeal. "Tell him about the list."

*No, no, no.* My eyes well with tears as Charlie asks, "What list?"

This will crush him, and Shannon has no idea.

"Her bucket list."

As Charlie's face changes, I know my world is about to implode. Shannon keeps talking, oblivious of the bomb she just detonated.

"Some of the things on it were fine. We sang karaoke, and that was fun. But we also took a road trip to Notre Dame, which her parents don't know about, and explored a cave, where she got another cut."

I would stare daggers at her, except my eyes are too blurry.

"And I know I enabled this," she continues. "I thought the risks we were taking were small enough, and that it was better to take a few, in case...in case she doesn't have a ton of time left. But now she wants to run a marathon, and I can't keep up with her training, so she started going without me, and I got scared." Shannon's voice drops. "I couldn't convince her not to run alone. I thought…I thought maybe you could."

When she finally stops snitching and acknowledges my presence, she looks sorry.

But the damage is done.

"What else was on the list?" Charlie's voice is barely above a whisper.

My crying gives it away, gives everything away.

"How could you? What we did—" he glances at Shannon, then lowers his voice even more. "That was one of the best moments of my life, and you were crossing something off a *list*?"

"No! It wasn't like that," I choke out. "It was one of the best moments of my life too. The only reason it was on the list is because it's something I've wanted to do with you for a long time—something I knew would make me incredibly happy, which it did."

"But we didn't do it until you convinced yourself you were dying." The fire goes out of Charlie's voice. "If you didn't have cancer, would we have done it?"

"…I…I don't know." I'm done with half-truths, but saying it out loud hurts because Charlie's face is so sad. "But I'm sure we would have done it eventually—I wanted you to be my first." The words tumble out faster and faster through my desperation to fix this. "It was special and perfect and everything I hoped it would be, and I know it was for you too. Can't that be enough?"

Charlie's eyes are glassy. "You kept secrets from me. I shared the deepest parts of myself with you and…and I thought you did the same, but you shut me out of this whole part of your life… That changes things."

He swipes roughly at his face, and I'm not sure if he's brushing hair or tears out of his eyes.

"Charlie…" I reach out a hand, but he takes a step back.

"I need some space, okay?" Without waiting for an answer, he turns and walks briskly to his car.

I sink to the ground and sob.

Shannon has the good sense to let me cry in peace. But when I finally lift my head and wipe away the tears and snot, she kneels next to me. "I'm sorry... I didn't think about what else might have been on the list."

*A lot of good that does me now.* I pop up and storm toward her car. As soon as she unlocks it, I get in, turn dramatically toward the window, and don't say a word the whole way home.

# SILENT TREATMENT

I hole up in my room and send seven texts to Charlie that all go unanswered:

> I'm sorry I didn't tell you about the list. I was afraid if you thought I wasn't being careful enough, you would think I was giving up.

> I've never given up hope. Hope for a cure and hope for more time to do things that make me happy, so many of which include you.

> Please believe that what we did meant everything to me. I love you.

> Talk to me, Charlie. It's okay if you're mad, but don't shut me out. Please.

> I won't run alone anymore, I swear.

> How can I fix this?

> You're scaring me. Are we going to be okay?

I seriously consider going to his house, because the silence is making me so anxious I'm queasy.

Matters aren't helped by the fact that my phone keeps buzzing, raising my hopes over and over, only to dash them like ships on the rocks when, every time, it's Shannon:

> I didn't mean to mess things up for you and Charlie. Just wanted someone to get through to you.

> I kind of like you. Wouldn't mind you sticking around a while longer.

> How bad did I screw up? Is this, like, friendship Armageddon?

It's a lot of one-way communication.

Eventually, I leave my phone on my nightstand and walk into the hall. Bean is playing in her room and greets me with a smile when I pause in the doorway. "You want to play?"

"Sure."

She looks so excited that guilt washes over me for not doing this more often.

"Yay! You be Eliza." She pops up, gets the stuffed tiger, and hands her to me.

Once I sit cross-legged on the floor, Bean drops things in my lap—pants, a shirt, roller skates. Then she goes back to dressing her pink bear, Hannah.

"They're ready for an adventure." I point to the roller skates and the skateboard that wait for the stuffed animals.

"They're going to the park. Hannah is going to teach Eliza how to skate."

After both animals are dressed, Bean crawls around on her knees with one hand holding Hannah and the other holding the skateboard.

"Come on, Eliza!"

That's my cue to mimic with the tiger. I twist my torso left and right as Eliza skates from side to side.

"You have to make her fall down."

*That's right—she's learning.* I swing her to the front, then smush her face into the carpet. "Oof."

Bean giggles and moves Hannah to Eliza's side. "Are you okay?"

"I don't know how to skate. Will you teach me?"

"Sure. Skating is easy. You do it like this." Bean takes one of Hannah's back paws in each hand and shows how to move one leg in front of the other. "Now you try."

I whisper to Bean, "Does she know how to skate now, or do I make her fall again?"

"You make her fall again," she whispers back.

But the third time's the charm, and then the two friends have a grand time skating together. I kneel next to my sister, and we put the animals' arms around each other.

"They're BFFs," Bean says.

"Clearly."

"It's good to have a BFF."

I nod and smile, even though it twists the knife in my heart.

---

After dinner, I decide confronting my phone is preferable to more Build-A-Bear. (*How many times can you undress and dress a tiger?*)

Still no reply from Charlie, but at least Shannon took the hint:

> I get that you're pissed. I'll leave you alone. But whenever you're ready to talk, I'll be here. You can even scream at me if that would make you feel better.

It's eighty degrees outside, and the sun won't set for another couple hours, but I change into pajama shorts and a tank top, then pull on one of Charlie's sweatshirts. Once I lie on the bed, I tuck my hands into the sleeves.

*What would you have said if I had told you about the list?* I ask him in my head. Maybe I should have tried harder to make him understand. Maybe I could have convinced him that living for today is just as important as fighting for more tomorrows.

It's too late for maybes.

I do nothing but stare at the ceiling until Mom comes to say good night. She closes my blinds, insulating me against the darkness, but only the kind that exists outside my mind. As I take off Charlie's sweatshirt, I inhale his scent, then climb under the covers and turn off the light.

Although it's probably a lost cause, I call him. When it goes to voicemail, I don't hang up like I normally would.

"Hey… I can't remember the last time I left you a message. I don't know if I've ever left you a message. And you don't have to call me back or anything. I just miss you and wanted to talk, even if I'm the only one saying anything. You know what I thought about tonight? The ducks. I was playing Build-A-Bear with Bean, and we made the animals go to the park. The rug was a pond, and she put her rubber du—"

*Beeeep.*

Guess my message is done. I consider calling back to finish the story, but I'm sure he remembers. It was after school one day last spring. We took a walk and saw a momma duck leading her three babies across a parking lot. She walked over a grate, but the babies were too small. When they followed, they dropped—*plop!*—*plop!*—*plop!*—one by one between the slats. Charlie lowered himself into the drain to retrieve them. The momma waddle-paced the whole time, then once the last baby was out, off they went.

I call Charlie again. Not to talk about the ducks, but because it's better than lying in bed alone with my thoughts.

"Do you remember the first time you showed me your pictures? Not when you showed me, like, the whole collection, but the very first time, when you clicked through the ones on the camera that you'd just taken. You wanted to prove how funny I looked in that ridiculous hat I thought was cute, but I knew you sharing your photographs was a big deal…" I pause to yawn. "I still have that picture in my—"

*Beeeep.*

I tap the call icon a third time. "I like winter better than summer. You know why? Cuz I can wear your sweatshirts. I had one on earlier, but it's too hot to sleep in. …It smells like you. Isn't that weird? That you can know someone's smell? But it's not just that—I know your walk, and your sneeze, and your cough, and your hand… You could blindfold me, and I could pick you out of a lineup based on any of those things. I like that…"

*Beeeep.*

By my fourth message, it's harder to keep out the feelings that have been threatening to overwhelm me all night.

"…I'm sorry I messed up." I'm on the verge of tears. "The idea that I could be dead in, I don't know, a matter of months, even a year…it's terrifying." As I sniffle, I reach toward my nightstand for a tissue, which I hold up to my nose. "I don't know how to deal with it… So, I made the list. It was stupid. It's not like I'll do enough to make up for missing out on the rest of my life. But I figured it would be better than missing out and not even doing a few fun things first. Still, I'm s—"

*Beeeep.*

I'm sleepy now but call again anyway.

"I love you… More than anything… And what we did made me love you even more, if that's…" *…even possible.*

*I'm a balloon. A giant, red, heart-shaped balloon. Floating in the air, traveling across the sky. I observe the houses beneath me—my house and Charlie's house and a castle that rises into the sky.*

*And now I'm Juliet on the balcony, with Charlie, my Romeo, kneeling on the cobblestone street below.*

*He climbs to reach me. I extend a hand, but he's too heavy, and I tip forward over the railing. I cling to the iron, but I'm too light, much too light now, and I can't hold myself back.*

*So, I tumble,*

*And spin.*

*Down...*

*Down...*

*Down.*

When I startle awake, it's two in the morning. I have one new text:

> I'm here. Just give me a little more time. Good night, Dell.

I hug the phone to my chest and sleep like that the rest of the night.

# #12: MAKE A CANDLE

The next morning, I'm sipping chamomile tea at the island when Laine brings her cinnamon raisin bagel over and sits next to me. "You okay? You kind of disappeared last night."

I meet her eyes and debate what to say, how much to tell her. "Shannon and I are fighting again."

"About the list?"

My eyes dart around, but Mom and Dad are nowhere in sight. "Pretty much."

Laine is quiet for a minute, then says, "Is there something on it we could do today? Ooh, any chance one of the items involves shopping?"

I smile. "Actually, I want to make a candle. You know the—"

"Yeah, yeah, the new place at The Landing. Let's do it."

We head to the outdoor shopping center, and thankfully, since things smell normal again, I don't gag when we walk into the candle store. I actually don't smell anything. Shelf after shelf of white candles line the walls, each candle labeled with its scent. The lids on the jars keep the smells contained, a smart move since walking into an earth-bacon-lilac-peppermint-wasabi-strawberry–scented store would probably repel any customer.

It's not very crowded. Toward the back, an adorable couple works together to open jars while holding hands, one guy picking up a candle and the other twisting off the lid. On the other side of the store, a mom offers her daughter different scents for consideration, crouching in front of her wheelchair to hold them under her nose. Each time she smells one she likes (which is almost all of them), she squeals in delight, filling the small space with joy.

Being here lifts my spirits.

An employee gives us a short overview of the process. She hands us each an index card–sized piece of paper and tells us to write down scents we like, with the ultimate goal of choosing three that are complementary.

The number of choices is overwhelming. Laine, the most methodical Marshall sister, starts at the beginning, picking up the jar of Almond Macaron and removing the lid. She sniffs, then sticks it under my nose. Maybe I shouldn't write down the first one I smell, but I do anyway. Then I skip ahead and reach for Banana Nut Bread.

Since I've never smelled Black Coral and Moss in the wild, I don't know what it's supposed to smell like, but if the accuracy of Black Raspberry Vanilla and Blueberry Cobbler are any indication, I'm guessing coral and moss lovers will be satisfied.

"That's hilarious." I point to Fruit Loops, and we both reach for it. It smells exactly like the cereal.

A few minutes later, Laine taps Lemon Pound Cake. "I'm using this one for sure."

I nod, then breathe in Library. Once we've evaluated all the choices, we sit on metal bar stools and place our cards on a tall wooden table. I study Laine's selections. "Most of yours are summery, so I would nix Hot Apple Pie."

She draws a line through it, which leaves Coconut Lime

Verbena, Hazelnut Coffee, Lemon Pound Cake, Strawberries and Cream, and Toasted Coconut.

"These three are similar." I point at the coconut and the citrus scents with my short pencil. "And coffee doesn't fit. I say go with Lemon Pound Cake, Strawberries and Cream, and Toasted Coconut."

"You are wise in the ways of candle making." Laine crosses off the other two, then focuses on my list. "Are you really considering Fruit Loops?"

"Oh, not only considering it—I'm building my olfactory profile around it."

Laine rolls her eyes but smiles. "Then your choices are easy —Fruit Loops, Strawberry Champagne, and Papaya."

She's right. The others I wrote down—Almond Macaron, Campfire Marshmallow, and Snickerdoodle—won't work.

We take our cards to the counter and settle in there. The woman working the Fragrance Bar, Nina, instructs us to fill measuring cups with the scented oils and stir them, then take a whiff to make sure we like the combo. We add drops at a time to get the balance right. Next, Nina pours liquid wax into our empty candle jars, and we stir the oils in while holding the wicks upright.

Our last job is drawing labels on the stickers Nina gives us. After a few minutes, I show Laine my toucan.

"Impressive."

Since the wax will take a couple hours to set, what choice do we have but to shop?

As we walk into one of our favorite stores, Laine says, "Do you ever shop with Shannon? I need to know if my shopping buddy status is being threatened." Her expression suggests this is her not-so-subtle way of getting me to talk.

"She's not the retail-therapy type."

"Good. That's my job." Then she forgoes subtlety. "So...you want to tell me what happened between the two of you?"

"Not really."

Laine looks at me, a gentle challenge in her eyes.

"Later, okay? For now, can we just shop?"

In a sign of acceptance, she holds up a slouchy one-shoulder top. "This would be cute on you."

We comb the racks until we're both carrying so much our forearms hurt. Once I'm in the dressing room, though, I realize this was a huge mistake. I've lost so much weight that nothing hangs right on me. And it doesn't matter anyway, because what's the point of buying things I may only wear once, or may never wear? I hurry out and stick everything on the discard rack.

I focus on not hyperventilating until Laine emerges from her dressing room.

"Can we go?" I demand more than ask.

With concern in her eyes, Laine sets down her clothes. "Sure."

I speed-walk to the entrance and don't slow down even after we're outside. Laine keeps pace but stays behind me, giving me space to stalk off my emotions. Tears prick my eyes as I rush past shops, and the tears fall as I turn a corner and squint into the sunlight.

Before I can head for the car, Laine puts a hand on my shoulder and nods toward a bench under a tree. A little embarrassed, I sit and wipe the wetness off my cheeks.

Laine sits beside me and waits a few seconds, then says, "Dee, we need to talk."

"I'm sorry, I didn't expect shopping to be triggering, but I'll be fine."

She holds up her hand. "I have to tell you something."

*Wait—what?* Am I not in the hot seat?

"Don't tell Mom and Dad I told you," she says. "And tomorrow you have to act surprised, okay?"

I'm confused, but I nod. "Okay..."

"We're taking you to the beach."

"What?"

"Mom had the idea to rent a house in Virginia Beach next week, before you start radiation."

My heart flutters. *See the ocean.* It's been my dream vacation since I was old enough to answer Mom and Dad when they would ask during hypothetical *Where would you go if you could go anywhere in the world* conversations over dinner. "Are you serious?"

Laine nods. "Matt will drive over from Nashville, and—"

"Isn't that way farther than him coming here?"

"It is. But Mom suggested it, and I asked him, and he said yes, so…"

Although I'm still processing what's happening, I'm glad for my sister. "Aw, Laine, that's great."

Her strained smile says otherwise. "Yeah, but she invited Charlie too."

Now my stomach sinks. And the expression on my sister's face tells me she knows something about the reason why.

"He texted me this morning and said he thinks it's best if he doesn't come…"

I look at the ground, the cracks in the sidewalk blurring.

"Did he say why?" I sniffle.

"He said to ask you." Laine puts a hand on my knee. "So, I'm asking. What's going on? Talk to me, Dee."

The tears come in full force now, and I nuzzle into Laine's shoulder. She rests her cheek against the top of my head and lets me cry while I tell her everything. *Everything,* everything.

"I don't know how to fix it," I say at the end as I dig in my tote bag for a tissue.

Laine shakes her head. "I'm so sorry."

After blowing my nose, I ask, "Why are you sorry? I'm the one who messed up… Are you going to tell Mom?"

My sister's huff of an exhale reassures me that she'll have my back no matter what. "No, I'm not gonna tell Mom. I'm sorry because you're in a shitty situation and there's no easy answer." She gazes over the plaza. "I don't blame you for wanting to have some control over this. And if the people around you didn't get that, what were you supposed to do? I'm sorry I made you feel like you had to keep the list a secret from me too."

"You didn't." I want to return her support, but even I hear my lack of conviction.

"I did. I gave you a hard time about coming to Notre Dame and told you not to do something like that again. You tried to tell me what you needed, and I didn't listen."

Her compassion cues another round of waterworks. "Thank you."

We sit quietly and watch people walk past, listening to the rise and fall of their voices, the sounds of their footsteps.

"What do I do now?" I ask.

"Talk to Charlie."

*If he'll talk to me.*

We pick up our candles, and on the way home, I text him again.

> Laine told me about Virginia Beach. Can we talk?

> Please?

Yeah. I'm here if you want to come over.

He meets me at his front door, but rather than invite me inside, he comes out and sits on the stoop. I do the same. Since his house doesn't have a porch, we're sitting in the sun. We won't be able to stay out here long, but then I realize, sadly, that's the point.

Neither of us says anything at first. Eventually, I say, "I hate when you're mad at me."

"I'm not mad." He sighs. "Well, I'm a little mad, but that's not what I'm struggling with."

"…What is?"

With his elbows resting on his knees, he looks across the cul-de-sac. "Why didn't you tell me about the list?" He opens his mouth like he wants to say more but leaves it at that.

I don't answer right away, taking time to figure out how to be honest without blaming him.

"I wanted to. But I was afraid you'd worry about me, or think I was being reckless."

After a few seconds, he asks, "Do you think you were?"

Everything is jumbled in my head. I can't unravel my thoughts from those being filtered through Charlie's view. But to fix things with him, I need to be as transparent as I can. I take a deep breath and say, "Maybe, sometimes. Things didn't feel reckless at the time, but maybe I convinced myself I wasn't doing anything wrong because that's what I wanted to believe."

Charlie picks at his nail. "And the things you did—they mattered enough to be worth the risks?"

The reasonableness of his questions forces me to confront some uncomfortable truths. I swallow hard. "Yes." I sit with the memories to help me explain. "After I found the lump, I felt like the odds of being cured were equal to the odds that no treatment would work." Charlie may not want to accept this, but it's the only way to understand why I did what I did, so I continue. "Hodgkin's lymphoma usually responds fast and well, except when it doesn't. And in those rare cases, the prognosis isn't good. I know this is hard to hear…but I think I'm one of those cases."

In the silence that follows, I watch two kids kick a ball back and forth in a yard down the street.

"What if you're wrong?"

"What if I'm right?" We look at each other. "And if I am, I'll keep getting worse. This may be the best I feel ever again, and if

I don't do the things I want to do now, I may never get the chance."

Empty minutes stretch between us as we bake in the sun. Since it's too hard to confront the disappointment and sadness in Charlie's expression, I focus on the neighbor boys. One is much taller, and he keeps sending the ball flying over the other's head. The shorter one scampers off to retrieve it every time.

I shift on the cement, pulling my T-shirt away from my back as a bead of sweat runs down my chest and into my bra. My eyes rove over our shoes and up Charlie's body until I manage to meet his gaze.

"I know I haven't exactly embraced the idea of preparing for your…" His voice hitches. "…of doing things in case you…you know." He takes a breath and sits up straighter. "But from the day you told me it was cancer…I thought we would go through it together." Before he continues, he shifts toward me, but when our knees touch, he turns back. "I'm sorry if I've been too optimistic, but was that reason enough to leave me out?"

His pain is so visible, my breath catches in my throat. "You've said, repeatedly, you don't want me taking risks. And I admit sometimes I did. Shannon went along because she accepted that I could be dying—she's the only one who accepted it—and she understood why that justified the risks." I use as gentle a tone as possible when I ask, "If I had shown you the list, would you have supported it?"

He shakes his head, seemingly more upset with himself than with me. "I don't know. Maybe not… But knowing you had this thing without me? It's destroying me." Tears swim in his eyes, which makes mine well up too.

"I never meant to hurt you."

With a small nod, he says, "I know. And I wish I didn't feel this way. I keep trying to convince myself it's good you have Shannon, that she's not replacing me."

I wipe away the tears that fall. "Of course she isn't." I take his hand and am grateful he doesn't pull away. "I love you. I couldn't do this without you."

"But you did," he whispers, his anguished eyes ripping a hole in my heart.

I press my forehead to his and watch through blurry vision as his eyes close, a tear slipping out and down his cheek.

After a minute, he stands. "Thank you for explaining. I understand better now. It just still hurts, you know?"

I swallow the lump in my throat and stand too. "How can I fix this?"

"Give me more time to process. Go to Virginia, have fun with your family. We'll talk again once you're back."

Panic rises in me, and I grab at his hands. "No, you have to come. Please come. We can talk there." In desperation, I add, "I've never seen the ocean before, and I want to see it with you."

He keeps ahold of my hands, but his voice is firm. "I have to work through this alone. You did what you needed to do for yourself." Probably afraid this sounds like an accusation, he quickly adds, "It's okay, I promise. But I need to do the same." He kisses my forehead, then goes inside, shutting the door and leaving me alone on the stoop.

# #3: SEE THE OCEAN

I'm greeted Sunday morning by a knock on my door, which opens to reveal Mom, Dad, Bean, and Laine, all smiling.

"What's going on?" I sit up and avoid looking at Laine, afraid her face will reveal what a bad actor I am and I'll break.

Mom sits beside me. "Since you've been feeling decent and there's a week until you start radiation, we thought—"

"We're going to the beach!" Bean bounces up and down on my mattress.

With a hand on Bean's shoulder to stop her from shaking me, Mom says, "We thought it might be nice to have a family vacation."

"We've rented a house in Virginia Beach." Dad grins.

"It's right on the ocean," Laine adds.

"Are you serious?" I can't decide whether to laugh or cry.

Mom leans forward to give me a hug. Then Laine leans into me. Dad kneels on the bed and wraps us in his arms, and Bean burrows her way into the middle and squeezes around my waist.

"I love you all so much," I say as I wipe my eyes.

"Let's get you packed." Laine jumps up and opens my closet.

Dad leaves with Bean, and Mom stands. "Take your time, and let me know if you need anything." She pauses in the doorway. "We invited Charlie—I'm really sorry he couldn't come."

I nod until it's just me and Laine, then ask, "What did you tell her?"

"That he's sick—just a cold, and I said you hadn't seen him in several days so she won't worry about you catching it."

"You're the best big sister. You know that, right?"

"Oh, I know." Laine winks, then pulls out several hangers.

The sound of the waves welcomes me to the coast as soon as I open the van door. I spin in a slow circle, the warmth of the late-morning sun on my face. The air smells salty and fishy and nothing like the air in Ohio.

Matt beat us here and approaches as Laine closes the distance between them. She takes his hand and leads him toward the rest of us. "Everybody, this is Matt."

Dad extends his hand. "Neil. Good to meet you."

"Same. Thanks for letting me tag along."

Mom hugs him. "Sylvia. We're so glad you could join us. Elaine has told us wonderful things about you."

Matt smiles at Laine. "She's said great things about all of you too. You must be Jill." He crouches in front of Bean. "I hear you like Build-A-Bear."

Bean nods eagerly.

"You know, I have a little sister too. She's a few years older than you, but she also likes Build-A-Bear and thought you might want this." He reaches into the back pocket of his jeans and pulls out a wristie, a coconut with a purple plush straw sticking out, an orange slice on the rim, and an orchid on the side. "Since we're at the beach, she thought one of your animals might like a tropical drink. That is, if you brought any animals."

Like Bean would go on vacation without Hannah and Eliza. She clambers back into the van to get them, and I say to Matt, "You just won her over."

"All part of my plan—Dell, right? It's nice to meet you too." Matt opens his arms for a hug, and I lean in, grateful he's keeping our first meeting a secret from Mom and Dad.

Now that we've taken care of introductions, everyone bustles about, unloading bag after bag and tons of food. Matt slings his duffel bag over his shoulder, then helps Dad haul suitcases into the house.

An image of Charlie with the two of them pops into my head, but I shake it loose. I won't let what's going on between us ruin this trip.

Once Dad locks the van and picks up the last box of snacks, I follow him inside. The flurry of activity has migrated here, with people choosing their bedrooms, delivering suitcases to the proper locations, and unpacking food.

I turn toward the huge windows spanning the living room and stare at the ocean.

But seeing it isn't enough. I slide open the back door and step outside, inviting all my senses to be part of the experience. On the deck, the waves are louder, *whooshing* in and out. Seagulls squawk as they fly overhead, and a warm breeze flutters my skirt and sleeves as the smell of the water greets me.

As I lean on the railing to take off my sandals, the door opens again and everyone else spills out. They remove their shoes, then we file down the stairs to the shore, where I wriggle my toes into the sand.

The sun glints off the water, making it sparkle and reflect beautiful, blinding flashes. Each influx of the sea swirls on the beach before being enfolded into the Atlantic. I move closer so when a wave comes in, water pools around my feet. It's colder than I expect, and I let out a little gasp. My toes sink into the sand, which sucks them deeper with every cascade of water until I'm buried up to my ankles. As we all gaze at the ocean, I offer a silent expression of gratitude to the universe: *Thank you.*

---

We pull chairs close to the water's edge and set up umbrellas to protect us from the sun. I spend the whole afternoon here, sometimes reading, sometimes talking, often just staring at the ocean or the people (and dogs) playing in the waves or along the beach.

Dad makes a lap-friendly dinner of sausage rigatoni and garlic bread so we can eat outside. As the sun sets, the sky transforms, turning pink, orange, and purple. I can't help thinking what an amazing picture it would make for Charlie.

Laine snaps me out of my moment of sadness when she leans closer and asks, "How you doing?"

"It's gorgeous."

She nods.

"And huge," I add. "I've never felt this small before." Aside from the stretch of beach we're on, everywhere I look is endless water.

"It does put things in perspective."

Bean works on a sandcastle, licking her lips as she concentrates. When she catches me watching her, she gives a little wave, and I smile. The turret she's building keeps collapsing, so Dad kneels in the sand to help. A minute later, Mom disappears into the house and comes back with two cups, which she uses to construct towers.

Laine, Matt, and I head inside to rummage for more vessels we can pack with sand, and soon all six of us are working together to create a giant castle. The tide creeps toward us, and Dad digs a moat around the perimeter of our fortress.

As darkness descends, we add the finishing touches—seashells stuck into the sides like colorful windows—and stand back to admire our work. The water comes within inches, and I hold my breath. After another couple ins and outs, the tide comes up far enough that water flows into the moat, but the castle remains unharmed, and we all cheer.

<hr>

The next morning, I'm more tired than a day at the beach should have made me. I'm late getting out of bed, but apparently, Laine slept in too. She and I eat the last of the French toast casserole together, then head outside to find Matt and Bean in the sand.

They're by the water's edge and don't notice us. We lean on the deck railing and watch. Matt slices his hand sideways through the air, keeping his arm straight, then studies Bean as she imitates him. He raises her arm at the elbow so it's parallel with the ground.

"Do you know what he's doing?" I ask Laine.

"Teaching her Tae Kwon Do."

*Ah, that's right.* "Cool. Is he a black belt?" That would be badass.

"Yeah, a first degree."

"Seriously?" I didn't expect her to say yes.

She nods. "He's hoping to test for his second-degree black belt this summer."

"Damn, Laine. He's hardcore."

"He started as a kid and really took to it." She lifts her hand to her forehead to shield her eyes from the sun. "With his mom and everything she was going through mental health–wise, this made him feel calm and in control."

*I get that, now more than ever.*

Matt has shown Bean several moves in combination, and

now she tries them on her own, her tiny fist raised, her small foot kicking out. When she finishes, Matt breaks into a grin and puts up his palm. Bean jumps to give him a high five.

"He's good with kids," I say.

"He is. He teaches at the school he trained at."

I study Laine watching Matt. "Have you guys talked about kids?"

"Yeah." She smiles at me. "We both want two or three."

I nudge my shoulder into hers. "Do you think you could get married in the next few months so I can be around for it?"

Her expression turns stone-cold serious, and I shake my head. I did *not* mean to take us there, so I mumble, "Sorry," then greet Bean as she runs onto the deck. "You were awesome!"

"Matt's teaching me the white belt form," she declares proudly. Then she leans conspiratorially toward Laine, jerks her thumb at Matt behind her, and stage whispers, "This one's a keeper."

I'm still worn out the next morning. Bean wants to check out the town (despite our insistence that there won't be a Build-A-Bear store), and Mom and Dad take her, with the promise to bring me back a pastry if they stumble across a bakery.

Since Laine and Matt are scarce, I make myself a cup of tea and take it outside. Being careful not to spill, I hold the mug in one hand and use the other to drag a chair where I want it—the sand here was covered by the tide all night but is now drying in the rising sun. It's soothingly damp and cool and gritty.

I burrow my toes deeper and deeper until it's like I'm wearing shoes. Then I lift my feet and do it again, while the world comes to life around me. In the distance, two women do yoga, mirroring each other in their tree poses. Closer to me, a man and a woman walk leisurely along the water, the woman stopping to cuff her pants so they don't get wet. And in the ocean, an older man swims freestyle until he decides to change direction and drifts the other way on his back.

The rhythmic comings and goings of the waves lull me into such a relaxed state that I close my eyes. But not for long, because the scene around me is too beautiful to miss.

I imagine myself in a tiny boat in the middle of the ocean. So exposed, so vulnerable. To the ocean, I'd be nothing. A speck. Hundreds—thousands? Tens of thousands?—of creatures would be swimming beneath me, all with their own struggles and life goals. Granted, for most, that's probably to have babies before they get eaten, but still. It's something to accomplish before they die. I guess we all have a bucket list, whether we recognize it or not.

A shadow falls over me, and I see Matt holding a mug and another chair. "Mind if I join you?"

"Not at all."

He takes a sip of coffee, the steam curling into the air. "You looked pretty deep in thought when I came out. Is whatever you were thinking about something you care to share?"

"Oh." I stare at the water again. "I was thinking about the vastness of the ocean and all the life that's in it and how inconsequential we are, comparatively."

"Hm." He lifts the mug to his lips. "Those are some heavy thoughts before breakfast."

I smile and shrug, expecting our conversation to shift to a lighter topic, but Matt surprises me by saying, "Laine said she told you my mom was sick a lot—depressed—when I was growing up, before she finally got help?"

I nod and hope he's not upset about what she shared.

"Yeah, well, I spent a lot of years believing what she was going through was all about me—what I had done to make her sad, or what I hadn't done and should have. But eventually, I came to accept that I played a tiny part in what she was dealing with. I learned to have a wider perspective." He meets my eyes. "That took some of the pressure off."

It's easy to understand why Laine is falling for this guy—he wears his heart on his sleeve. "It's good you found a way to be okay with it," I say. "I'm sure it wasn't easy."

"No, but necessary, if I was ever going to have a healthy relationship with my mom."

"And she's doing better now?"

"Much better." Matt takes another sip, then wraps both hands around the mug and rests it in his lap. "And I'm glad for her, obviously, because I know now how much she was struggling. Dealing with her own kind of pressure, you know?"

While I don't know what her challenges with mental illness were like, I do understand having a huge weight on your shoulders. No matter how I choose to handle having cancer, it doesn't affect only me.

"Do you have someone you can talk to?" Matt asks softly. "About everything you're dealing with?"

Several seconds pass as I watch white and gray birds scuttle about on the sand. "I don't know."

Matt must think I'm brushing him off, because he says, "I'm sorry. That was too forward of me. I shouldn't have asked."

"No, I don't mind that you did. I just…genuinely don't know how to answer." I give him a tight smile. "Death is an unpopular conversation topic."

"For a lot of people, yes." Matt crosses his legs, sand spilling out of his flip-flop as he rests his ankle on his knee. "But I can tell you from experience that having the hard conversations usually benefits everyone involved."

*It didn't with Charlie.* But maybe that's not entirely true. As much as I wish our last talk had ended with him deciding to come here with us, I suppose it did end with each of us understanding the other a little better.

When I don't respond, Matt says, "I know it's difficult, but so is what you're going through. It's important you find someone you can really open up to."

I nod and let his words sink in. "Thanks." We're both quiet as we gaze at the waves. "Laine does this too, you know."

"Does what?"

"Gets all insightful and gently pushes me to do what she knows will be good for me."

Matt smiles. "One of the things I love about her."

I try to read between the lines, to parse the full meaning of *love*.

He raises his eyebrows teasingly and stands. "Speaking of your sister, I should see if she's up."

For all the texts I draft to Shannon and then erase before finally sending one, you'd think I would come up with something better than, *Hey*.

But it gets the job done; she replies with a *Hey* of her own.

> I'm sorry I blew up at you.

Totally justified. Sorry I screwed things up for you and Charlie.

> You just told him the truth. I'm the one who screwed up.

Not like I've never screwed up. We're good.
What about C? You two okay?

I'm not sure how to respond to that.

> Too soon to tell. I hope we will be.

I'm sure of it. That boy loves you something fierce.

I stare at my phone for a minute. Then I close the text app and video call her.

"Where are you?" she asks, and I tell her about Virginia Beach, and how Charlie didn't come.

"Seeing how hurt he is reminded me I'm not the only one struggling with this." *Did I really need a reminder? Maybe Charlie wasn't the only one with his head in the sand.* "While I've been focused on the dying part I have to do, I haven't thought so much about the grieving part everybody else has to do."

"There's definitely no easy side." Shannon frowns.

"I know this is selfish, but imagining how hard it will be for them makes it worse for me. I want some reassurance that Charlie and my family will be okay."

"Define *okay*."

"You know what I mean."

Shannon nods as she gathers her thoughts. "When a young person dies, people grieve differently. If your grandma dies, you're sad because all your memories of her remind you that she's gone. But when someone young dies, people are also sad about all the memories they never got to create." As an afterthought, she adds, "Plus, it feels like a cosmic injustice because young people aren't supposed to die."

"But they do."

"I know. But it's harder to come to terms with that."

"So, how do you?"

Something I've noticed while having cancer is that everyone speaks slower, like they're choosing their words more carefully. With my parents, I think it's because they're deciding how much to tell me, or how to share something in the least scary way possible. But Shannon uses her silent moments to figure out the most truthful way to answer.

"First, it takes time—a lot of time." Shannon tucks her hair behind her ear—revealing a new piercing. Before I can comment on it, she continues. "And it depends on the person. A lot of people we met when Noah was sick were involved with The Leukemia and Lymphoma Society or another charity. So, they had a cause. That can help—if you find a way for someone's death to have meaning."

"Is that the case for your parents?"

"No. They shut out the friends we made at LLS, even though I wish they hadn't." Like every other time her parents come up, Shannon's expression darkens. "My mom clings to religion, which helps some people find closure, but she uses it to stay in denial. I don't know what my dad does. He never talks about Noah. It's like he's trying to forget he ever existed."

I pause before asking the next question. "What about you?"

She sighs. "I'd like to say I've accepted his death." Her face on the screen is obscured as she rubs her forehead. "But if I'm being honest, I haven't. I don't know how to."

We're both quiet. Her take isn't what I was hoping for. But as usual, her dose of reality gives me a little relief too. It breaks my heart to imagine Charlie and Laine, Mom and Dad, and Bean struggling to move on after I die. But trying to convince myself they'll be okay is exhausting. So, maybe I have to acknowledge that I can't control how or whether they come to terms with my death. I say as much to Shannon.

"You can't control it," she agrees. "But for what it's worth, I think they're closer to accepting it than you give them credit for."

"What do you mean?"

"They let you do the run. They're giving you this magical family vacation."

Surprised, I consider her words. "You think this trip means they understand I could be dying?"

"Seeing the ocean was something they knew you wanted to

do, right? Did they take you before now? Trust me, they're coming around."

Our last night here, I wake up with night sweats. It's not so bad I have to change the sheets, but I put on new pajamas and, since I'm too hot to sleep, slip out of my room.

The rest of the house is dark. I quietly flip the lock on the back door and slide it open. The night sky is untarnished by suburban light pollution, and it's incredible how many stars are visible. I sit in a chair and crane my neck to stare heavenward.

After a while, that position gets uncomfortable, so—*Why not?* —I lie on the deck, the wood smooth beneath my legs, arms, and head. Innumerable bright stars connected by trails of dimmer ones fill the inky sky with pinpricks of light.

I'm startled by the back door opening. I prop myself up on an elbow and make out Laine.

She sits in a chair. "Whatcha doin'?"

"Looking at the stars." I settle on my back again.

Laine lowers herself to the deck. "Scoot."

I scoot, and she lies next to me. We're both quiet for a few minutes. Her head turns in my direction. "So, we said it—the *L* word."

"What?!" I say too loudly. Laine shushes me, then giggles. I shift onto my side. "Tell me everything."

She rolls over so she's facing me and rests her head on her hand. "It was simple, which was perfect. When we were walking on the beach after dinner, he thanked me for inviting him to come here with us and told me how much he likes our family, that he's really enjoyed getting to know all of you. He kissed me and said meeting me is the best thing that's happened to him, and then he said he loves me."

I take Laine's free hand. "What did you say?"

"I said I've never known someone who makes me feel the way he does and told him I love him too."

"Awww, Laine..." The tears that worm their way into the corners of my eyes are welcome for once. "I'm so happy for you."

Before we go inside, I find the brightest star in the sky and make a wish: *Let Laine and Matt be each other's person, and let them have a long and joyful life together.*

# BACK TO NORMAL

I n the first few days after we return from Virginia Beach, I have three text exchanges with Charlie:

**1. I let him know we're back.**

> Home safe.

> Did you have a good time?

> Yeah. Missed you, though.

> I'm glad you had fun.

I ignore the fact that he doesn't say he missed me.

**2. He checks in after my first radiation appointment.**

> How did it go?

> Quick. Much easier than chemo.

He replies with a thumbs-up emoji.

**3. I try to figure out where his head is at.**

How was last week for you?

I send the text after breakfast, and by dinner, he still hasn't responded. I consider adding, *That good, huh?* but follow my better judgment and refrain.

It's not until I'm in bed that my phone finally buzzes.

You up?

As soon as I reply that I am, he video calls. "I thought this would be easier than texting."

"It's good to see you, to hear your voice." I've never gone this long without hearing it, without seeing him, even if it's only on a screen. And this weekend, he's leaving for his own family vacation, which means another week apart.

"I'm sorry I didn't answer your text. I was still…thinking."

"And…?"

He sighs. "I love you, Dell—"

My stomach clenches at his tone as I wait for the *But* I'm sure is coming.

"—and in my head, I get where you were coming from. I'm not mad." He pauses. "But in my heart, it feels like things between us are different now."

Tears pool in my eyes, then spill out, making my pillowcase wet and warm. "Why?" I whisper.

Since the lights in his room are off too, it's hard to make out his expression, but given the pain in his voice, it's better that it's dark. "What kept me from falling apart over you being sick was believing we were in it together. I guess I felt like my job was to be there for you, and if I can't do that—"

I start to protest, but Charlie keeps talking. "I understand that Shannon has gone through something none of us has, and I'm really happy you have her. Truly. I'm just struggling to figure out how I fit now if I'm not the guy to help you through this."

"Of course you're that guy." I sit up. "And Shannon is that girl. And Laine and my parents—I need all of you."

He's quiet as he runs his hand through his hair. "You're right —logically, I know that… I don't know why I'm having such a hard time letting this go."

"What can I do?"

"…You don't have to do anything. Let's just go back to normal."

Hesitantly, I ask, "How do we do that?"

"We take it one step at a time. Are you up for hanging out tomorrow? I could come over after radiation."

"I'd like that."

The amount of thought I put into Charlie's visit is ridiculous. *Do I stay in my room where we can be alone and talk or go in the family room to keep things light and avoid the pressure to talk? Do I kiss him hello or wait for him to make a move? Should I tell him about Virginia Beach, or will it make him sad he wasn't there with me?*

I shuffle back and forth between bedroom and family room twice before settling on the couch because I'm too tired to move again. When the doorbell rings, I drag myself to the door.

"Hey." Charlie steps inside and gives me a quick, chaste kiss.

"Hey." As I lead him into the family room, I pull my hands into the sleeves of his sweatshirt I'm wearing, grateful the air-conditioning allows me this comfort.

I sit in my usual spot in the middle of the couch and wait for him to sit in the corner so I can snuggle up to him. My stomach drops as he glances at the chair, but then he occupies the space next to me.

Only after he puts his hand on my knee does a little bit of tension leave my body.

"Tell me about your trip." Since his tone is inviting enough, I give him the highlights—the ocean, the beach, the stars. Getting to know Matt, and the fact that he and Laine are in love.

Charlie smiles and looks like himself again. "That's a big deal. I'm excited for them." Because Charlie spends so much time with my family, I know he's genuinely happy for my sister.

"Me too." Although I'm careful not to pour salt in the wound by showing him pictures of gorgeous sunsets or our communal sandcastle or the various wildlife I saw on the beach, I do pull up a shot of Laine and Matt so Charlie can put a face with the name.

He takes my phone and studies it. "That's a good picture. It captures their love." Our eyes meet.

I still can't read his expression. Neither of us says anything, and the silence quickly becomes unbearable. "What did you do last week?" I ask.

"Took lots of pictures." He smiles sheepishly. "I thought I'd take some for my portfolio, but I couldn't focus on that. I just shot whatever I felt like. Kind of helped to clear my head."

I nod, expecting him to reach for his camera on the coffee table, but he doesn't.

"Do you want to show me?"

His eyes flit to me, but then settle downward. "Maybe another time."

*He doesn't want to show me his pictures? What does that mean? Are they all reflections of the pit of despair I've plunged him into*—ominous storm clouds and dead flowers and abandoned animals?

I'm so flustered by the fact that he doesn't want me to see them that even though I'm aware he's spoken, I didn't catch a word of what he said.

"Dell?" he prompts.

"What? Sorry."

"It's okay. I just asked if you want to watch something."

*Great—things are so off between us that we're resorting to TV to fill the space our conversation can't.*

"Sure." As I pick up the remote, I try not to cry. We've watched TV together before. *We do it all the time*, I tell myself. This is us going back to normal.

Except Charlie was right—things are different now.

When I scoot down to rest my head on Charlie's chest, I place my sleeve-covered palm between his T-shirt and my cheek so he doesn't feel the wetness of my tears.

# #1: RUN A MARATHON—PART 2: RACE DAY

On Sunday, the day of the marathon, I decide to pity myself.

Because succumbing to my heartbreak is easier than ignoring it, I drive the van downtown to immerse myself in the dream I was forced to give up.

It's after eight by the time I navigate the road closures and find a place to park, eight-fifteen when I reach the course. The fastest runners pass by me at mile 10, and my body thrums with adrenaline. Despite my sadness, and the fact that radiation fatigue means I'm almost too tired to stand, I'm not immune to the electricity in the atmosphere as I join the crowd of onlookers.

Clouds move swiftly through the sky. With the sun covered, there's a temporary respite from the steadily increasing heat, then the shadow lifts and I'm once again bathed in sunlight, a push and pull, yin and yang, that continues throughout the morning.

A certain rhythm accompanies the race—the rise, crescendo, and fall of the spectators' cheers each time a runner or group passes.

Although I keep myself at a distance, I'm close enough to see the runners' faces. Most look like they still have plenty of energy in the tank. Many smile. Some wave or offer high fives to kids who stick out their hands.

*What would I do?*

With each person who runs by, it becomes harder not to picture myself on the course. *Where would my cheering sections have been?* My family and Charlie would have been among the throng at the start, and they probably would have moved around to see me multiple times. *Would they have stayed together or broken off into pairs or small groups?* They all would have been there at the end.

It's so vivid in my imagination, it's like I'm experiencing it—crossing the finish line, then everyone running up to me to clobber me in a group hug. Sweat drips down my face and back, and my legs wobble, but I forget my pain at the sight of the pride on my parents' faces, the love in Charlie's eyes.

I brush tears off my cheeks and walk along the course. To focus on something else, I read the signs people have made: *WE'RE SO PROUD OF YOU, SAM!* on neon green poster board covered in sparkly purple foam letters. *YOU'VE GOT THIS!* No name—is the sign holder confident their runner will recognize them or the sign, or are they here to provide support to everyone? *WE LOVE YOU, JAXON* surrounded by a border of hearts filled with photos of, presumably, Jaxon and his loved ones.

I maintain a tenuous hold on my emotions until I reach mile 11—Angel Mile.

I read about it on the website, and seeing it now hits me like a ton of bricks. This mile of the marathon, which is organized by the children's hospital, honors kids who have died. My chest tightens, and despite being outside, the space around me suddenly feels very small. Maybe coming here was a mistake.

Near blind with tears, I back away from the course and sit

on the grass, pulling my knees toward my chest. It's hard enough to watch people accomplishing something I never will. But to be reminded of all the other kids who will never achieve their dreams? It's too much.

As soon as my tears clear enough to walk, I stand and tug down my shorts. But before I turn toward the van, another sign catches my attention: *WE WILL ALWAYS LOVE YOU, LILA*. The beaming face of a little girl sitting atop her dad's shoulders fills the other half of the poster.

The man holding the sign has a few more gray hairs than he does in the photo, but his smile is the same.

I take a tentative step forward. His voice carries, and it's easy to hear him call out to the runners who pass.

"Thank you for choosing this race!

"This marathon helps sick and injured kids!

"You're making a difference!

"I appreciate you!"

My eyes well up again. Still, I move closer and read another sign, this one with a picture of a baby: *NEVER FORGET*. And one of a girl who looks to be twelve or thirteen, bald, with a huge grin. Her mom, I'm guessing, stands before me, cheering for the runners beneath a message that reads, *WE CAN DO HARD THINGS*. Her eyes meet mine, and she gives me a warm smile.

As I stare at the pictures and the people cheering on the runners, I fixate on their happy faces, soak up their uplifting words. And cry.

I cry for them, for their loss. I cry because we live in a world in which some parents have to watch their children die. And I cry because one day, my parents might be among them—another year, I might be the face on the sign.

But mixed in among the sorrow, I also cry from hope. Tears for the families who continue to find meaning and purpose in life despite their grief. Tears for those who choose to inspire others. Tears for the people I love who will mourn me if I die but who, I believe, will hold space for me in their hearts without letting my death consume them.

While I wipe my cheeks with one hand, I reach into my tote with the other. Although it's a poor substitute for poster board, a pad of Post-its will have to do. I pull it out, along with a pen, and start writing.

One square at a time, I craft my message until I have a long strip of Post-it notes that I carry to the edge of the course. I thrust out my hand and let the notes hang down for the runners to read:

*MY DAYS MAY BE NUMBERED, BUT I'M GRATEFUL TO BE SHARING THIS ONE WITH YOU.*

# ICU

The night after the marathon, I wake up sweating, but this time I'm shivering too. Mom drives me to the hospital.

Even after I'm settled and morning rolls around, I don't text Charlie—no sense ruining his vacation by making him worry. With the antibiotics I'm on, I'm sure I'll be home before he is. I'll tell him when I see him.

Dad brings Mom and me some things we didn't think to grab, including a couple books I've been reading. I like the classics, but in my fevered state, *The Grapes of Wrath* is a slog to get through. Eventually, I put it down and pick up *Great Expectations* instead, but it isn't much better.

When Shannon visits, I happily set Dickens aside.

"You up for some company?"

I swallow a few times to make sure I can speak without coughing. "Yeah, thanks."

She drags a chair closer to my bed, then waves her hand over my body. "How are you doing—they fixing you up?"

"I have pneumonia, but the antibiotics should work soon."

She nods and is quiet. After neither of us says anything for a minute, I ask something that's been weighing on me. "Did Noah know when it was time?"

With a deep breath, Shannon leans forward and rests her elbows on her knees. "He knew when he was ready." As she talks, she twists one of the rings on her finger. "It was a weekday afternoon. My dad hadn't gotten off work yet, so it was just me and my mom with him in the hospital…"

Whether she's conjuring the memory or summoning the courage to share it, Shannon waits several seconds before continuing. "He'd been drifting in and out of consciousness all morning… I went to the bathroom, and when I came back, I overheard Noah say he was tired of fighting… He asked our mother if he had to fight anymore."

Shannon reclines in the chair and stares at the ceiling as she crosses her legs and bounces her foot. I can tell this is the hardest thing she's talked to me about. Once she composes herself, she leans forward again. "He knew the end was close. He was ready to let go."

"What did your mom say to him?" I ask quietly.

"She told him how strong and brave he was. Said he had to keep fighting." Shannon pierces me with her eyes. "He wanted permission to die, and she wouldn't give it to him."

I swallow hard.

"Later, when it was just the two of us, I told him it was okay, that I understood. That he should do what he needed to do… But he wanted to hear it from her."

We look at each other until I cough. Then I say, "Is that part of why losing him was so hard—because he felt guilty, and you couldn't convince him not to?"

Shannon tilts her head. "You trying to make me cry, Marshall?"

"Sorry. It's just…you don't talk much about your feelings, besides, well, being pissed at your parents."

"That *is* my dominant emotional state."

"Yeah, but if you ever want to talk about the other stuff, we can. If you need someone to listen, I'm here. At least, you know, as long as I'm actually here."

The small smile she offers tells me she won't answer my question.

Our conversation is interrupted anyway by a coughing fit severe enough that Shannon heads for the door to get a nurse. I hold up a hand. "I'm…okay."

"You sure?"

I nod. *Okay enough.*

---

Normal sleep cycles disappear in the hospital.

This time when I wake during the day, Mom sits in the chair, reading a printout with "Licenses and Permits" across the top.

"What's that?"

She sets the papers on the floor. "Sorry, I didn't realize you were awake."

"I just woke up. What were you reading?" I ask again.

With a hesitant smile, she tucks one leg under the other and shifts so she's facing me. "Well, your dad and I had an idea. This whole experience with cancer has been eye-opening—I know I don't have to tell you."

*Nope, you certainly don't.*

"We recognize how fortunate we are in a lot of ways in which other families struggle, and one of those ways is with food." The spark in Mom's eye makes me sit up and pay closer attention. "Seeing how hard it's been for you to find things to eat that are nutritious and appealing and that sit well, while also knowing many families don't have time to cook specially designed meals…we thought there might be a business opportunity."

"For Dad?" He loves his restaurant—I can't imagine him doing anything else.

"For both of us. We would offer chemo-friendly meals prepped and ready to cook. People could customize their order so the cancer patient gets exactly what they need and want, and caregivers and other family members could add or modify dishes to suit their tastes." Mom waves her hand as she says, "Obviously, Dad would handle the food, and I would manage the business side of things."

*Huh*. My parents creating a business together... Because of me and the fact that I have cancer... Because they want to help other people, to make this experience a little easier for them.

I remember what Shannon said about grief being more manageable for people who have a cause, and my heart swells. "That's amazing. I love this idea. Is it weird to say I'm proud of you?"

Mom reaches for my hand and gives it a squeeze. "The other day, we talked briefly with a nutritionist here at the hospital, and she's interested in helping. And we've reached out to some organizations that might help offset the costs for patients."

Tears pool in my eyes. "You both are incredible."

She kisses my head. "You're the incredible one."

I cough in reply, but hopefully she understands it means, "Thank you."

---

Overnight, things go from bad to worse. I wake up with chills, my skin clammy. My pulse races, and I struggle to take even quick, shallow breaths—the more I attempt to get air into my lungs, the more panic sets in.

Mom presses a button on my bed and says, "It's okay, baby. Just relax." She strokes my arm, her head bent close to mine.

A nurse and the on-call doctor come in and test my oxygen

level, then decide to give me supplemental oxygen to help me breathe. They also want to move me to the ICU.

While they prepare to transfer me, Dad drives to the hospital. Laine, who stays home with Bean, texts a bunch of heart emojis.

> Hang in there, Dee. I'll come first thing in the morning.

> Love you.

Once Dad arrives, he kneels next to Mom and takes my hand. I close my eyes, and a tear slips out.

I replay my conversation with Shannon in my head. *Do I think it's time?* I'm definitely not ready, so hopefully that means this isn't the end.

Now that this is more serious, I regret not texting Charlie two days ago. What if he feels like I've kept another secret from him? I can barely do anything right now except try to breathe, but in between my shitty inhalations, I manage to say his name.

"We'll let him know," Mom assures me.

*What if it's too late?*

That thought threatens to open the floodgates, which will do no favors for my breathing. I focus on Mom and Dad—Mom rubbing my back like she did before bed when I was little, Dad sandwiching my hand between both of his.

During the move, both parents stay by my side. My heart still hammers, and I wheeze with each breath. I close my eyes and listen to the hospital sounds around me—the beeps of machines and the rolling wheels, the ding of the elevator, the whispered voices in the nighttime.

I concentrate on getting air into my lungs. *In...out—in...out—in...out—in...out—in...out.*

When we reach the ICU, I open my eyes, but seeing the machines and tubes makes my vision go a little dark around the edges. I close my eyes again and direct my effort toward not passing out. While the tubes are positioned on my face, I squeeze my eyes shut tighter.

Thankfully, it doesn't take long to get the tubes settled in my nose and over my ears. Then the activity around me gradually subsides—the nurses leave, and my breathing quiets, and finally it's just me, Mom, and Dad in my new room in the ICU at 4:00 in the morning.

My fever goes up the next day, and I can't stop shaking. When a coughing fit overtakes me, which happens more and more frequently, it's absolute torture.

The ins and outs of my broken sleep remind me of a toy picture viewer, the kind with a lever on the side that you click to make a new picture appear. Every time I drift off, I open my eyes to a different set of people surrounding me. Sleep. *Click.* Mom and Laine. Sleep. *Click.* Laine and Shannon. Sleep. *Click.* Dad and Laine. Sleep. *Click.* Mom and Dad. On and on throughout the day and night.

In my fuzzy consciousness, I'm pretty sure I ask repeatedly for Charlie, but I'm too out of it to comprehend the answers. Or maybe I only think I'm saying his name.

I must be speaking aloud some of the time, because after one of my plaintive cries for him, someone squeezes my fingers. Once I manage to open my eyes, I see Laine holding my hand.

"He's on his way."

It's a long night, made longer by the fact that every hour that passes without Charlie sends me into an emotional tailspin. *Why isn't he here? Is he still convinced I don't need him? Surely now he'll accept that I could die—like, at any moment. Or does his refusal to admit it mean he's willing to risk not getting to say goodbye?*

"Charlie..." I'm not sure if I'm lamenting or asking.

My mother's voice: "He's in West Virginia. He'll be here in a couple hours."

*West Virginia?* Then I remember—he was in Florida. He's driving across the country to be with me.

At some point, I say his name again, half conscious, but this time, his voice replies, "I'm right here."

My eyes pop open. Charlie has moved a chair so close to my bed that his knees are pressing into the side, and my hand is clasped in both of his. I start to sit up, to reach for him, but he presses on my shoulder and gently guides me back down.

"No, don't." He rubs his thumb over my skin to soothe me.

"I'm...so...sorry," I say through labored breathing and hiccupy sobs. "I—"

"Shhh..." He bends close and presses his forehead against mine. "I'm the one who should apologize. The most important thing is that you get what you need, whether it's me or someone else who can give it to you." His eyes close. "I got scared that if you didn't need me, then maybe somehow you wouldn't fight as hard to stay with me, and I can't stand the thought of losing you..."

He doesn't get it—how much I need him. "Before you came...I was so...upset and scared...that I would die...without seeing you...and fixing things... I love you...so much!"

I want to say more but cough so violently that one of the machines I'm attached to makes a sound it wasn't making before, then the door opens and hospital staff hurry in.

Though I'm preoccupied with not hacking up a lung, I realize they're trying to make Charlie leave.

*They can't take him away.*

With one hand on my stomach, I reach out with the other, grasping at the air and searching for him. In the spaces when I can open my eyes, I see him arguing with a nurse who has his hand on Charlie's chest, preventing Charlie from returning to my side.

My parents rush in. Mom hurries to me and Dad joins the argument between Charlie and the nurse. Another nurse shoos Mom out of the way and does something with one of the tubes going into my arm.

"I need to…talk to Charlie," I beg my mother, then promptly cough again.

"Sweetheart, you need to calm down. They're giving you something to help you relax."

They're going to make me sleep—they're going to stop me from talking to Charlie, and what if he leaves, and what if I don't wake up, and how could Mom let them do this to me? I have to talk to—

*Charlie.*

*We're running together, but not for fun. Running from something.*

*We're side by side until we come to a narrow path. He pushes me in front of him, but I glance over my shoulder at the sound of an animal behind us.*

*The quick feet—four feet—sound louder as I hurry between tree trunks and shrubs. When I break into a clearing, I look back again. Charlie is right there, but not far off, something races through the underbrush.*

*A flash of orange and black.*

*A tiger.*

*Charlie and I run straight ahead until he grabs my hand and yanks me to the left.*

*He's found a small cave. We sink to the ground, scoot toward the back, and pull our knees up to our chests. Our breathing is heavy, but we stay quiet.*

*It's difficult to hear the tiger moving over the rush of blood in my ears. But then a blur of orange and black streaks by as our pursuer chases something that is not us.*

*Charlie exhales and leans his forehead against mine. "I'm so glad you're safe."*

*"Only thanks to you," I whisper. Our eyes meet. "You saved my life."*

*"I'd do anything to protect you."*

---

When I wake up, the room is quiet (relatively, anyway). It takes a second to get my bearings. Without a window to check, I determine it's nighttime by the dim lighting, lack of activity, and Mom sleeping in the chair. As soon as I remember being separated from Charlie, my eyes fill with tears. I almost wake Mom to ask when I can see him again since calling him isn't an option—no phones in the ICU.

The drugs must still be in my system, because I quickly fall asleep again. Sometime later, I'm rudely awakened by the worst coughing spell yet. I bolt upright as my whole body convulses. Mom puts a hand on my back for a second before my body jerks away.

Once I can take a shuddery breath, I lie back down and close my eyes.

Between whatever they're giving me and the fact that I'm not getting any meaningful stretches of sleep, time becomes surreal. In one of my lucid periods (Sleep. *Click.* Mom), I ask how long I've been in the hospital. I probably shouldn't be surprised but still am when she tells me, "Five days."

"Why aren't I…getting better?" I can understand cancer taking me out, but shouldn't pneumonia be cured by antibiotics?

Mom gently pats my sweaty forehead with a cloth, seeming to struggle to meet my eyes. "Dr. Mastro wants to do another scan. He's afraid the cancer may have progressed."

I thought the lump was a pretty clear sign that it had, but if he didn't want to do a scan then and wants to do one now, he must suspect it's worse than that.

"When?"

"Tomorrow."

My heart beats faster, and I close my eyes, trying to calm my body. *Please let this not be the end*, I pray. *Even if the cancer has spread and I don't have much time left, let me get over the pneumonia. Let me leave the hospital and talk to Charlie and have a little more time with my family. Please.*

---

Somehow, I manage to hold my breath and not cough for the 10 seconds it takes to do the CT scan.

Both Mom and Dad are in the room the following morning when Dr. Mastro comes in with the results. While I listen to him tell us how aggressive my cancer is, I fixate on how much time I have left.

"...spread to additional lymph nodes, which we (*How long?*). And unfortunately, it has also spread (*How long?*). When the liver (*How long?!*), it tends to (*How long? How long? How long?*)."

In the silence that follows, I ask in a voice I barely recognize as my own, "How long...do I have?"

Dr. Mastro presses his lips in a straight line. "We don't like to give exact numbers, because we can't know for sure. And there are still other treatments to try—other therapies, and even clinical trials." He holds my gaze for a second before looking at Mom and Dad. "But if we don't get this disease under control, we're likely expecting months, not years."

# MEMORIES

After Dr. Mastro leaves, Mom and Dad sit close by my bed, and we cry.

With a loud sniff, Mom reaches for my hands. "I would give anything to fix this."

Dad's eyes are glassy as he runs his rough thumb under my eye, wiping away my tears. "We would do anything for you."

"I'm sorry I...couldn't beat it," I whisper.

"Do not think for a second that you have anything to be sorry about." Mom raises her eyebrows and points her eyes at me. "You did everything you needed to do."

*Did I?*

"You sacrificed so much," Dad adds. "No one could ask anything more of you."

The tears come harder. "But after I...found the lump...I knew the cancer was spreading...and I thought that meant...I wouldn't be cured. What if...by believing it, I made it happen?"

I pull my hands from Mom's and cover my face. She lets me wallow for a few seconds, then gently lifts my fingers away. "Adele, look at me. I'm all for positive thinking, but you can't will cancer away, and it's not waiting for an invitation to progress. Nothing you did or didn't do caused this."

*What about the pneumonia?*

*What about the list?*

*Where did I come into contact with the bacteria that made me sick this time? Was it at the marathon?*

My silence must tell Mom I don't believe her.

"You went through hell and back with the treatment your doctor prescribed for you," she continues. "That's exactly what you were supposed to do. What more could you have done?"

*Not push myself so hard.*

*Taken it easy when my body said it needed rest, instead of crossing something off a stupid list I didn't even finish.*

After my next coughing fit, I say, "I'm tired," as another tear runs down my cheek. My parents seem to understand I mean so much more than needing sleep, because both of them squeeze some part of me before I close my eyes.

During one of the periods I can keep my eyes open for longer than a few seconds, Laine comes in, and I cry again.

"Oh, Dee." She sits and brushes away her own tears before taking my hand.

"Does Bean know?"

Laine shakes her head. "Not yet."

"What about...Charlie?" My breath catches. "Why isn't...he here?"

My sister holds my gaze. "He knows. He'll be here as soon as they let him—right now, they're only allowing immediate family."

"I have to...apologize again...for the list." Angrily, I shake my head back and forth on the pillow. "It was stupid...and made Charlie...think I don't...need him."

"Don't do this to yourself. The list wasn't stupid. Everyone has things they want to experience in life. There's nothing wrong with doing things that were important to you."

"But there's so much...I didn't—won't...get to do... Maybe the list...is even why...I'm here." Coughing prevents me from saying more, but nothing is worth saying anyway. There's nothing I can do now.

Once I relax into the bed, Laine says, "I hope it's okay—I told Matt what's going on. I was afraid—" She pauses and looks me in the eye. "I was afraid you'd blame yourself, and since he struggled with guilt over his mom, I thought he might have some insight. Can I tell you what he said?"

I nod, not expecting it to help, but knowing an argument won't either.

"People do things for a reason. Even if you regret some of what you did, when you did it, it filled a need. Maybe there were other ways to meet your needs, I don't know, but you had to meet them somehow, and you did it the best way you could find at the time."

*Maybe.* "I thought the list...would be my win...even if I... couldn't beat cancer... But I still feel...like I've failed."

Laine puts her arms around me, as awkward as it is with the bed rails and tubes. Her hair is soft against my skin, and I breathe in the smell of her coconut conditioner. After several quiet minutes, she says, "Don't forget about the special moments you shared with people because of the list. I, for one, am grateful you came to Notre Dame—that's a memory I'll cherish."

A hint of a smile touches my lips, the first I've managed in several days. "Me too."

Laine sits up. "I'm sure I'm not the only one you affected."

I suppose she has a point. If I hadn't made the list, would I have done the fun run? I'd like to believe some of the people who came out to support me felt inspired, that being a part of the event was a positive experience for them. I definitely wouldn't have sung karaoke, and Shannon and I are so much closer because of that and all the other things we did together. And being with Charlie—even now, knowing about the list, I hope he doesn't regret sharing that intimacy.

---

Minute to minute, hour to hour, day to day, everything is the same. Broken fits of sleep interrupted by coughing or beeping machines or doctors and nurses poking and prodding me. Mom, Dad, and Laine keep a steady presence, but since I can't say more than two words without coughing, we have one-sided conversations or none at all.

Still, nighttime is the worst.

Amid the darkness, I'm smothered by a loneliness so deep, it takes everything I have to not rouse whichever parent is sleeping by my side.

During one such instance, in the light that seeps in from the hallway, I notice something new: a scrapbook.

I quietly open it. A Post-it note in Laine's handwriting graces the inside cover.

*The list of things you've done may be too short, but the effect you've had on us is immeasurable. We love you.*

Her name is signed beneath the message, but it's not the only one—next to it is Charlie's in his blocky style, and beside that, Shannon's in narrow slanted letters, Mom's elegant cursive in one corner, Dad's neat printing in another, and Bean's large letters sandwiched between them.

My eyes fill with tears, and I wait several seconds before turning the page.

The first picture is of Mom holding me the day I was born, tucked up on her chest beneath her hospital gown, snuggled under her chin. Next to the photo, she wrote, *Words fail to express how much I treasure the memory of meeting you for the first time.*

On the right, I'm sitting in a highchair with strained peas splattered all over my face, and Dad is mid-chuckle. His caption reads, *You've made me laugh more times than I can count, and your laugh fills my heart with joy every single time.*

I flip the page and find not a photo, but a ticket stub, to the first Taylor Swift concert Laine and I went to, the Red Tour. *Sharing this show with you was the first time I felt like we were friends, not sisters, and you've made me feel that way a million times since.*

Next to a picture of me holding baby Bean and her grinning at me, she wrote, *You're the best big sister (don't tell Laine).* A sobby laugh escapes and I wait to see if Mom wakes up, but she doesn't stir. I wipe my eyes and turn the page.

Me and Mom on the trail. *You pushed me to be a better runner. I'd never considered a marathon before we started running together.*

And Charlie. A whole spread full of pictures. I can't imagine how he chose which ones to include. In the top left corner is one of us kissing. *Our first kiss was perfect—I wouldn't change a thing about it (or any of our other perfect firsts).* I blush, hoping Mom and Dad didn't read what everybody else wrote.

The picture at the bottom of the page surprises me. I'm making a funny face at Charlie, my eyes crossed and tongue sticking out sideways, but I smile when I read what he wrote: *You let me take your picture a lot, and I appreciate that.*

A single image sits in the center of the next page. It was taken at the end of homecoming sophomore year. Because it's close-up, only the top of my mauve dress is visible. My hair is disheveled, strands that escaped my updo sticking to my sweaty neck. Even in the dim lighting, it's clear my eye makeup is smudged. But I'm staring into the camera with a profound happiness, basking in the glow of the words Charlie and I had just exchanged for the first time. On the scrapbook page, he wrote, *Because of you, I know what love is.*

I'm crying too hard now to not wake my mother, but the concern in her expression melts when she notices what I'm holding. Carefully, she squeezes into the bed beside me, then hands me a wad of tissues before putting her arm around my shoulders.

"Thanks," I squeak.

Shannon gets the next spread. No pictures, just words—a list.

*Though these weren't on your list, here are 10 more things you've done in the time we've hung out:*

1. *Became my best friend (haven't had one of those in an embarrassingly long time)*
2. *Gave me a reason to get out of bed in the morning*
3. *Let me live vicariously through you—you checking things off your list made me slightly less bitter about Noah not getting to check things off his*
4. *Reminded me of some good memories with Noah*
5. *Made me take a hard look at how much time I spend on TikTok (I might be writing poetry again—yes, I write poetry, and no, you can't read it)*
6. *Got me thinking about my future—Notre Dame is pretty, plus it's far away from my parents, and I already know a cool girl who said she would hook me up if I get in*
7. *Reignited my desire to sing karaoke (still not doing choir or anything that people-y)*
8. *Turned me into a runner—kidding, but I have been walking on the trail, and nature is, you know, nice*
9. *Made me believe DMing Angie Markel wasn't a terrible idea, and we've gone out for coffee twice*
10. *Inspired me—you're a badass, Marshall*

I close my eyes, and tears stream down my cheeks.

It's almost six when Mom returns to her chair so I can get some rest. I must sleep for hours, because the next time I wake up, it's bright in the room.

Immediately, I know something is different. The sheets are drenched—my fever has broken.

This isn't the end.

# PART III

# CELEBRATION

Now that an antibiotic is finally working, my fever goes down until it disappears. My breathing is still shit, and I'll probably have this cough forever, but at least the cough no longer threatens to turn my body inside out.

Once it's clear I've stabilized, the hospital room door opens, and Charlie's beautiful face appears.

I smile and cry, but these tears are manageable. The panic from before is gone, I guess because I'm not on Death's doorstep. Just Death's driveway, or sidewalk, maybe.

Charlie cries too, but I bet his are also tears of relief. After he lifts the camera strap over his head and sets the camera on the table, I scoot as close to the bed railing as I can and motion for him to lie beside me.

"You sure?"

I nod, still afraid of talking too much and exacerbating my cough.

When we're face-to-face, inches apart, he holds my hand against his chest. With my other, I brush the hair out of his eyes.

"I've missed you—missed us," he says.

"Me too," I whisper. "Now you know...how much I...need you, right?"

He squeezes my hand. "We need each other... So, what am I supposed to do without you?"

I sink my fingers into his mop of brown curls and swallow hard. "I know you'll be sad...for a while."

His expression both warms my heart and crushes it. Clearly, "sad" is an understatement. I push forward. "I know you'll be...a little sad...forever... But don't let that...stop you from being... happy again someday."

"How do I do that?"

I lift my head toward the camera. "You keep finding...the truth. At first...it will be sad... But one day you'll forget...for just a moment...and see something...that makes you smile... Take a picture... And let yourself...be happy. Don't feel guilty... for moving on."

The words catch in my throat. Charlie puts his hand on the side of my face. "Dell." His voice is wavery, and when I meet his gaze, his eyes brim with tears. "I love you more than anything."

Since even this short conversation has worn me out, I snuggle further into him, then turn over and close my eyes. With his arm draped over me and my hand clasped in his, I sleep—the best I've slept in weeks.

---

A crowded van takes me home, with Dad driving and Mom in the passenger seat, me and Charlie in the next row, along with my new portable oxygen tank, and Laine and Bean in the back.

Dad plays "I'm Still Standing" by Elton John, and when I meet his eyes in the review mirror, he winks. Bean brought both Hannah and Eliza, dressed to impress, to celebrate my homecoming. She keeps plunking one or the other onto my shoulder, dancing to the music, and their fuzzy fur tickles my neck.

Once we're all settled in the family room, we grin at each other. I don't know why we're so giddy—well, okay, I do know why: I didn't die. At least, not yet. I may be on borrowed time, but I will take as much as the bank of life will loan out.

Laine casually swings her legs, which are slung over the side of the chair, as she says, "We should have a party."

"Excuse me?" Mom asks, her tone light.

"Not a big party. Something low-key. Just us, and Shannon. To celebrate."

Mom silently confers with Dad, next to her on the love seat. A slow smile plays on his lips. She turns back to Laine, to me. "Okay."

"Wait—what? Are you serious?"

"Low, low-key," Mom continues quickly. "Mellow. Verging on boring."

Laine pops up with an "Okay!" then everybody springs into action. Dad heads to the grocery while my mother and sisters get ready to hit the party store.

"Don't let her leave the couch," Mom directs Charlie.

"I'll make sure she's a model patient."

"Keep your phone handy," Laine tells me as she grabs her purse. "I'll send you pictures so you can weigh in."

Once the garage door closes, Charlie kisses the side of my head. We're snuggled together, careful of the tubes in my nose, but cozy with a soft blanket tucked around us, even though it's scorching outside. My internal temperature is still recalibrating, a matter further complicated by the weight I've lost.

"Do you want me to do anything for the party?" Charlie asks.

Inspiration strikes. "Ooh, we should have an Independence Day theme since I was in the hospital on the 4th." *And leaving the hospital is my personal independence day.* "You can get our decorations from the basement."

"You got it." He stands.

I put my feet on the floor, but Charlie points his finger at me. "You stay. Just tell me where to look."

Like an obedient puppy, I tuck my legs in again. "In a bin—red, I think—on a shelf in the back corner by the treadmill."

He disappears, and while I wait, I text Laine, Mom, and Dad my theme idea.

A few minutes later, Laine replies.

No 4th of July. What about these?

She sends a picture of plates and napkins with pineapples and tiki mugs and *Aloha* written across them.

Aloha—hello and goodbye.

Perfect.

I switch to my text thread with Shannon and invite her to the party as Charlie pushes the basement door closed with his foot.

"Are we decorating inside or outside?"

"Let's go out." Our yard is shady enough—a summer party belongs outdoors.

He nods, then elbows the back door open and sets the bin on the patio. Next, he moves a chair under the big oak tree next to Bean's play set.

When he comes back in, he picks up my oxygen and offers me his hand. "You ready?"

Once I'm settled in the chair, Charlie opens the bin and holds things up for my consideration, starting with a bunch of flags.

Now that we've swapped 4th of July for Aloha, I have to rethink the décor, but I'm pretty sure we have some summer decorations too. "What else is in the bin?"

Charlie sets the flags aside and pulls out colorful plastic pinwheels. They'll work with the tropical theme. I decide to group them together like flowers. "Put them all in that back corner, in front of the pine tree." There's not much wind today, but every now and then a breeze blows, and the pinwheels spin and flash in the sun.

An hour later, Charlie is attaching a multicolor pennant banner to the gutter when the door opens and Mom, Laine, and Bean step out.

"It's so festive out here." Mom smiles up at Charlie on the ladder, while Bean runs over to the pinwheels.

"What did you get?" I peek into the many bags Laine brings over. "I thought you were just getting plates and napkins."

Laine has a glint in her eye. "We got a little carried away."

In addition to plates, napkins, and cups, they got a tablecloth, cardboard centerpieces, and confetti.

"I'll be back." Mom disappears into the house and returns with giant bags of balloons—two dozen, I count after she frees them from the plastic. While Mom and Laine untangle them, I'm surrounded by teal, pink, and lime green latex, like I'm in the middle of a colorful, happy tornado.

As I watch the goings-on—Laine arranging groups of balloons on the patio and in the yard, Charlie clipping weights on the tablecloth, Mom assembling centerpieces, Bean straightening the napkins and plates—my heart feels too big for my chest, all end-of-the-movie Grinchy.

Dad slides open the door and steps out carrying his grill set. "Wow, this is amazing." He cleans the grill, and I check the time on my phone—Shannon should be here in twenty minutes.

In the meantime, everybody bustles in and out, opening bags of chips and mixed fruit containers, setting a pitcher of lemonade on the table, sticking torches in the ground, and moving more chairs into the yard.

I smile at Shannon's surprised expression when she arrives.

She crouches by my chair and wraps her arms gently, but firmly, around me. The unexpected gesture makes me a little weepy, but she beelines for the food before I can say anything. A minute later, she sits next to me, while Charlie takes the spot on my other side.

"I can't believe you did all this in a few hours," Shannon says before popping a chip in her mouth.

"The Marshalls don't mess around," Charlie says.

"Oh, you don't have to tell me."

Mom puts a hand on my shoulder. "Can I get you anything?"

"I'll take some fruit, thanks."

Food tastes especially good to me today, probably because I've been subsisting on hospital meals. I chew a juicy piece of watermelon as Bean runs around the yard waving a baton, a purple shimmery ribbon trailing behind her.

*Click.* Charlie lowers his camera, then reaches across the space between our chairs.

I slide my fingers between his, then use my other hand to pick up a wedge of cantaloupe.

At one point when it's just me and Shannon, I thank her for what she wrote in the scrapbook. "About that poetry…"

Her face is comically aggrieved. "No—no! I said I'm not sharing it. It's crap anyway."

Knowing it's futile to argue with her (about being allowed to read it or its quality), I switch topics to another item on Shannon's list. "Then tell me about Angie."

Shannon blushes but can't stop the corners of her mouth from turning up. Before she speaks, she messes with her hair, twisting it into a messy topknot, then letting it fall back to her shoulders. "Mmm…maybe she's had a crush on me since middle school…and maybe she was excited when I messaged her…and maybe I'm kind of liking hanging out with her."

I smile slyly. "Maybe, huh?"

"It's too soon to commit." Around a mouthful of guacamole, she mumbles, "She is a person, after all. You know how I feel."

I shake my head as Dad calls, "Chow time," and carries a platter of burgers and hot dogs to the table.

After the chaos of serving subsides, Dad raises his cup. "To Dell."

The six people I love best in the world gaze warmly at me, their drinks held aloft. I lift mine in return and stare into their faces until Bean tires of the sentimentality and takes a giant bite of her burger, making the rest of us laugh.

I finish my hot dog, smothered in ketchup and onions. Dad raises his eyebrows when I ask for a second, but happily puts it on my plate. By the time he and Mom clear the table, I'm stuffed. I can't remember the last time I felt full.

The back door opens, and Dad appears holding a blueberry pie—my favorite dessert. He eyes me as he sets it down. "We thought maybe you'd be up for a little piece."

This isn't a store-bought pie. I know Dad made it, but it doesn't make sense. "How did you do this? There wasn't time."

"I made it and froze it a while back, with the hope we could enjoy it together."

My stomach hasn't had this much in it in months. I'm wary of the price I might pay, but it's worth the risk—this is the world's best blueberry pie, and as Dad cuts it, I have to work really hard not to cry.

This pie has marked so many special occasions for our family. For my sweet sixteen party, I didn't want cake—just Dad's blueberry pie.

When Charlie met my parents, Dad made the pie. Charlie was so nervous, but Dad's cooking was an easy icebreaker. Charlie gushed over the pie, and later Dad gushed over Charlie.

I was thirteen the first time I helped Dad with this recipe, and making the dough was one of the most relaxing things I'd ever done—squeezing the pieces of butter between my fingertips, adding tablespoons of ice water to the flour and butter mixture, and folding the dough like a letter. I was so proud when it came out just like Dad's.

My earliest memory of this pie is when I was nine. It was the dessert Mom and Dad brought out before telling me and Laine we were going to be big sisters. We were ecstatic.

They say your life flashes before your eyes when you die, but apparently that's also sometimes true when you eat pie.

Once I can't take another bite, I waddle back to the yard, where Laine and I slouch in our chairs. Shannon swings with Bean, then the two of them disappear inside. They return carrying Bean's stash of bubbles. Charlie picks up his camera as they wave the wands.

The scene before me could come from a Pinterest board—the colorful decorations, the balloons, and now the bubbles.

I close my eyes and listen to the talking, the laughter. Then a tiny dot of moisture lands on my arm, my cheek. I'm surrounded by bubbles—Bean and Shannon on either side of my chair, fanning me with their wands. Laine picks up another tube and joins in, and I observe from behind the soapy curtain swirling around me. Charlie circles us, clicking away.

Like raindrops, bubbles pop on my skin. My sisters and Shannon dance around me until I'm actually wet. Two of the wands are empty, and Bean flourishes hers until it too runs out.

Mom grins as I hold out my arms, then gets me a towel. While I rub myself down, Charlie sits next to me and pulls up the pictures to show me.

I drop the towel on the grass and take the camera. I'm in the center of the photo with bubbles surrounding me, some clear, some blurry. The balloons and other decorations are fuzzy in the background. The expression he captured shows exactly what I was feeling—surprised, happy, grateful, loved.

"Put this in your portfolio." I look him in the eye as I hand back his camera, and he leans forward to kiss me.

As dusk darkens the sky, fireflies twinkle above the grass. Bean dashes around the yard to catch them, and Charlie sets one on my arm—it tickles as it crawls along, lighting up twice before flying away.

Despite nixing the Independence Day idea, I'm startled by the *boom...crackle* of fireworks. I tilt my head in confusion but then remember that the gated community near our subdivision has an annual summer party, complete with fireworks. I've never paid much attention to when it happens, but based on the colorful light bursts above the trees, I assume it must be tonight.

Dad and Charlie line up chairs in the grass, and we all sit side by side—Mom, Dad, Laine, Shannon, me, and Charlie. Bean sits on Dad's lap, leaning against his chest, her eyes heavy.

We watch in silence, except for when Shannon leans close and whispers, "Your family is awesome."

I glance at her, then peer down the line at everybody else. "I know."

With a gravity to her voice, she adds, "They'll be okay."

We can't hear the music from the party, just the festive thunderclaps. As the crescendo builds, noise and color fill the night. A green starburst sizzles into trailing gold light. A flare of red shoots off purple streamers that streak across the sky. *Pop! Pop! Pop pop pop!!!* Yellow! Red! Pink, orange, blue!!! A barrage of light and sound bombard us before everything goes dark and quiet.

Everyone is still as the silence settles like a blanket. Then people stir—Mom stands and holds out her arms for Bean, Laine turns to Shannon to say goodbye, and Charlie picks up my oxygen and offers me his hand.

"Thank you all," I say.

Even though I can't see their faces, I know they're smiling at me.

# LETTING GO

The following week, Shannon and I sit in my room. Ever since the party, I've been increasingly gloomy without being able to pinpoint why, so I'm hoping Shannon might have some insights.

"It has to be hard settling back into regular life," she offers. "You were in the hospital for a long time, then the party was this fun, meaningful celebration, and now it's just your everyday existence. Maybe it's a letdown."

"Maybe... But it feels like more than that, like being in the hospital changed things."

"Well, it made everybody else more realistic about your future, didn't it?" Shannon kicks off her sandals and stretches out her legs, resting her feet on my bed. Her toenails are painted teal, a brighter shade than I'm used to on her.

"I guess it gave me a reality check too." I sigh. "More than before, I understand now that there are a lot of things I won't get to do."

"List things or other things?" One of Shannon's best qualities is knowing what I'm getting at before I'm even aware myself.

I give her a small smile. "Other things. Now that my doctor

is saying I don't have a ton of time, I can't stop thinking about the experiences I'll miss out on, all the special moments I won't get to share with people."

Shannon nods. "Letting go of dreams or expectations or hopes for your life is ridiculously hard… But also probably necessary if you want to find some kind of peace."

"So profound." I smile, but the weight of her words is heavy. "How do I do that?"

I don't expect Shannon to have an answer, since it's personal and unique to each person, but she surprises me by saying, "You could do something symbolic."

"What, like, write everything down, then cross it off?"

"No more lists."

*Fair point.*

"How about throwing darts at pieces of paper on a dart board?"

Despite my appreciation of Shannon's efforts, I scrunch my nose. "I suck at darts." Turning my regrets into something tangible is appealing, though. "Have you heard of lantern festivals?" I ask. "I've always liked that tradition—writing a wish on a lantern and sending it into the sky. Pictures online are gorgeous, and releasing your hopes into the air seems freeing. Too bad I can't do that with my regrets."

Shannon cocks her head, her wheels clearly turning. "You up for a short walk?"

I nod, but short walk or long walk, it's an ordeal. I haven't gotten used to the portable oxygen, and although my cough is better, the slightest exertion aggravates it. We make our way outside and to the end of the street with the speed of two turtles.

At Shannon's direction, I settle comfortably, albeit awkwardly, close to the pond while she gathers rocks and pebbles into a pile. The blades of grass scratch my legs, and I adjust my shorts.

When the breeze blows, the leaves on the tree above me rustle, shifting the bright and shady spots so the sun's rays warm different parts of my body.

Once Shannon is satisfied, she sits next to me, knees bent to keep her thighs off the grass, and picks up a rock. She rubs it between her thumb and index finger, then offers it to me. "Tell me something you'll regret not doing, then let it go."

I gesture toward the mound she created. "How many regrets do you think I have?"

"Your short-term bucket list was long enough—if you're mourning the next sixty years, I doubt this will be enough." Shannon raises her eyebrows in mock concern.

Pointedly, I toss a rock into the grass, not the pond. "That *was* going to be my regret about missing things with you—being college roommates or something—but suddenly I'm not so sad about that."

With a wry smile, Shannon says, "You'll need that whole pile for things with me you'll miss."

I dig through the pile for a pebble. "This is my tiny regret that I'll never read a poem you write about me. Although I'm not sure how flattering you'd be, so maybe it's better I never read it."

"All my poems speak the truth, so how flattering I would be depends on how nice you are to me." She takes the pebble from me and throws it into the pond. "You know it's eating you up, not getting to read my poems."

"It actually is. Despite your opinion of them, I bet they're really good."

Shannon holds my gaze for a second before playfully shoving my arm. "Okay, you sap. Do what you came here to do."

I take a deep breath. "Okay... I'm sad I'll miss graduation." After holding a stone in my hand a second longer, I toss it into the water. Rather than skip across, it *plunks* straight down.

"Being handed your diploma or the parties or what?"

"All of it." As I imagine the celebratory moments, a heaviness settles in my chest. "It's this closing of a major chapter in life. It would be exciting and bittersweet and a little scary and significant, and I'm sorry I won't get to experience it."

We sit in the silence of my imagined feelings, then Shannon hands me another rock.

"College. A new chapter." As I stare out over the water, I picture what it could have been. "I wish I knew where I would have gone, what I would have studied, how I would change during those four years."

Gently, Shannon asks, "What would make you happy, if you could know the outcome?"

"Mmm…I don't know. I always thought it would be OSU, but it wouldn't have to be. Maybe I'd be near Laine, or in some cool new city. Still with Charlie. And we'd get our own apartment." The more I envision it, the quicker the details come. "He would study photography, and I would study philosophy or literature—literature, I think. I'd get a PhD and become a professor, and we'd have smart friends who would have wine tastings and talk about books and art."

"Snob," Shannon jokes, and I nudge her with my shoulder.

I stare at the rock, then let this could-have-been go too.

I reach into the pile, scoop up a handful, and chuck them quickly. "Buying my first car." *Plop.* "Adopting a dog." *Plop.* "Being maid of honor at Laine's wedding." *Plop.* "Having a proposal of my own." *Plop.*

Tears prick the corners of my eyes. Once I swallow my sadness, I pick up a rock big enough to fill my palm, then hand it to Shannon. "What about you?"

"This isn't about me."

"Are you telling me you don't have regrets about Noah?"

"Of course I do."

I nod at the rock. "Let's hear them."

She doesn't meet my eyes for a long time, just stares at the rock in my hand. Finally, she takes it, turning it over and over before gazing out at the water. "I'm sorry his final days weren't more peaceful." The rock remains in her hand. "I wish I'd fought harder to get him what he needed...that I'd made my mom understand she had to tell him it was okay for him to let go."

Abruptly, she lobs the rock, sending it plunging into the water in the middle of the pond.

"Feel better?" I ask.

"No." Her mouth is set, but after a second, she sighs. "I don't know." She picks up another rock and thrusts it at me. "You go."

"...I'm sad I won't be a mom." I swallow the lump in my throat. "Or see my parents as grandparents. I assumed my family...that we'd always be an important part of each other's lives. Like, I have this image of us at Christmas." It takes a second before I can finish the thought. With a loud sniffle, I continue. "Laine and her husband and kids, and Bean and her family, and me and maybe Charlie and our kids, and my parents —this big, happy family full of love and energy and chaos and laughter."

*Splunk.*

Right now, I regret not bringing tissues. I compose myself, then hand another rock to Shannon.

"It hurts that I can't even imagine Noah as an adult." She stretches out her legs, resting her hands and the rock in her lap. "He was so young when he died that I don't know if he would have married a woman or a man, if he'd get married at all, or if he would have had kids or where he'd live or what he'd do on the weekends. And I get that it sucks to have plans for your future that don't play out...but it also sucks to have this black hole of an unknown."

This rock goes even farther than the last one.

I hope it's cathartic to share these regrets about Noah, but I want her to open up about herself too. "What about you—what will *you* regret?"

Her eyes show genuine surprise. "Didn't I just tell you?"

"You said things about Noah that make you sad. What about you, your life?"

"You really do want to make me cry, don't you?"

"Would that be such a terrible thing?" We lock eyes, and I can tell she's deciding whether to take down her wall. I know how hard a decision it is, because if she goes for it, there's a lot she's going to unleash.

She picks up a rock, plays with it, stares at it. "I'm scared I don't know how to be happy anymore."

*Splash.*

"I'm tired of being angry. All. The. Time."

*Splash. Splash. Splash.*

Shannon grabs a handful of rocks and gets to her feet.

"You know why I don't do any activities? Because no one would come see me if I did. My parents lost a kid, and yeah, that's awful, but they still have me, and I'm goddamn sick of being ignored."

*Splash.*

Glancing down at me, she jiggles the rocks in her fist. "I told Noah I'm a lesbian. He was totally cool, way cooler than my parents were, or are. And now I've lost my ally, and that blows. Maybe with him, I could have had the picture-perfect family Christmas too, maybe he would have made it okay for my parents. But without him, I want to get the hell out of Ohio and never look back."

She pauses, then it's like a fireworks finale, with many in rapid succession—

"I dread dating because it will always lead to the question, 'Do you have any siblings?'" *Splash.*

"And if I date anyway, I'm scared I'm so messed up, I won't be able to love someone because I'm too afraid of getting hurt." *Splash.*

"But in spite of all that, even if I am willing to date and if somehow I fall in love, I don't know if I can ever be a parent because I'm scared shitless of losing my kid too." *Splash.*

Shannon flings the remaining rocks into the water, then drops to the ground. With her knees pulled in tight to her chest, she swipes roughly at the tears that fall.

I slowly scoot closer. When she doesn't move away, I get on my knees and wrap both my arms around her. At first, she's completely still. But then she shakes from crying so hard and throws her arms around my waist.

# PROM

Walks with Charlie become one of my favorite things. Because of my lungs, we move slower, which is conducive to the stop and go of his picture taking. His focus is gratifying, because I no longer view photography as his hobby—I believe it will be his salvation after I'm gone.

We take to driving around the city, starting someplace new, then walking whatever distance my body will allow. One day we visit a rose garden. My favorite area is the formal garden with its symmetrical patterns, while Charlie prefers the variety in the perennial garden.

Another day we go to an "urban oasis" where we watch kids splash in the fountains, then stroll along the promenade, stopping to snuggle up on one of the swings overlooking the river.

But the best is the morning we explore Columbus College of Art and Design. As soon as we set foot on campus, Charlie fits in so naturally, it's like he's already a student. He shares the history of the "Art" sign, the neon-red, block-letter sculpture that he proudly informs me was conceived of by a photography professor.

His enthusiasm warms my heart. "You'll definitely apply, right?" I confirm.

He nods as he takes my hand. "It's what I love. I figure I owe it to myself to try to make a career of it."

"I'm glad." We approach one of the buildings. "And your parents are okay with you going to an art school?"

"Yeah, they keep saying how important it is to pursue my passion."

We look at each other knowingly—life is too short to not chase your dreams.

On our self-guided tour, we see fashion sketches of brightly colored garments, as well as student paintings and photography equipment that makes Charlie drool.

Once we're back in the sunshine, I say, "I'm sorry I won't be with you while you do this."

He squeezes my hand. "Me too."

"I'm sorry for all the things I'll miss." Although sadness has crept into my voice, Charlie is surprisingly perky.

"Maybe there's one you don't have to."

I raise my eyebrows at him.

He turns to face me and takes both my hands. "There's something on *my* bucket list that I think we can still pull off."

"What's that?"

"Prom."

"Uh…the odds of me making it to April aren't great." In the hospital, Dr. Mastro gave the impression that nine more months would be a miracle.

"A different kind of prom. A prom just for us."

I tilt my head in confusion, but Charlie is quick to explain.

"Your Dad and I will decorate your house, and he'll handle the snacks and music. Your mom and Laine want to take you dress shopping."

*Prom.* I can't believe it might actually happen…

"We'll do it before school starts," Charlie continues. "If you like the idea, we could do it this—"

Before he can finish, I throw my arms around his neck and kiss him. When he pulls back, a huge grin spreads across his face.

The following day, Mom, Laine, and I go shopping.

"Don't touch anything," Mom reminds me as we walk in the store. "Point to dresses you like, and we'll get them for you."

Since my immune system is largely nonfunctional at this point, I also wear a mask—a small price to pay to be here.

Given my too-thin frame, I'm not sure what will look good on me. I pick several different styles. Mom and Laine add some to the pile too. Once we've gone through the whole department, we all cram into a fitting room.

Mom sits on the bench and unzips the dresses. Laine slides them over my head and zips them up. The first option is a long, peach chiffon gown with lace cap sleeves, fitted in the torso and loose and flowy the rest of the way down. The A-line design hugs me in the right places without calling attention to how underweight I am, and the material is soft and delicate against my skin. It's perfect. But no way will I commit right out of the gate and miss the rest of the trying-on fun. Laine hangs it on the "maybe" hook while Mom prepares another.

I don't fill out a short, shimmery gold strapless dress, and my lack of curves makes a floral tulle gown droop. A black woven dress is okay, and a teal embroidered tea-length gown makes it onto the maybe hook, but the "no" hook quickly fills to bursting.

We exhaust the possibilities, but all agree that none comes close to the first. After I'm back in my regular clothes, Mom gives me a quick side hug before opening the door.

"Do you need jewelry?" Laine asks.

I could probably find or borrow pieces that would work, but

I want something new. With instructions not to lift anything off the carousels, Mom lets me shop for jewelry as well.

When we finally leave, Mom carries my dress bag and Laine holds a shoe box in one hand and a bag with a necklace, bracelet, and earrings in the other. I slump happily in the van, tired but not minding one bit.

On Saturday, Mom and Laine sequester me upstairs while Dad and Charlie transform the family room.

All I have to do is put on the dress, then I sit and rest. Mom fastens the chain around my neck, and Laine does my makeup, turning me away from the mirror until she's done. At last, she tells me to stand, and I stare at my reflection.

My hair is growing back—a thin fuzz that's short enough to appear patchy on my scalp. But without hair to hide them, my earrings catch the light and sparkle. Behind the oxygen tubes, Laine has kept my makeup light and natural, which makes my eyes appear bigger and greener, and somehow makes my smile look even happier. "I love you both."

We share a group hug before moving into the hallway. I wait at the top of the stairs while Mom and Laine make sure everything downstairs is ready. Butterflies flit with anticipation in my stomach.

Charlie appears below, wearing a suit and grinning up at me. He's so put together, except for his hair, which will never be tamed. The unruly mop of curls frames his face and accentuates the sparkle in his eyes. He maintains his intense gaze as he mounts the stairs, and the love between us is so strong, it almost makes my chest hurt. He extends his hand and escorts me down.

The scene takes my breath away. Silver, gold, and cream balloons float everywhere. Some are tied close to the weights, near the floor. Others are scattered about at waist height, and more reach up to the ceiling. As I walk into the family room, it's like wading through a sea of balloons.

Silver streamers line the fireplace and bookshelves. Dad and

Charlie moved the couch to make room for dancing. They even rolled up the giant area rug to expose the wood floor and hung a mirror ball from the ceiling fan. A punch bowl and several plates of food sit on the coffee table, which has been pushed against the wall. Music plays, the lights are dim, and candles illuminate the hearth and mantel. Regardless of how decked out the school gym will be in April, it can't be any more magical than this.

"This is beautiful. Thank you all."

Laine kisses the side of my head before she walks out. Mom gives me a squeeze. "Let us know if you need anything."

Dad envelops me in a hug. "You knock my socks off," he whispers in my ear.

Once everyone has left, Charlie holds out his arms, and I take his hands. He pulls me toward him and wraps me in his embrace. "You're stunning."

"You look incredible too." I tuck a curl behind his ear, but it springs right back.

Almost stranger than Charlie in a suit is him without his camera. But then I notice his tripod in the corner, aimed at the wall. "Why is your camera there?"

He leads me over to a box on the floor that contains various party accessories—metallic Mardi Gras masks, silly glasses, plastic tiaras, sparkly headbands, a top hat and cane, and a feathered boa.

"Fun—whose idea was this?" I reach for the boa, the black feathers both soft and scratchy against my neck.

"Your dad's." Charlie dons the top hat and leans on the cane. He sets the timer on his camera, then steps into place, offering his arm for me to hook mine around.

We play with the props for a while, taking silly pictures, striking glamorous poses, and getting some nice shots too. I'm still laughing as Charlie removes his pig nose and asks, "Can I get you something to drink?"

"Sure." I sit on the love seat and take the cup and plate Charlie hands me. Even with finger foods, Dad's on his A game. I end up eating two baked feta bites, several meatball parm skewers, and a tomato-fontina tartlet.

After we finish the snacks, Charlie asks, "Are you up for dancing?"

Standing, I offer my hand. "Who doesn't dance at prom?"

We sway to the music. Charlie's breath is warm on my neck when he says, "You're the most amazing person I know." He pulls back and smiles at me, but we keep our bodies pressed together. "I've been thinking a lot about all our firsts…and our lasts, and everything in between."

To hide from the sadness I'm afraid is coming, I nuzzle my head under his chin.

"I'm going to miss—" Charlie starts, but I press my finger to his lips.

"Can we not? Not tonight."

"Okay. Then I'll say, I *love* holding your hand."

I thread my fingers through his. "And I love—" (not *I'll miss*, even though that's what we're both saying) "—resting my head on your chest and listening to your heartbeat."

He pulls me close, and there it is—*beat-beat, beat-beat, beat-beat*.

"I love—" (*I'll miss*) "—waking up to a text from you," he says.

"I love—" (*I'll miss*) "—you taking my picture."

Vindicated, he teases, "Ah, so all those eye rolls I've gotten were fake. You *do* like being the star of my photos."

"Sometimes. And, you know, you do it anyway. It's become so familiar that it feels wrong if you're not doing it."

Charlie removes his camera from the tripod, then holds it directly in front of my face. *Click.*

"Are you pleased with yourself?" I ask as I smile. "We were having a nice moment."

"Oh, we're still having a nice moment."

"Who decides if it's nice?"

He sets the camera down. "Are you saying it's not nice? Is it a naughty moment?"

My giggles prevent a retort, but it doesn't matter, because Charlie puts his hand on the back of my neck and kisses me. Since I'm still half-laughing, it's a tight-lipped kiss, which makes me laugh harder.

"Are you pleased with *yourself?*" He tilts his head in mock annoyance. "We were having a steamy moment, or rather, I was trying to."

"*Steamy?*" I ask. "Who says *steamy?*"

With another chuckle, I sit on the couch. Charlie sits next to me and says, "I love—" (*I'll miss*) "—the sound of your laugh."

I scoot closer so our knees touch, the stiff fabric from his pants brushing against the smooth chiffon from my dress. "I love playing with your hair, and kissing you, and the way my heart lifts when you walk into the room." *I'll miss, I'll miss, I'll miss.*

He caresses my cheek with his fingers and stares into my eyes. "I love you."

"I love you too."

*I'll miss you so, so much.*

# BEYOND

In early August, it seems like Death might be coming to collect.

The cough that returns gets progressively worse, to the point that I refuse to go downstairs anymore because my last trek up sent me into such a spasm that Mom rushed in to make sure I was okay. Still, despite doing nothing more than lying in bed, I wake in the middle of the night to a coughing fit that severely limits my breathing even after the coughing stops.

Sitting in the dark, I put my hand on my chest and concentrate on getting air into my lungs. *In...out—in...out—in...out—in...out—in...out.* Time to alert Mom.

She obviously heard me coughing, because when I open my door, she's there in the hallway. "Shoes," she says before ducking back into her room.

"I'm sorry," I say once we're in the van.

"Never apologize. And don't talk if it's not necessary."

In the ER, Mom checks me in while I drag myself to a chair and close my eyes. A few minutes later, someone sits next to me. I'm too tired to part my eyelids and confirm it's Mom, but I don't have to—I recognize her fingers closing around mine.

With each painful breath, I keep a mental tally to focus on something other than my misery. I've counted to six hundred thirty-two when a nurse says, "Adele Marshall?"

Mom stands, and I lean on her as we walk, because my muscles are like jelly.

After I'm settled in a room, she drags a chair next to the bed and takes my hand again. I muster the energy to give her a little squeeze, hoping it's enough to convey how thankful I am for everything she's done throughout all of this. There's no way I could have coped without her, and I pray I get the chance to tell her before my time runs out.

---

This time, the fever follows the cough. And while I have a steady stream of company, I'm rarely able to socialize. My eyelids weigh two tons, and forcing them open demands all my energy, leaving none for anything else.

Charlie visits. Mom rises from the chair and puts a hand on his arm before she leaves.

As he walks toward me, I scoot over to make room in the bed, but he says softly, "It's okay. Stay where you are."

Once he sits, he sandwiches my hand between his. I drift in and out and have no idea how long he stays—several hours at least, since I'm aware of refusing dinner. I've dozed off again when his voice startles me awake.

"I'm sorry, I have to go."

I crack my eyes open.

"I'll be back tomorrow." He stares at me for several seconds, then leans down and kisses my forehead. "I love you."

*I love you too.* I don't know if I say this out loud or only in my head.

---

Both Mom and Dad are with me when Dr. Mastro gives us an update. My eyelids flutter open and closed throughout the exchange, providing glimpses of the doctor shaking hands with Dad and putting a hand on Mom's shoulder. He stands near the foot of my bed and rests his hand on my shin in between gesturing.

"The cancer has spread to the lymph nodes in her lungs. And she has pneumonia again." Hand off. "We'll keep administering the antibiotics." Hand on. "Unfortunately, the oxygen isn't helping as much this time." Hand off. "A morphine infusion is our best bet for symptom relief." Hand on.

Mom's voice: "Should we be concerned about giving her an opioid?"

"At this point, I'd like to make her more comfortable, and morphine is very effective at reducing shortness of breath."

*Yes, please, let's do that.*

Dad's voice, addressed to Mom: "She's clearly suffering."

No one says anything, but I assume Mom nods, because Dr. Mastro's hand disappears again and I hear the door open and close.

---

Once the morphine kicks in, my breathing improves, my body relaxes, and *I sleep*. Sleep, sleep, and more sleep, until (quick check of my phone) 1:18 a.m. *Not sure what day.*

My phone confirms it's Tuesday. I've been here for three days, and I haven't eaten in that time. That can't be good.

As my eyes travel around the room, a few things catch their attention: Mom's overnight bag propped against her chair. A piece of paper on the table next to my bed—a drawing from Bean with the words, *I love you, Dell.* Next to the card, the scrapbook everyone made for me. And Fuffers, my stuffed rabbit who normally lives on a shelf in my bedroom—

That's when I know I'm not going home again.

I lie quietly and let this thought sink in. It's not as awful as I feared it would be. I guess part of accepting that it's time to die is not having the energy left to fight.

Saying goodbye will be hard, there's no denying that. My stomach churns just thinking about talking with Mom and Dad, Laine, Bean, and Charlie, knowing it's the last time. There will be too many words I want to say and not enough time to say them.

A tear escapes from the corner of my eye, tickling as it rolls down my temple and settles in my ear. I reach for Fuffers and hold him to my chest. I don't know who thought to bring him, but I'm glad they did.

---

My fever stays high, my cough gets worse, and despite the morphine, my breathing becomes more labored. Mom, Dad, Laine, Bean, and Charlie spend the whole day at the hospital. Shannon visits too, everybody taking shifts.

Once they up the morphine dose, I live in a toy picture viewer again: Sleep. *Click.* Mom and Dad. Sleep. *Click.* Laine and Bean. Sleep. *Click.* Charlie. Sleep. *Click.* Mom and Laine. Sleep. *Click.* Shannon. Sleep.

---

I haven't eaten in six days. The pneumonia is stubborn, the fever persistent, and I exist in a constant state of near combustion. Breathing takes my whole focus, and my lungs threaten to be the first body part to surrender.

In the morning, I can tell from Mom's red, puffy eyes that she's been crying. She tells me they're going to intubate me, to put me on a ventilator.

"Dr. Mastro said your body is spending its energy helping you breathe, instead of fighting the infection. This will let your lungs rest."

My heartbeat quickens. "Will I come off the ventilator?"

A tear rolls down Mom's cheek. "If your lungs get better."

*So, probably not.*

Mom takes my hand. "We don't know what else to do."

I nod, and she finishes explaining what this means: once I'm intubated, I won't be able to talk, so they'll sedate me. An induced coma. Until my lungs can function on their own again, or until Mom and Dad decide to take me off life support.

It's time to say goodbye.

Mom goes into the hallway, and I'm alone for a few minutes. Although I can't take a deep breath, I imagine taking one to steel myself for what's ahead.

The door opens, and Shannon slips in, then sits next to my bed.

"I'm sorry you're...having to go through this...again," I tell her.

With an eye roll, she says, "Please. Do not apologize to me. Life is shit sometimes."

I give her a small smile. "You helped make this...less shitty."

She exhale-laughs. "I didn't do anything."

"You listened... You told me...the truth. That means...a lot."

After a moment, she nods. "The reason sucks, but I'm really glad I got to know you."

I offer my hand, and Shannon squeezes it.

"Anything you...want me to...tell Noah?"

"What, you believe you'll see my brother in the afterlife?"

"Who knows what's...waiting for us...in the great beyond... Maybe I can...pass on a message."

Shannon stares at me for—well, I won't say an eternity, but for a very long time. Finally, she swallows. "Tell him I love him —I'll always love him. I miss him. And I hope he's okay."

Through my blurry vision, I watch her exchange places with someone outside the door.

My stomach flip-flops as Laine comes in. She laces her fingers through mine. "Damn, Dee."

Sobs escape in hiccuppy bursts. "This is hard."

In a strained voice, Laine says, "I know. And I know nothing I can say will make it any better. So, I'll just say you're the best sister I could have asked for and I got majorly lucky that you're my best friend too."

"I can't imagine…my life without you."

We stare at each other, then she delicately wraps her arms around me and holds me while we both cry.

"I love you," Laine chokes out.

"I love you too."

Laine wipes her eyes as she walks toward the door.

Bean steps slowly into the room. I know she understands what's happening by the fear in her eyes.

"Sit here with me." I pat the sheet and try not to lose it completely even though my pulse throbs in my ears and my body temperature has climbed another five degrees.

Carefully, Bean snuggles next to me, and I lean my head against hers. "Do you remember…when you would…climb in bed with me…in the morning?"

She would tiptoe into my room and crawl into my bed. We would talk in whispers until we heard footsteps in the hall. Occasionally, I would tickle her, and her laughter would wake the rest of the house.

"I loved when…you did that… It was nice having…some time…just the two of us."

"Mommy wouldn't let me come in until seven."

"You definitely came in…earlier than that." I give her a gentle poke.

We're quiet. *What am I supposed to say now?*

Suddenly, my brain stops worrying about saying the right

thing and my heart does the talking. "You're the best...little sister, Bean... You're sweet and funny...and smart and caring... and I love you...so much."

With a sob, she turns sideways so she can wrap her arm around my other side. It's an awkward hug with all the tubes, and it hurts where one is being tugged, but I squeeze my sister with all the strength I can muster.

"I love you," Bean whispers, her breath hot on my ear.

We stay in our embrace until Mom opens the door, then Bean extricates herself from the tubes and slides off the bed. Her expression when she turns back and Mom's expression when she puts her arm around Bean about destroy any resolve I'm managing to maintain.

Despite knowing better, I take a deep, shuddery breath, then withstand the coughing fit that ensues. Once it's over, I stare at the door until Dad appears.

He sits on the edge of my bed and takes my hand.

"When you were two, you ran into a revolving door. Your mom went after you but ended up in the next section. The door kept moving, pushing you, and you got scared and screamed." After a pause, he clears his throat. "Mom yelled for you to go out, but you kept reaching for her. Once you finally turned, I was afraid you wouldn't clear the opening before the door closed it off, so I ran out the emergency exit and grabbed you from the outside."

With glassy eyes, he says, "I'm so sorry I couldn't save you from this."

My heart breaks—because he can't save me, no matter how desperately we wish he could; because my parents are dealing with a generous helping of guilt on top of all the other hard emotions; and because we live in a world where some parents have to watch their children die.

"I love you, Daddy," I manage through my tears.

Dad wraps his arms around me. "I love you, Adele. I will

always love you."

Probably trying to collect himself, Dad stays like that even after I drop my arms. He kisses my head before he gets up.

Mom and Dad don't look at each other when they trade places in the doorway. Mom's eyes are red, and she wipes away tears as she sits next to me. "Hi, baby."

We reach for each other, both sobbing. How do I put a lifetime of thank-yous into a sentence? There aren't enough words—or rather, there isn't enough time for me to say the words—to express my gratitude for every time Mom lay with me in the middle of the night after a bad dream, for every note she packed in my school lunches, for every run we shared. I can't begin to tell her how much I appreciate all the times she made me a cup of tea and listened to me talk, or how much I admire the way she cares for our family, or how much I'll miss her smell.

When I think I can get a few words out, I pull back. "If it's… seventeen years with you…or a lifetime…with some other mom…I pick you."

Mom's face crumples and she folds me into her embrace. A minute passes, then she separates herself and stares at me. "Adele." She swallows. "I am so incredibly proud of you—your determination and resilience, your openness, your warmth." Her closing words are barely intelligible, but I have no trouble understanding them: "I love you very, very much."

We hold each other for several minutes. Once our sniffling subsides a little, Mom rubs my back, then stands to go.

I prepare myself for the final goodbye. Charlie approaches slowly, then sits by my side and leans his forehead against mine.

Neither of us speaks until my cough forces us apart. "I have something…for you." I turn to the table by my bed and reach for the cardboard sleeve holding a picture I had printed.

Charlie's face shows his surprise as he pulls out the photograph—I've never given him a photo before. It captures him taking pictures at our aloha party. He looked so purposeful, so fulfilled, so *Charlie*, and this will remind him of the peace he finds behind his camera.

"Do what...you love...and you'll be...happy."

He cries openly, and I pull him close.

"I love you with...all my heart," I say.

"And I love you with all of mine."

Through our tears, we share one last kiss.

---

My family and Charlie surround me when it's time for the ventilator. A nurse injects the sedative and tells me to count back from one hundred.

*One hundred...ninety-nine...* I gaze at everyone. *Ninety-eight... ninety-seven...ninety-six...* Mom holds one of my hands, Charlie the other. *Ninety-five...ninety-four...* Dad rests a hand on my ankle, Laine on my shoulder, and Bean on my side...

*When they brought Bean home from the hospital, her skin was so soft.*

*Ninety-three...ninety-two...*

*Like a flower petal, silky and delicate. White petals rain from the pear trees in April. Snow in the springtime.*

*Ninety-one...*

*I'm walking on the snow...except it isn't snow. It's a blanket of petals. I spread my arms wide and fall backward, and when I land, I don't feel a thing.*

*Voices. I hear them, but don't know if they're real or in my head. Now I'm riding on a fluffy cloud. Bean is with me, and we're searching for animals—look, a rabbit! Fuffers is in my hand, but Laine pulls him away. I protest, but from behind her back, she produces a tiny top hat that she places on his head before returning him to me.*

*I feel a kiss. So many kisses. Kisses from my parents, my sisters, Charlie. Kisses every day, every night. Everyone should have so many kisses. I blow one from my lips, and when my hand leaves my mouth, a red heart floats into the air. It joins other hearts, all the kisses people have blown, and the hearts are playing, racing.*

*I'm running with the hearts, and I'm happy. This is the race to beat all races. It's not a normal race, though. This one is special because there will be no more races, this is the last. My family is here—Mom, Dad, Laine, Bean—and my friends—Charlie, Shannon. They're cheering, my ears fill with the sounds of their support, but they're not encouraging me to go faster. There are no places in this race, no first, second, third, fourth. Only feelings—peace, love, joy, laughter.*

*One of the hearts—Love—is on my left, falling back, then skipping ahead. Laughter somersaults through the air in front of me. Joy and Peace, on my right, entwine and separate and come together again.*

*Gratitude overcomes me as I join the revelry. I dance, because this race is a celebration of life. Joy, Laughter, Peace, Love, and me—we tumble into each other as we bound forward. With a full heart, I raise my arms to the sky as I cross the finish line.*

# ACKNOWLEDGMENTS

I am tremendously grateful for everyone who has supported me and my writing and for those who helped get this book across the finish line, especially:

The Highlights Foundation Writers Workshop at Chautauqua and my fellow Workshop alums Lisa Amstutz, Bill Burton, Jennifer Florentin, and Carly Schuna. My week at Chautauqua was transformational, and when I took the advice to "write what scares you" by pursuing this project, you gave me the encouragement I needed to keep going.

My Navicor colleagues—working with you launched my career; helped me find my place in a new city; introduced me to the science, hope, and heartbreak of Hodgkin's lymphoma; and gave me lifelong friends. Special thanks to Susan Albert, Jamie Bowers, Don "Diesel" Davis, Jason Ferguson, Phil Ferguson, Keith Flint, Veronica Karingada, Bruce and Belinda Nicoll, Karen Sanford, Kathy Strausser, and Laura Wall.

Michael Dolan, whose support of authors is a shining example of what publishing can be. I am extremely fortunate to benefit from your vision, respect, and care.

Vanessa Lanang—I am thrilled to have an editor I trust, admire, and like. Collaborating with you on this book was every bit as delightful as the first and profoundly improved the final product.

My fellow WRDS authors, particularly Jessica Foster, Charleigh Frederick, and Sarena Straus for the wisdom and friendship you've shared.

Rejenne Pavon, whose book covers are among the best in the business. This one is gorgeous and fills me with joy.

Jillian Hunt MSN, APRN, FNP-C, AOCNP; Cincinnati Cancer Advisors, for your keen medical eye and thoughtful observations about the clinical aspects of the novel.

Lenae Walters—I am honored by your willingness to share your story with me and touched by your open heart and your kind words about this manuscript.

My author community: Kristy Boyce, Becky Gehrisch, Annette Hashitate, Jason Lady, Kathryn Powers, Debbie Rigaud, Jennifer Ann Shore, and Erik Slangerup. Time with you all fills a cup I didn't even know I had.

Friends who supply me with a steady dose of fun, laughter, and warmth: Jurgita Fumo, Will and Riley King, Al and Gloria Marcinonis, and Steve and Betsy Wonderly, as well as Melanie Amato and Lynn McConnell, who were among the first people to read Dell's story.

Kelli Rex, for the thoughtful attention you give to my writing, as well as your thoughtfulness in life.

Julie King—I am grateful for everything, always, but specifically for this book, thank you for the Notre Dame insights and the James Dean Museum memories.

My family, for a lifetime of love:

Shawn Wilkoff—my heartfelt appreciation for your encouragement and support of my writing over our years together.

Audrey Dodson, whose influence still guides me, and Dale Dodson, for your unwavering interest in my writing; Sue Fillers and Pat Smith, for the excitement with which you greet my literary endeavors.

Denise and Tom Stout, who never seem to tire of listening to me talk about books (or anything else). I don't know what cosmic lottery I won to get you for parents, but I know how lucky I am.

My child, Elise—as you grow, it becomes more deeply fulfilling each day to share this journey called life with you. I love you beyond measure.

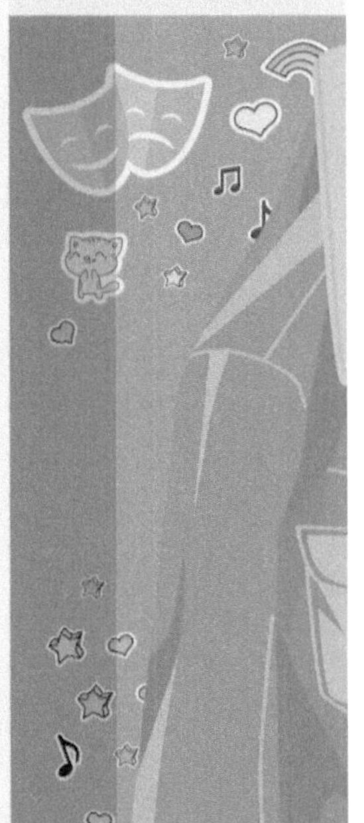

BRIEANNA
WILKOFF
I'LL
BE
THERE
FOR
YOU
'80S ROCK

# I'LL BE THERE FOR YOU

Rae is grieving the loss of her '80s rock–loving dad. Can Mac, who thinks any problem can be solved with a show tune, help heal her broken heart?

Turn the page to read an excerpt from Brieanna Wilkoff's award-winning debut young adult novel, *I'll Be There for You*.

# "NEVER SAY GOODBYE"

I like to pretend my father's mortician was Jon Bon Jovi's grandfather. Granted, we didn't go to Bongiovi Funeral Home because we don't live in Raritan, New Jersey, and Bon Jovi's grandpop is probably dead too, but if somehow Mr. Bongiovi had buried my dad, it would have made him happy.

He loved '80s rock. (My dad—I don't know about Mr. Bongiovi. But I figure if your grandson is the front man of a famous rock band, the music can't help but grow on you.) Journey, Def Leppard, Mötley Crüe, Guns N' Roses, AC/DC— their songs were all regular fixtures in my house growing up, but none more than Bon Jovi. They were Dad's favorite.

Shamelessly, he took every opportunity to tell people about the 23 times he'd seen them in concert. My mom and I would roll our eyes at each other whenever he started in. But it was an eye roll of loving indulgence, which is why I stop outside Mom's room at the sight of a Bon Jovi shirt on top of a pile of clothes on her bed.

"What are you doing?"

She doesn't answer. When I step through the doorway, I see the earbuds. I move closer and wave my hand to get her attention as she drops another shirt—the Slippery When Wet Tour—onto the stack.

Startled when she finally notices me, my mother wipes quickly at her eyes and then stops whatever she's listening to.

"What are you doing?" I ask again, an edge to my voice.

With a sigh, she sits on the bed, her shoulders hunched forward. "Going through your dad's stuff. I figured it was time."

Arms folded across my chest, I demand, "What are you doing with it?"

"Donating what I can, pitching the rest."

I note a hole at the collar of the SWWT shirt and stare at the pile in horror. "Is this the trash?"

Mom sticks her finger through the seam. "Does this look like something I can donate?"

Maybe not. I dig through the rejects—countless (*okay, exactly 23*) Bon Jovi shirts, along with a bunch paying homage to other rock gods. "How can you get rid of these? They're Dad's Bon Jovi shirts."

"I know what they are, Rae." She shrugs. "What would you have me do with them?"

My heart beats faster. "I don't know. But you can't throw them away—Dad loved these."

"We can't keep them forever. It's been a year since—"

"No, it hasn't! Not till Tuesday."

"You're right," Mom says as she rubs her forehead.

Once she meets my gaze again, I dare her with my eyes to pick up the trash bag on the floor. Instead, she brushes her fingers over the shirt, no fight left in her. I grab the pile from under her hand and storm out.

---

My dad died on Monday, October 22. I tried really hard to not remember the date. For weeks after the accident, every time the date would pop into my head, I'd say other numbers to fuddle my brain. *October 22...25...20...27.* I hate the idea of a death-iversary. But despite my best efforts, the date was insistent, and now I'll never forget it.

The day before the one-year milestone (*death-iversary*), I try unsuccessfully to focus on other dates teachers deem worthy of my attention, but none of them can drown out *October 22* muttering in the background.

After last period, I look at one more date: October 24. Above it is a single word: AUDITIONS. I've stood before this poster every day since it went up two weeks ago. The theatre department is putting on *It's a Wonderful Life: A Live Radio Play.* Last fall they did *Peter and the Starcatcher.* I had signed up to audition. Then my world fell apart.

By the time *Little Shop of Horrors* rolled around in March, I could have auditioned, theoretically. But I wasn't ready to sing again. I don't know if I'll ever be.

"You signing up?" A voice intrudes on my thoughts, and I turn to find a boy whose most striking feature—despite nice eyes and invitingly tousled hair—is his shoes, which sport a collage of Playbills.

"Um...I haven't decided yet." I refocus my attention on the wall.

"You should. It'll be fun."

I hesitate before I turn to him again. "Are you auditioning?"

The look he gives me refutes the "There are no stupid questions" credo. "I don't act. I'm the student director. Name's Mac."

He stares at me expectantly until I say, "I'm Raina—Rae."

"You a freshman, Raina-Rae? I haven't seen you in our theatrical environs before."

"I'm a sophomore."

"Same. Why didn't you try out last year?"

I study the *Les Mis* waif on his foot. "It didn't work with my schedule."

"Then now's your chance. And come on, who doesn't like *It's a Wonderful Life?*"

"It's not at the top of my list." I'm not trying to be difficult, but seeing George give up so much throughout the movie makes me sad.

"No? Watch it again. I'll admit the first couple viewings are painful—the situation looks so bleak. But once you're one hundred percent positive things will turn out all right in the end, it wins hands down for feel-goodness."

I'm rusty at this talking to new people thing, so I don't know how to end the conversation. I go back to the poster, hoping Mac will disappear as suddenly as he materialized, but I can tell he's still here, waiting. "Do I have to prepare a monologue or something?" I ask.

"Nope, just read from the script." He raises his eyebrow. "So, I'll see you Thursday?"

"Maybe." I start walking away.

"I'll give you the moon, Raina-Rae!" he calls after me.

That evening, I descend to the basement to watch the Frank Capra classic. Forgoing the couch, which faces the TV, I sit in Dad's recliner, pulling his knobbly fleece blanket over me as the black and white title sequence appears on the screen. I don't mind the old movies—I grew up watching Julie Andrews in *The Sound of Music* and Frank Sinatra in *Guys and Dolls*. My grandma died before I was born, but my grandpa lives right down the street, meaning movie nights are a regular occurrence, so the simple filmmaking fills me with comforting nostalgia.

During the scene when Harry returns home from college,

Mom comes down the stairs carrying a laundry basket. "A little early for Christmas movies, isn't it?"

Given that she continues past me into the laundry room, I don't feel the need to respond. I turn up the volume to mute the rhythmic *swish* of the washing machine.

She returns empty-handed and sits on the couch, perched on the edge of the cushion. "Can you pause it a minute?"

I turn toward her with a sigh, swinging my legs over the side of the chair.

She rubs her hands together and looks at her lap. "So, we haven't talked about tomorrow."

And just like that, it's ten degrees warmer in here. "What about it?"

"I understand it will be a hard day for you, for us. What can I do to help?"

Squirming, I look at the floor. "I don't know."

"Do you want to skip school?"

"And do what?" Like it matters. School, home, freakin' Disney World—tomorrow, any of them will be the unhappiest place on earth.

"Whatever you need—talk, cry."

"Haven't we done enough of that?" You could fill a bathtub with the tears I've shed.

Mom reaches her hand out, but I stand, the blanket falling to the ground and burying my feet. "I know you're hurting," she says. "I wish I knew how to help you."

"You can't help me because nobody can fix this." I move toward the stairs, but Mom blocks my path.

"I'm not saying I can make everything okay, but sometimes… sometimes I'm afraid you're not really processing what you're feeling. Of course, you're struggling. But you have to work through those emotions."

I cross my arms. "Oh really? Is that what I need to do?"

Mom's face takes on a pinched look that's equal parts

exasperated and wounded. "I don't have all the answers. But if you would talk to me, share what you're going through, tell me what you want—"

"What I want?" The heat that flashes through me must melt my filter because words spew out. "What I want is to go to school tomorrow and come home and have dinner with my parents. I want to go to bed and know they'll both be here in the morning. What I *want* is to not be having this conversation. I want to rewind time and pretend the last year didn't happen. And no matter what I do tomorrow, or the next day, or the day after that, it won't be the tiniest bit okay because I won't see my dad, and I hate that he's gone!"

Rushing past Mom before she can stop me, I race up the stairs and slam my door. I sit on the floor, reach for Dad's New Jersey Tour shirt, and hold it close to my heart as I sob.

For the past 364 days, I've woken up and missed the smell of coffee, which I don't even like, because Dad was always the first one up. At night, I've longed for him to raise his hand, pinky and index finger up, and say, "Rock those dreams." I'd give anything to hear him ask about the most interesting part of my day or, if I was being snarky, the least interesting part. Every time I've heard one of his favorite songs on the radio, my heart has ached to not see his excitement, and it hurts to imagine all the Bon Jovi concerts he'll never attend. I miss the smile in his eyes and his one crooked tooth and the ridiculous high-pitched sound he made when he was laughing so hard he could barely breathe.

The past 364 days have been the worst days of my life.

And the very worst part of all is knowing my father died because of me.

# ABOUT THE AUTHOR

Brieanna Wilkoff (she/her) is an award-winning author of contemporary young adult stories about friendship, romance, and family that tug at the heartstrings, including her debut, *I'll Be There for You*. In her day job, she works as an editor for an oncology advertising agency. Outside work and writing, Brieanna loves reading, going for walks (not running), and musical theatre—a Playbill cruise is high on her bucket list. She lives in Westerville, Ohio, and can be found online at brieannawilkoff.com.

www.ingramcontent.com/pod-product-compliance
Lightning Source LLC
Chambersburg PA
CBHW020917060726
47591CB00004B/1289